The Biggest Door

Les Russo

Amy & Ray
Hope you like
The Biggest Door.
2/3/12

The Biggest Door

ISBN: 978-0-9847215-2-8

Library of Congress Control Number: 2011942102

Cover by All Things That Matter Press

This book is dedicated to Petie,
who's still as beautiful as that first time I saw her
walking across the quad.
The Biggest Door is possible because of her.

Acknowledgments

To Petie, Lou, Noreen, George, John, and Carmel. Thank you for your immediate and complete acceptance, support, and enthusiasm for The Biggest Door and me. It fills me with pride and is another reminder that my family is incredible.

Deb and Phil Harris, my publishers at ATTMP, for taking a chance on a new writer. Deb, thanks for your wise counsel.

Marvin Wilson, my editor, for his excellent suggestions.

My parents Les and Sheila Russo, Petie's parents, Margaret and Jack O'Connor, the Russo's and O'Connor's for helping to shape me.

My early supporters and friends – Colleen Detjen who always had coffee ready for our Saturday discussions, Maggie Roche for her continuous encouragement to move forward, and Celeste Soden, the best cook I know, who cheered me on every step of the way.

My writer friends, Patrick Creevy, Jerry Blitefield, Floyd Sullivan, and Laura Nelson for all their helpful hints.

Jody O'Connor, my great pal, for her photos. Jods, see you in the corner.

The laughs and stories the "Running Club" always provided.

Whitney Jenner for setting me straight on the Kennedy's.

Maggie Raynard and Kate Soden for never refusing to help.

The Carmelites of Des Plaines for their example and inspiration.

And, Debbie McGowan, for her life advice and friendship

ONE

I am standing, waist high in water, in a large isolated lake surrounded by majestic pine and cedar trees. It is peaceful and quiet. As I reach up my hands to thank God for this gift, I notice the water is rising, causing me to worry. When it gets to my chest, panic builds; my fear of drowning is overwhelming. Although I am momentarily paralyzed with fear, I know I must get out of the lake before it's too late. I finally find the will to half-swim, half-tread out of the water.

Once on shore I begin to walk, then jog, and finally run frantically toward a glass building I see at the end of a path that runs through the trees. I must get to the building because Debra is there waiting for me. When I arrive, wet and out of breath, she is outside sitting at a table, reading from a black notebook. She is calm as she looks up at me, motions for me to sit, and says, "Let's have our meeting outside today."

I look around, see people close by, and it unnerves me. I don't want anyone to know I have been seeing Debra on the sly. I hesitate, fidgeting, then take a seat next to her and we start talking. I am at once more relaxed just being with her. In a matter-of-fact tone, I tell Debra, "I'm one hundred percent sure my business will fail."

This is the dream I had the night I realized the manufacturing company I owned for ten years was going bankrupt. The only reason I recorded the dream is because Debra makes me write down all my dreams. Debra is my therapist. She's a perky five-foot-four inch, good looking middle-aged blonde from Los Angeles who sometimes during our sessions will say fuck, shit, or prick. Not in a bad way, but in an amusing and sexy way. There are only a few women who can pull off swearing and Debra is certainly one of them. After telling her about someone who aggravates me, she might say, "Shit, Ken, that guy's a real prick, isn't he?" Almost every time she uses a dirty word, even if I am in a bad mood, I muffle a laugh or let out an immature giggle.

I also like the way that halfway through a sentence she sort of pops out of her chair and comes back down sitting cross-legged. Debra is what we Catholics call a WASP. She is, however, married to a man of Irish descent who was not only raised Catholic, but attended Catholic grammar and high school. Her office has a statue of the Blessed Virgin Mary and she keeps a Bible on one of her tables. Debra is like a Catholic without the guilt; in my opinion the perfect personality combination. She is as honest, moral, and spiritual as anyone I have ever met, except for the person who introduced us. Incidentally, this person has no idea that Debra and I see each other once a week for an hourly session. This has been going on for at least a year.

I wish I'd known Debra when she was in college. I'll bet she was the life of any party she attended. I imagine her sitting at a bar wearing sunglasses and smoking a cigarette surrounded by guys who would love to be her boyfriend. When I enter the bar she would yell, "Hell, yeah, Ken, 'bout time. Now get yourself over here," and treat me like I'm the most important person in the room. I love being around Debra. She reminds me, not in looks, but in personality, of Audrey Hepburn as Holly Golightly in the movie *Breakfast at Tiffany's*; sexy, eccentric, and a little wild, but someone who always makes you feel at ease when you're around her.

TWO

My story really started when I moved out to the Midwest. Shortly after graduating from Manhattanville College—a small liberal arts school outside of New York City—in 1978, I drove to Chicago to be with my girlfriend, Frances 'Francie' Madigan. I tried to convince my family and friends it was only going to be for a couple of months, sort of a like a long road trip.

I told them, "I'm just going to have a little fun before I start my 'real job'. I'll be back before you know it."

My friend Murph kissed me on the cheek during my bon voyage party and said, "You're not coming back. You'll stay in Chicago. Francie is the woman you're going to marry."

I remember with great clarity the first time I saw Francie. I'm not completely sure, but when it comes to Francie, I like to think I was hit by the proverbial love at first sight thunderbolt. Until our first encounter, I was on the lookout for her because at least three friends let me know that we were perfect for each other. Can you imagine, the semester had hardly started and I was being told there is someone out there that was perfect for me? This kind of intrigued me, so naturally I kept an eye out for Francie during the early part of the 1976 fall semester. It got to where I pestered friends every time a girl entered a room, "Is that Francie," I'd ask.

Seeing as I was having no success in meeting her, I decided to make a few curious inquiries. I learned that because of a sister's wedding she would be arriving on campus late. Since Manhattanville is a compact, walled-in campus with a small student population, I figured as soon as she arrived we'd have to run into each other. But, typical of my somewhat neurotic personality, the anticipation of meeting Francie created anxiety in me, yet also gave her an air of mystery. About three weeks into the semester, I finally had the opportunity to meet my future wife. A bunch of my new college friends decided earlier in the week to take a jaunt into New York City. As we were preparing to leave, one of the guys let us know he had asked Francie to join us. We were to meet her by the quad in five minutes.

As we sat in my car waiting, I looked across to the far side of the open space and noticed a five-foot-eight inch tall, thin, more than okay endowed, strawberry blonde woman in a tight fitting striped sweater walking toward our car. Because of the distance, I couldn't clearly see her face. As she drew closer to my beat-up, four-door gold '68 Ford Torino, her features came into focus. I was not disappointed; in fact, I was awestruck. The freckles, high forehead and small smile portrayed a

Rockwellian childlike innocence. Funny as it sounds, her wrists and hands looked the most perfect. I think they unconsciously showed her gentleness. I was too young to formulate a life together; rather, horniness took over. At a minimum I wanted to madly kiss this woman like the heroes do in movies. I hid my lust as she jumped in the car beside me, extended her hand and announced, "Hi, I'm Francie."

Two years later I was on my way to Chicago, with a savage hangover, in a cramped VW bug. At the end of the fifteen-hour drive, approaching the house that Francie grew up in was mind boggling. It was the largest house I had ever seen. It had more bathrooms than my mom and dad's apartment had rooms. I dated Francie for two years at Manhattanville and had no idea her family came from this much money. Having grown up poor, I was instantly in awe of her family and their lifestyle. They did not worry about money or how the electric bill was going to be paid next month. They didn't make decisions based on price. For me every decision I ever made was based on money. The schools I attended, the clothes I bought, everything depended on cost. Early on, I remember going to dinner with the Madigans; everyone ordered steak. I was questioned when I ordered a hamburger. "After all, Ken," I was informed, "You can never go wrong with steak."

It was as close to seeing the entitlement I had read about and discussed in my college sociology classes. But it wasn't just that they all ordered steak. Their lives were seemingly carefree. They were satisfied, worry-free, and happy. I was naïve enough to see money as a means of obtaining this happiness.

A few weeks before Christmas 1979, the year before we were married, Francie's dad asked Francie and me to buy the family Christmas gift: roller skates. Without question we went to a large Chicago sports store, pulled out Mr. Madigan's credit card, and spent a ridiculous amount of money on thirty-five to forty pairs of the most kickass roller skates you've ever seen. Arriving at the Madigan's home on Christmas day along with Francie's six sisters, two brothers, a host of in-laws, and grandchildren was absolutely awesome. Adults and children alike were recklessly roller skating throughout the downstairs of a house large enough to accommodate the insanity. I wove in and out of rooms, past future in-laws, while children whizzed by, almost going through my legs. The Madigans were singing Christmas carols as they shot out the front door in a Conga-like line onto the cobblestone, tree-lined street on Chicago's warmest December day in decades. God of course made sure of that. Up and down the street we skated waving and wishing passersby our sincerest Merry Christmas. It was a scene right out of anyone's favorite feel-good movie. As I clumsily skated along I thought to myself, who does this? Is this for real? My God, I can't tell my childhood friends this story. If they did believe me, they certainly wouldn't understand.

I was being seduced by Francie and her family's way of life. My childhood of apartments and bills was fast becoming a hazy distant memory. Roller skating through the fancy North Shore neighborhoods of Wilmette and Kenilworth that Christmas was spellbinding. The houses were so large, the yards so well kept, and the owners so young. I wanted to be a part of this world. I knew I was on my way to fulfilling Murph's prophecy of marrying Francie and staying in Chicago.

Right after Francie and I were married, I watched my father-in-law direct my older brothers-in-law toward owning small companies. I also watched with amazement as their fortunes, houses, second homes, and vacations grew. Shit, they made it look so easy. I knew that I would eventually succumb to my father-in-law's wishes; I would take advantage of his generosity and accept his help in buying a small manufacturing concern. Why wouldn't I? Dammit, I was going to be the rags to riches story that people read about. "Yeah," everyone would say, "can you believe his mom and dad never owned a house, now he owns three, one of which is in France?"

I was obsessed with becoming this person. I wanted the money, as well as the power and respect that came with wealth. I wanted to walk into a room and watch people point to me and whisper about my accomplishments as I passed by.

During the early years of our marriage, which now seem to have been a lifetime ago, Francie and I lived in the garage apartment behind her parent's house. I worked for a benefit consulting firm and Francie was a clerk for three options traders at the Chicago Board of Trade. At night she would tell me with great enthusiasm how her bosses taught her to trade stock options. All three were highly successful and willing to take the time to tutor their clerk. When Francie made a trade we watched stock prices with excitement, imagining our future riches. She explained that their method of trading was to 'spread' trades. Basically, they bought and sold the same stock option at different maturity dates when there was an imbalance or spread in the price. This method minimized risk and pretty much ensured a profit. Francie played with tens of dollars while her bosses played with thousands. It was a fairly common method of trading.

One day while working for the consulting firm, I was offered a ride home by two senior consultants. On the way home they asked probing questions. This led to, "Does your wife work? What does she do?"

Feeling unusually open, I told them, "She is a trader at the Board of Trade." I tried to beef it up a little. You know, make Francie look good. I figured since she had started making small trades, I wasn't really lying.

"What kind of trading does she do," one of the consultants asked.

"Well, she trades stock option futures," I answered fast and with confidence because I was proud of Francie and how well she was doing in this male-dominated field.

Still curious, he said, "Does she have any particular trading method that she uses?"

So, naive and incorrect, I answered, "Oh, yeah, she and her associates have come up with a stock option trading method called eagle trading."

Why and how I came up with eagle trading I will never know. It just sort of popped out. So, I told the two consultants about a form of trading that I had inadvertently made up.

As we continued driving I directed them to my home. Seconds later we pulled into Francie's mom and dad's driveway. There they sat parked in a long circular driveway in front of one of the largest houses in Wilmette; a house I then realized the two consultants thought I owned. When I reached the front door of the house and looked back at the car, I will never forget the looks on their faces, wide eyed with jaws dropped in disbelief. I knew their opinion of me had just risen tremendously because they thought I was sitting on a pile of money. They had to be thinking Francie had cracked a trading code and made millions of dollars. I will always remember the way those two treated me at work after that ride home. For the first time in my life I was able to sense firsthand the power and respect that came with having money. After that incident, I often imagined the two consultants inquiring at trading firms about eagle trades. I wish I could have seen their reaction when they were told, "We've never heard of this eagle trading you keep talking about."

That night I told Francie what had happened and my reaction to how the associates acted toward me when they thought I owned a mansion. How I loved the feeling of being respected by the senior consultants. I could tell she did not understand my feelings. For her, having grown up with money, it wasn't something to worry or think about. It was the first time I realized how different her approach to life was from mine. Years later, when my company went broke, she confided in me that it had never occurred to her that I wouldn't make a lot of money. I, on the other hand, grew up dreaming of making millions, but never expected it to happen.

As Francie and I purchased our first house and began having children, I managed to hold down a series of good, solid, conventional office jobs. But Francie and I both wanted more. My salary was never enough to support the lifestyle we envisioned for ourselves and our children. Having obtained middle class status with a mid-level position was no longer good enough for us. This fueled me toward asking my father-in-law for his support in purchasing a company. It was freely and immediately given.

I was now the poor boy about to make the leap into a world that was foreign to me. I knew to enter this new world I would have to remake myself and live outside my comfort zone. I had to leave behind the world I grew up with. I had to be interested in things that hadn't interested me. But I was young and cocky enough to think I could easily make the transition. I wanted so badly to be accepted into the Madigan family that I never gave a second thought to the move I was about to make. What I didn't realize was, with the change came a price—anxiety and depression. Looking back, I often wonder if subconsciously I never completely escaped my past, perhaps sabotaging myself in a way.

I was determined to find a strong existing company to purchase. This mission is what drove and sustained me. After a five-plus year search and a two year courtship I found the perfect situation: a seventy-year-old company owner with six children, who was looking to retire. He had a large family, like me. He sent his children to a Catholic grammar school, like me. He went to a Catholic high school, like me. And, according to the owner, he had married an Irish woman who was from a large family, again like me. "And we know what that's like, right, Ken?" He saw a younger version of himself in me.

None of his six children showed any interest in continuing in the company and besides, it would be too difficult to divide the company up six ways. The owner planned to live off the interest from the sale proceeds. He reasoned that when he passed away, the children could divvy up the money.

The best part was the company was affordable and, most of all, profitable. On January 7, 1998, I, Ken Sabino, the forty-four-year-old eldest son of an electrician, purchased Milbank Packaging Company, a manufacturing concern for 1.5 million dollars. I was on my way to realizing the American dream.

THREE

Two years, maybe longer, before I met Debra, my sister-in-law Annie Madigan gave me her telephone number. Annie and I, having both married into this ridiculously large Irish Catholic Chicago family in the same year, had formed a tight relationship. My wife Francie and Annie's husband Dan were two of nine siblings who all lived within ten miles of each other. The nine Madigans, all married to their first spouse, had a total of forty-nine children and fifteen grandchildren when my company, Milbank Packaging, failed. Francie and I added six children to the number. One of our six, Patrick, died of SIDS at three months.

At family parties Annie and I would always find each other and talk about anything and everything. We discussed our children, likes and dislikes, but mostly we discussed the Madigans and how overwhelming it was trying to fit in with this enormous, dynamic, and highly successful family.

I knew when Dan and Annie had a fight: I also knew when and how they made up. I once said to Annie after an argument with Francie, "Sometimes I just don't know how to end the fights."

She immediately replied, "Oh, I know how to end them," and gave me a little mischievous wink.

I consider Annie my best friend. She is my savior from the lovable Madigan madness. As an eldest child, I was used to having my stories listened to, or being asked for advice. Being married to the youngest Madigan put me at a completely different level of importance. I was, along with Francie, considered the baby of the family. I am by nature an introvert and have trouble with large groups. So, to walk into a gathering and have Annie there to talk to kept me sane in the mayhem that was swirling around me.

Francie's family recognized that Annie and I needed each other. Often toward the end of a party, I'd look up from one of our intense conversations and realize we were the only ones left in the room. I confided in Annie more than anyone except Francie. She was the first one to know about my anxiety over Milbank Packaging. We were at a family function when I pulled her aside and said, "Annie, I'm really worried."

Before I could finish my thought she smiled and said, "Ah, c'mon Ken. We're all worried, god, the kids, money—geez, you name it."

She then laid into a story about her own anxiety and how she deals with it. She said that when her fourth son in five years was born she felt overwhelmed and stressed. To relieve the stress she tried to run every day. Half way through the run she usually found herself crying uncontrollably. One day she again had the urge to cry but, instead, without thinking, she half closed her eyes and stretched out her arms as she continued running. A smile came to her face as peace engulfed her body.

She said, "Ken, I felt like an angel, it was as if I was flying, with Jesus looking down on me. For that brief moment my worries left me. I knew they would come back, but for those five minutes I was heavenly."

Ignoring her message of spirituality or running—at the time I was not quite sure which—helping her to relieve tension, I said, "Annie, MPC is struggling." I purposely used the word 'struggling' instead of going broke. I couldn't quite bring myself to admit complete failure, even to Annie.

She looked at me, puzzled. I'm not certain if she truly understood the significance of what I said and I didn't encourage more conversation.

Annie was a family buffer for me. I was truly intimidated by my wife's family. There were times when I felt completely stung by something that happened to me at a family event. It could undo me for months. I was constantly worried about fitting in and very aware of how different my background was from the Madigans.

I'll never forget when my daughter Rose turned thirteen. Not for the happiness of the event, but because of something that happened at her birthday party. As guests began arriving for Rose's party her godfather had not yet called to wish her a happy birthday. Francie was distraught and undecided on whether she should call and remind our friend that it was Rose's birthday. Even the dumbest man knows when his advice is not welcomed; this was one of those times. So, I decided to keep my thoughts to myself. Francie finally made the decision not to call him. After all, as Rose's godfather, Francie felt it was up to him to remember her birthday. This should be important to him.

During dinner, Francie's dad lost his patience with Francie and asked her why she was acting so crabby. Francie said she was upset because Rose's godfather hadn't called to wish her a happy birthday. Well, at this point, for possibly the first time in my life at a Madigan event I decided to say something. Being the good husband, I announced, basically repeating Francie's words of an hour earlier, that, "Francie shouldn't have to call Eric, it's his job to remember Rose's birthday."

Big mistake.

The reaction was quick and fierce. I felt like everyone in the room, including Francie, was now focused on me and felt obligated to explain to me why I was wrong.

"We all have busy lives."

"Eric will feel bad when he realizes he missed Rose on her birthday."

"It's unfair to think that you can remember everyone's birthday," and on and on.

As I tried to regain my composure and get myself under control, Annie grabbed my shoulder and drew me closer to her. She whispered in my ear, "That's what you get for having an opinion; why do you think I swim and exercise so much."

Yes, my savior Annie's kindness was unparalleled and it's what originally drew me to her. However, her rather pleasant looks didn't hurt in adding to my little crush on her. Like the Madigan sisters whom she was often mistaken for, Annie had the typical fair Irish complexion with freckles that danced across her nose when she squinted due to her poor eyesight. Her brownish red hair added to her fresh, wholesome outdoor look. She was so slender that her husband Dan often said it was Annie's waist that first caught his attention during their courtship. Only a man with seven well-endowed and leggy sisters can look past, well, a lot of things, to focus on a woman's waist.

During our conversations, Annie, knowing my anxiety, often told me about this person she was seeing who helped put balance into her life, imparting to her the fundamentals of understanding how to enjoy the things she has and to be happy. I thought the concept of being taught to be happy was insanely odd. I believed that happiness was the result of the events or things around me. I did not think I had control over my happiness. When things or events close to me go well, I am happy or pleased. When they go bad, I am unhappy. So the idea that there was a person who guided people toward happiness was foreign to me. Yet, I did not realize at the time that this person would in the future be responsible for saving my life. I finally relented and asked Annie for the person's name and telephone number. Annie told me her name was Debra O'Shea and rattled off from memory her office number. I wrote it in a perfunctory scribble on the back of a piece of cardboard lying close by. I never imagined I would use it.

When I arrived at work the next day, I threw the cardboard in my top right desk drawer. There it sat hidden among other desk collectables for at least two years. When I had a bad day or someone bothered me, I would open the drawer, pick her number up, look it over, consider a call to Debra, and then toss it right back into the drawer. I never followed through. Fifty-year-old men do not see therapists, especially female therapists. I love Annie, trusted her with my life, but every time I pulled the number out, I immediately knew it was too big of a jump for me. My knowledge of men seeing therapists was always marriage related. I know a number of guys my age who go to therapists with their wives for counseling. Middle-aged men generally are scared shitless of therapists and do not go, no matter how bad they feel. They're afraid of what they might say or worse what might be said to them. I am convinced that men only go with their wives because they are afraid if they don't go they will never get laid again. Just look at the man and not the woman when she tells you that, "Bob and I see Karen every Saturday morning and it has done wonders for our marriage." It's almost as if the man wants to shrug his shoulder and say, "Ken, it's nine in the morning, it's only for an hour, there are no sports on TV yet, and shit man, I really want to get laid on Saturday nights."

I am not sure what specific event made me break through my therapy prejudice and gave me the balls to call Debra. I've often tried to think back to the day or moment that made me pick up the phone and dial her number. Was it a customer call with bad news? A botched order? More likely it was my overall feeling of shittiness created by the impending doom of MPC that I did not quite recognize or fully understand yet. Although I may not have been fully aware of it, MPC had started its descent into chapter 7. Bills were slow to be paid and customer orders were decreasing.

As a result of the company's financial woes the previous two years, Francie and I had put a large amount of our own money into the company. When that did not work, we pledged our house and had the bank write a loan to dump more money into MPC. Finally, some family members helped out by putting money into the general company account. These repeated calls for capital finally caused my bank to decide I should step down as operational manager and concentrate on sales. A series of checks and balances were put in place to track the business's progress on a financial basis. After one year a reevaluation would be completed to determine the financial status of MPC. After the reevaluation the shares of the business would be redistributed and as a result I would lose a portion of my company.

"A smaller percentage of something is better than one hundred percent of nothing," I was told.

I was unceremoniously removed from running MPC. It made me feel extremely shitty about myself. MPC's situation may not have been the cause but it certainly helped bring to light the symptoms of my depression. Enough so that I finally pulled a two year old telephone number out of my top desk drawer and called a therapist for help.

I may not know the exact reason why I phoned, but I do recall most of the events leading up to and including my first conversation with Debra like it was yesterday. I was timorous just making the call. I remember closing my office door so I would not be heard by employees. Jesus, talk about spooking the whole company. I also know that I called at ten in the morning. I realized that once I made the call it would be hard to reverse the course I was setting out for myself. Ironically I got her answering machine. I left a short, timid message, "Hi, my name is Ken Sabino, and my number is 847-234-1212. Uh, please feel free, um, to call me back."

For the next hour or so, I went from hoping she wouldn't return the call to wondering what she looked like based on her voice. What kind of person would Debra be? I thought fat, skinny, old, young, nice or maybe crazy? What kind of person would Annie recommend? Now that I was past the initial phone call, it struck me as weird to be sitting in my office thinking about seeing a therapist. My only knowledge of this field was from books and TV. I had no idea what the true process would be like. Was I exposing myself to some form of goofiness I did not really believe in or understand? One thing I felt certain about was the call was an admission of failure. I wasn't smart enough to diagnose emotions. I just knew I felt like crap.

Was I wasting my time or her time? Was I really anxious or depressed enough to be seeing a therapist? I was fighting an incredible battle of uncertainty, working my fucking nerves into a frenzy once again. Was I being a big baby, concerned about my tendency to overreact to both physical and mental pain?

A recent series of medical tests I had on my stomach was reinforcement to why I had these feelings. My stomach had been sore and gassy for more than a year. With strong encouragement from Francie I went to see Dr. Oberson. During our first meeting, she suggested that I needed a basic checkup to get started. As most men know there are moments in a general physical exam that are humbling regardless of the doctor's gender. Since this was my first time with a woman doctor I was anxious about what I knew was the climax of the exam. I tried to make us both comfortable by telling a few jokes, but never got as much as a comment or smile. Well, finally the time had come for the part of the exam men have been laughing and joking about for centuries: the turn and cough, and the turn around and bend over grand finales.

Suddenly, Dr. Oberson got up and headed for the exit. As she was leaving the room, she asked me to undress from the waist down. No emotion, it was the same as when I asked an employee to weld two wires together. It was her job. Doing as I was told, I completely undressed except for a tee shirt. I stood there in all my glory, waiting for Dr. Oberson to return; it was a little nerve racking, to say the least. I was also hoping like hell I would be properly represented as a man down below, when in walked the good doctor. She went over to a cabinet, took out rubber gloves and put them on. Turning toward me Oberson looked me up and down, not skipping anything and said, "You have some really nice strong knees."

I still do not know to this day whether this was telling a joke or if she really thought I had nice knees. I do know my male friends laugh at the story and my female friends think I'm an idiot.

I saw Dr. Oberson for a series of exams over the next three months.

After every test she called to say the test was negative, and then she would suggest a new one. I had just about reached my frustration level, when Francie read about lactose intolerance in Marilu Henner's health book. She said the described symptoms were exactly like mine. During my next visit to Dr. Oberson, I asked about the possibility of being lactose intolerant.

She said, "Why not, we've tried almost everything else."

I stopped eating dairy products and the stomach pains ceased immediately. After spending ten thousand dollars on medical tests and having my wife discover that I should be taking tablets I can buy over the counter at Walgreen's for five dollars and ninety-eight cents made me cautious about calling another health professional—like a therapist.

I did not want to go through the same exercise in frustration with Debra, a female therapist for God's sake, that I went through with Dr. Oberson. I sat at my desk and convinced myself there were only two possible outcomes, I was sane and reasonably happy, and this is all life had to offer. Or, I was insane and depressed, so get ready for years of therapy and expense. The two choices seemed equally dismal.

During my lunch, Debra called me back. I felt like I was back in high school asking the queen of the prom out on a Friday night date. I was sweaty, nervous, and my voice cracked a bit.

Debra asked me a few questions. How did I find out about her?

"Annie, ah, yes Annie. She's a wonderful person, isn't she?"

What was bothering me? I told her about my work situation and how this situation has made me moody, anxious, and generally unhappy. It was also affecting my marriage, my relationship with my children, and my overall demeanor. It was preventing me from living a fulfilling life.

"Well, we can't have that, can we? Would you like to come in Wednesday at six?"

I thought about making an excuse, but somehow I sensed it was futile. Debra was not going to let me off the hook. I hesitated a second and then answered, "Okay."

So that was it? It was that simple and that fast. It was the start of my relationship with Debra. From that moment on, I was a person who felt he had enough problems to seek out a therapist.

FOUR

Driving north on the Edens Expressway that night, I told myself I was seeing a therapist and there was no turning back. I was anxious but surprisingly excited, and knew I was going to keep the fact that I was seeing Debra a secret, from almost everyone. To this day no one except Francie, not even Annie, knows that Debra and I have been meeting for over a year. It took me almost six-months to tell Francie and even that was done somewhat by accident.

Francie never asks me about my time with Debra. I'm sure she does not know where her office is, what she looks like or even her name. It's as if she senses that it's my way of staying sane as I watch my life completely unravel. I'm not sure if I'm ashamed about seeing a therapist or if I just didn't want this to be something that I constantly have to discuss.

Sports used to be my method of unwinding. At the gym, I ran around for a few hours, swore, argued, joked with the boys, and then returned home feeling revived. Tired, but revived nonetheless. Those were the days when problems were simpler, like being mad at a boss because my review did not go as well as I expected. I now felt my problems were much deeper, warranting help from a professional. I could no longer control my anxiety.

I wondered, before the first session: What we would talk about? What is the process? How do you get started? Am I really depressed? Am I crazy? I wondered if Debra would tell me that I am normal, go home and be a good husband, Dad, or friend. I again tried to imagine what Debra would look like? How would she act toward me?

While driving, I recalled how Annie, when we first talked about Debra, said, "She may be too womanish for you. Ah, but Ken, you think like a chick though, don't you?"

A lot of times Annie would introduce me to a female acquaintance and say, "You can talk to Ken, he listens like a chick." Annie was right; I loved talking with and being around women and listening to their stories.

College is where I first learned to be comfortable with women as friends. Until 1973, Manhattanville was a Sacred Heart Women's Catholic College. The school catered to the daughters of mostly wealthy Catholic families. Rose Kennedy, Eunice Kennedy Shriver, Jean Kennedy Smith, Ted Kennedy's wife Joan Bennett, and Robert Kennedy's wife Ethel Skakel all attended Manhattanville. Francie's mom and two of her older sisters graduated from Manhattanville, which is in part why Francie decided to go there. When I arrived in 1976, the school had not yet evened up the sides. There were four girls for every guy.

I loved college and remember how depressed I was right before graduation, knowing that I was leaving for good. Maybe that was a sign I should have been in therapy a long time ago. I was moping around, in my dorm room, when my friend Murph came by and said, "C'mon, let's go for a walk."

Manhattanville had a large wooded area directly behind one of the dormitories. The woods had paths with benches made of rock and religious statues scattered throughout.

During the walk, which was mostly silent, Murph glanced at me and asked, "Sabino, what exactly has you acting like such an ass?"

I told him, "Murph, I'm graduating and Francie's moving back home to Chicago. I'm not sure if I should get a job here in New York or in Chicago. I'm sorta panicked. I'm not ready for this real world shit."

He rubbed his cheek, nodded his head up and down a little and said nothing as we continued walking. Finally, impatience got to me so I turned to him and asked, "Well, Murph, don't you have any advice?"

He looked at me in all seriousness. "Yeah, as a matter of fact, I do. Always keep in mind that when you walk off this campus, you're going to be ugly again."

Truer words had not been spoken; I was living in a male's perfect dream world. Even ugly men get dates when the odds are four to one. It took me right out of my depression. All week long we chanted, "Ken is going to be ugly again. Murph gets ugly in 1980."

At a family wedding, years later, the photographer took group pictures. Both of the mothers were Manhattanville alumni. The groom's dad, and the bride and groom graduated from Holy Cross. The Holy Cross contingent gathered first in front of the stage. Thirty to forty people, mostly men, ran out to the dance floor, jackets off, beers in hand, hooting and hollering. After their picture was taken, the band leader announced, "Will all the Manhattanville graduates now kindly come to the stage area for a group photo."

Francie's eighty-year-old mother, followed by the bride's and groom's moms, my sisters-in-law, Francie's aunt, Francie and ten to fifteen other well-dressed women made their graceful way to the staging area. The photographer saw me and asked if I would kindly move to the side. I let him know that I was a proud Manhattanville graduate. He immediately got it and gestured me to take a place right in the middle. One of Francie's brothers saw this, leaned over to another brother-in-law and said, "Maybe Ken's not so dumb after all."

FIVE

Will Debra be able to give me advice as good as Murph's?—the kind of advice that will immediately put me in a proper frame of mind? Will she snap her fingers and pull me out of my depressed state and put enjoyment back in my life? Will she teach me to be happy? Well, I naively thought I was about to discover all this out in the next hour. I'll march in, tell Debra how I feel, what's bothering me, and let her recommend a cure or method to change my negative feelings to positive ones.

I exited the highway at Lake Avenue in Wilmette and was almost at Debra's. Her office is on Greenwood Avenue a half mile from my house. I had driven, walked, or run by her office thousands of time without ever dreaming it would someday become my sanctuary. I tried to park a little off the beaten path. I was worried Francie or Annie would drive by and see my car. Francie would wonder what I was doing home and Annie would know I was at Debra's. Even walking to the office filled me with anxiety. Being this close to home I was sure to run into someone I know.

"Hey, Ken, what and how are you doing?" would come the awkward query, with, "Oh, just fine, my company is going bankrupt and I'm here to see a therapist. How 'bout you?" being my equally inept and sorry reply.

I opened the door to her building and entered the little foyer at the bottom of the stairs. I looked at the row of mail boxes to see what floor Debra O'Shea's office was on. I walked up the stairs to the second and only floor accessible by this stairway. The first floor is a storefront. I have never bothered to see what type of store. Maybe it's because I always rush to get inside unnoticed. The second floor has four offices. Debra's is the one furthest down the hallway, room number four. The door, with her name and a bunch of letters indicating her degrees was slightly ajar. Should I knock? I decided to nudge the door open and walked into a waiting area. There was a couch against the back wall. In front of it was a table with a bunch of Time magazines and a book titled, *What my Therapist Thinks*. On the wall directly across from the couch were two photos: a city scene and a beach scene. Under the photos were two small chairs. A table with a bunch of fancy teabags sat between the chairs. I have since learned that the city is San Francisco and the beach is Carmel by the Sea. To my left I saw a bathroom. It was a simply decorated room. I stood there thinking how weird this was; *What My Therapist Thinks*? What the fuck am I thinking? Then out of a second door shot Debra, "Hi Ken." I saw the woman in whom I was about to entrust my soul for the first time.

First impressions are always great. I never see the person I was expecting. If I thought someone would be thin and dark, they usually turn out to be large and fair skinned. Although quite different than I imagined, Debra was not in any way a letdown. I'd have to say that she was the opposite. She is a rather attractive woman whom I could tell was a fox—do people still say fox?—in her day. But it was not her looks that jumped out at me. It was obvious she had an enormous appetite for life. Her whole manner, her walk, her voice, the way she dressed, reflected a life-is-good attitude. She had a spunk about her that was evident as soon as she popped out toward me. She extended her hand, shook mine and said, "Come in. Can I get you anything to drink?" A question I would get used to hearing every Wednesday at six p.m.

I cautiously entered the second room, which was twice as big as the waiting area. I half thought to myself, there is still time to run out of here. But then a feeling of peace settled over me as I scanned the room. There was a black leather couch against the far back wall. In front of and off to each side of it stood two upright chairs. A cheap-looking table, with a candle on it, sat in front of the couch and between the two chairs. Next to the couch on both sides were small side tables, one with a bible, the other a bowl of candy. Above the sofa was a large Japanese-like style of art. The furniture was okay, a little down to earth but practical. Opposite the couch, a four-tiered bookshelf was set against the wall.

If I sat on the couch, I would be looking at a number of books on the shelves, a great deal of them about and by Carl Jung. There were also Chinese statues, weird pictures, a figurine of Saint Teresa of Avila, and a funny looking doll. The doll is about twelve inches high, dressed in a long black formal gown with a furry white stole wrapped around her neck. Her hands are covered in elegant white gloves and on her head is a stylish black hat with a feather shooting out of it. What grabs you most is her totally frightening face. It is completely out of character with the rest of the doll. Even in an office with a lot going on, it's impossible not to notice this doll.

I finally let my eyes wander away from the doll. On each side of the bookshelf, diplomas, and certificates from different schools hung on the walls. A picture of Carl Jung was prominently displayed in between the many accreditations. Against the left wall sat a desk with a computer, printer, phone, a bunch of disheveled papers, and a statue of Mary on it. Next to the desk was a second door where patients could exit unnoticed. It was a relief to learn that Debra would not release a patient until the person with the next time slot was settled in the outer room.

Debra directed me to the chair furthest away from the desk and invited me to sit down. I could officially say I had seen a therapist.

SIX

On Wednesdays, throughout the day, I gave myself little pep talks to make sure I maximized my hour that night with Debra. All week long I jotted down notes of the things I wanted to talk about. Notes on how I felt, what bothered me during the past week, my relationship with Francie, anything that I thought would help Debra do her job of analyzing me. I came to the sessions with my dreams and notes neatly written down, with an extra copy for Debra.

When I arrived at Debra's building at six p.m., I would run up the stairs leading to her office, full of enthusiasm. When I came through the door into the outside office, Debra sometimes stood there waiting for me. Most of the time, however, she was sitting in her chair in the second office, reading a book or some of my past dreams. She always jumped up and asked me, "How are you doing," immediately followed with, "I ask you that every week don't I? It's such a silly question for a therapist. Can I get you something to drink?"

I would always decline her offer. My hour had begun.

"Well, Ken, how was your week?" she would say.

I'd slump in my chair and answer, "Fine. Uh, okay, I guess."

"Is there anything you'd like to talk about?"

"No, not really."

"Well, then, let's read a dream or two."

Debra's method of therapy was based on the teachings of Carl Jung. Jung, she explained early in our meetings, was a Swiss psychiatrist who was born in 1875 and died in 1961. He was a one-time friend and contemporary of Sigmund Freud. He broke with Freud because of a difference in how to understand a person's mental state. One of the ways that Jung thought a person should be analyzed was by exploring the world of dreams.

Since I was not offering much during the sessions, Debra made a point of making me read my dreams out loud. She always asked me to pick one or two. Sometimes, when I really was not talking, Debra made me read every dream. She listened intently while reading silently along. When I finished reading, Debra would slowly take her glasses off, put them on the table next to her, lean back in her chair, and look directly at me. She would then try to lead me into a discussion about the dream.

Looking back, I'm amazed at how tense and guarded I was with Debra during those early sessions. I sat across from her and found myself fidgeting with the papers that had my dreams written on them. I consciously avoided eye contact while answering certain questions. Most of all I was very careful and calculated with the responses I gave to

Debra. I was unsettled by the intimacy of some of her queries, especially so early in a professional relationship.

The dreams were Debra's chance to understand what my unconscious mind was thinking. For her they revealed secrets about me that I may have never thought about, let alone discussed openly. The dreams were meant to be the basis for discussion. Yet, I found myself clamming up right after reading them. It was arduous for me to talk about myself, especially about my problems and weaknesses. Debra was more of an open book. Over the course of our initial sessions I learned all about her. I knew where her husband Matt worked. I knew that she and Matt met at Stanford. I knew her kids' names, their ages, and where they went to school. I knew about her dad and how he made his riches when Debra was in high school. I knew about her eighty-year-old mom and her mom's boyfriend. About the time Debra said the boyfriend was a fucking ass-hole while riding in the car with her mom and discovering her mom's speaker phone was still on. How the boyfriend hung up on his end and never brought the subject up. I knew when and where she was going on vacation. I even knew they were going to the Stanford-Notre Dame football game the next weekend. I knew her favorite singing groups. But it was more than superficial things.

Debra assured me I did not have to be afraid to share my thoughts. I explained that part of my problem was I had been a forty-two regular my whole life. There are no great and exciting stories. She smiled and said, "That's not always bad."

After reading a dream during one session, there was complete silence. I did not want to talk and from time to time Debra respected that. There could be silence between us for up to thirty seconds. When I say thirty seconds it sounds like a brief time, but sitting in my therapist's office as she stared at me made it feel more like a year. Plus, my mind would instantly start racing, thinking mostly, at least for me, of negative thoughts. It was reminiscent of Sundays during mass when I was young, high school age, listening to the priest's sermon. Every once in a while our parish priest would purposely pause for effect during their homilies.

For example, he might say something like, "If you don't give generously during the collection you will rot with sinners in *hell.*"

Long pause.

I would immediately start to think, Shit, I only gave a dime last week. Now I'm going to rot in hell. Fuck, I thought of the word shit in church, now I'm really screwed. Oh shit, I thought of the word fuck. God, I know You can hear my thoughts. God, I'm really, really sorry for thinking of the words shit and fuck in church. Please forgive me.

I would then be startled out of it by the priest booming out, "So give generously to Saint Roch Catholic Church and your reward will be to sit by God and His angels in the kingdom of heaven."

Ah fuck, I only have a dime. "Psst. Hey, Marty, do you have a quarter I can borrow?"

I snapped out of my church thoughts when I noticed Debra looking down, and then looking directly at me again. I had now seen this enough to know she was about to tell me a story. I loved hearing her stories, they were always funny, entertaining, and out of character.

"Ken, when I first arrived at Stanford I met and fell in love with this man. His name was Henry. My husband Matt knows about Henry and loved him too. I actually thought that he might be the man for me. We were inseparable. We went out together, studied together, did most everything together. After dating or being with Henry for a month I began to wonder why he never tried to kiss or touch me. I was young and ready to be with Henry. I would try coming on to him from time to time and he would make an excuse. This was thirty years ago, so homosexuality was not as open or discussed as it is today. I never initially imagined that Henry could be gay. Finally, I confronted him about his lack of intimacy and he admitted his sexual preference. I was shocked, learning that the man I was in love with was gay. I was determined not to let it ruin our friendship. We stayed close through and after college. Henry contracted AIDS and died at the age of thirty-six."

I was half right. The story was out of character, but not funny at all. We both sat silently looking across at each other. I thought we both were going to cry.

Since the session was close to being over, I stood up and began to walk out the back door. Just before leaving, I turned to Debra and said, "I don't have a story like that, and you're right … that's not such a bad thing."

After leaving Debra's office I would get into my car furious with myself. I felt like I had just wasted an hour and a hundred and fifty dollars. I wanted to talk, to let her know my feelings, and tell her all about me. I wanted to let her know how hard work was, that even a ten to thirty percent chance of going broke was real and frightening. The story about Henry stirred an emotion in me. I was initially thinking of Henry, but then found myself contemplating my son Patrick instead. Why didn't I tell her about the hardship his death created? Debra gave me an opening, God damn it! Why didn't I take advantage of it? Ah, fuck it. I should've told her that, even though Francie and I got through Patrick's death, we still have our differences and argue. I'm leading a life I cannot stand. How could Debra tell me a story about her friend Henry so early on in our relationship? I should be the one telling her stories. At times I felt like I was going to have a nervous breakdown. At other times I wondered what kept drawing me back into the room every Wednesday to sit with the pictures of harmony and tranquility hanging on the wall behind me.

SEVEN

It was well into our sessions when the talking gradually switched from Debra to me. Thinking back, I now know why Debra told me her stories. She knew we had to become intimate. She even warned me that doctor and patient have to be careful not to cross the line. That they often end up having intimate feelings for each other. She was right. I soon grew fond of her and could see how I could like her even more. Part of my problem with opening up to Debra was my fear of showing my weakness, or giving her a reason to not like or respect me. She knew she would have to expose herself to me. There was nothing subtle about it. She might as well have walked into the room nude. She was baring her soul. She did not hesitate to tell me intimate stories, sad stories, happy stories, anything she felt like. Debra was never embarrassed during or after a story. In one early session I, half as an aside, sort of mumbled that Francie and I argue once in a while.

"That's normal isn't it, Ken? You know, I once threw a pan at Matt," she said and then started laughing at her own recounting.

I tried to talk myself into believing it was worth the time and money to just go and sit with Debra. To hear her laugh, tell stories, and give me the opportunity to discuss what was on my mind. She often gave me books to read. One of the earlier books was about interpreting dreams. Another was *Eat, Pray, Love* by Elizabeth Gilbert. I read them voraciously, making sure I had read the whole book before our next session. I jotted down notes and tried to remember important events. I did not want to disappoint Debra. I was always amazed at how appropriate the book was for that particular moment of my mental and physical state.

I'd say, "How'd you know to pick that book?"

She'd answer, "Oh, my niece thought I would like it, so I thought you would like it."

I always wondered, Was it an arbitrary selection? Was it really only her niece thinking *Eat, Pray, Love* was a book Debra would like? It was too perfect.

I also wanted to be perfect with my dream recording. I trained myself to wake up after each dream and, without disturbing Francie, run into the bathroom and write as much of the dream down as I could remember, with as much detail as possible. I felt like I'd let Debra and myself down if I did not have plenty of dreams to discuss. I was disappointed if I arrived on a Wednesday with only two or three dreams. I always wanted to have seven and was only satisfied with at least four. But it's hard to record dreams. I am amazed at how many times I had a dream, remembered the dream, woke up and reviewed it in my mind, only to have the dream totally escape me the next morning. I wanted to be the perfect 'insane, depressed' patient. Debra often said to me, "Ken, don't worry so much about your dreams. Even if you came in here with one or two lines from one dream, we could discuss that. You can come here with no dreams at all and we'd be okay."

She had the same attitude about everything we did. Debra might recommend a task for me, such as, "Ken, for next week, why don't you write down one happy event in your early life and one sad." I'd pull out a piece of paper and intently write down the task, like it was a homework assignment.

She'd look at me amused and say, "Now you know, you can come here having written a lot, a little, or, if you want … nothing at all." There were no rules, no obligations.

After each session I went home and tried to figure out the process. What was going on? Was I hindering the procedure by my inability to open up? How long does this take? Am I depressed, insane, sane, sad, or normal? Not knowing the answer was driving me crazy. Why aren't there rules? Why is she recommending books she thinks I will like and not ones to help me get cured? Is she not taking me seriously?

The process was all foreign to me. I believed that seeing Debra initially increased my depression. I was depressed about being depressed.

A number of times I thought about quitting my sessions with Debra during those early months. But something kept drawing me back. I know I was worried sick about MPC and its possible ruin, but it was more than worry that made me return every Wednesday. I had to sit in that office with Debra. It became a sanctuary. It became my place. No Francie, no children, no work, nothing. Just Debra and me telling a few stories and working out a few problems. It was like meeting an old friend for coffee on a Wednesday afternoon before going home to see the wife and kids. The big difference was I paid a lot for the cup of coffee and I was keeping our meetings secret from everyone … including Francie.

EIGHT

One session, trying to mollify me, Debra blurted out, "You do understand that you're not responsible for the World Economy?"

She was right; a lot of MPC's problems were exacerbated by the movement of manufacturing, particularly packaging production, to the Far East. After 9/11/2001 there were two significant events that helped lead US manufacturing down this path. One of the sidebars to the terrible tragedy of the terrorist attack on the US was we were dragged into the emerging global economy. The second and lesser known fact that occurred around this time was the Republic of China signed the World Trade Agreement and, like the USA, became a part of the global economic community. The country with the largest population in the world not only decided to become a part of the world economy, but to become the dominant partner.

The Chinese were quick learners. In virtually no time they were able to build an infrastructure and a number of factories that manufactured a wide variety of products. As a result of the low costs of their never-ending labor supply, they were able to offer manufactured goods to the world markets at a fraction of the cost of US and European manufacturers. Any US manufacturer that produced labor-intensive goods was at a major disadvantage when competing directly against Chinese manufactured goods. All packaging goods are labor intensive and as a result they were one of the first industries to be threatened by Chinese manufacturers.

I looked up at Debra and said, "Still, I saw and understood the Chinese threat and didn't react to it. It was my managerial missteps that got me relegated to the role of a salesman in my own company."

MPC was in bad financial shape as the end of 2006 approached. It barely paid vendors, its accounting records were in a shambles, and it had trouble meeting customer deadlines. All these issues had me sliding more and more into a depressed state when MPC accidentally happened upon a big revenue source from a large marketing company. While designing a new display project, the company uncharacteristically hired an outside engineer to assist with ideas. The engineer's wife worked as a teacher with Francie.

The company ended up giving us an order that was the largest in MPC's history and more than enough to compensate for the loss of revenues going to China. The order had the potential to double, possibly triple over the next two years. We laid all our hopes on this one new customer. It was the biggest—and really the only—thing that had to be tracked over the next six months. Would MPC be able to handle an order this size and would the order make money? It would ultimately decide whether MPC remained open or had its doors closed forever. We needed the order to either immediately generate cash flow or to at least put MPC in a position where it could make money on the anticipated reorders. One thing we all knew was MPC could not continue to run in place; it needed to start becoming profitable.

But, to me, the timing was bad and an event that should have been joyous was not. So in spite of market conditions, MPC was in a position to succeed. But I was angry I'd have to share the rewards. I had secured the potentially large customer, after my company was reorganized.

In spite of the order, I was still confused and worried about MPC's chances of survival. I was upset about losing power within my own company. And, I knew that landing the new customer masked fundamental problems at MPC and within our industry.

During most sessions Debra would ask me, "What do you think the percentage is that MPC will succeed?"

My answer depended wholly on how I thought the new order was going or what I saw as the potential of it increasing in the future. If I was informed our raw material purchases were high or if the customer gave me an optimistic forecast of an anticipated order increase, I'd answer, "Maybe, ninety plus per cent."

If there were purchase complaints, distribution problems, or a pessimistic tone from the customer, my percentage would be lower. I always tried to answer with what I really thought the company's chances of survival were. It was always a thought out answer. In the case of negative feedback, I usually estimated that MPC had a seventy to eighty percent chance of survival.

No matter what I answered, Debra looked at me and would rhetorically ask, "Well, that's good isn't it?"

It was. It wasn't until well into our sessions that I started to have serious reservations about receiving an order increase from our new customer.

NINE

I use to love the fall. It was like a new beginning. I know that most people associate spring with this feeling, but not me. I love the start of a new school year, the new football season, the start of baseball playoffs, fall parties like Oktoberfest, hockey and basketball beginning anew, and the beginning of a new holiday season starting with Halloween continuing through Thanksgiving. Each fall I looked forward to when the *Chicago Tribune* printed the poem 'Indian Summer' by John T. McCutcheon. They first printed the poem in 1907, but had to discontinue it in 1992—I learned it was because of its offensive nature to Native Americans. I never knew it was offensive because I never read the words closely. I just remember the cartoon picture of the little boy with his dad or granddad watching a pile of leaves burn. It reminded me of fall days growing up, being with my dad while he raked and burned leaves. Like the poem, burning leaves is a tradition I will never be able to share with my children.

Each Halloween, Francie and I invited a number of friends and relatives, mostly relatives, and their kids, over after trick or treating for a big soup fest and candy exchange. If we were lucky there was a college or professional football game on TV.

Unlike most kids, I always considered Thanksgiving, not Christmas, as my favorite holiday. I remember the Macy Day Parade, *The March of the Wooden Soldiers* with Laurel and Hardy, watching and listening to my dad and uncles discussing football, especially those "god damn, shitty New York Giants," a meal with family and friends, and finally ending the day by sitting and watching *It's a Wonderful Life* with Jimmy Stewart and Donna Reed. The classic film by Frank Capra was made in 1946. At the time of its release the movie did not do as well as expected and was considered a flop. Yet, years later it began turning up on numerous TV stations throughout the United States, mostly around Thanksgiving and Christmas. It began to get a cult following and I understand now it's listed number eleven on the American Film Institute list of the hundred best American movies .

During one session, Debra asked me to pick a movie to compare to my life with. I picked *It's a Wonderful Life* thinking of all its sad parts, the building and loan almost failing, and George Bailey being depressed enough to want to kill himself. It all seemed so real to me now and not as funny as when I watched with my parents and then my children.

Debra, after I answered, said, "God, that's great Ken. What a great movie to pick. See, you have hope. Everything works out at the end of the movie. I'm positive it's going to work out for you."

All I could say was, "I hope I find my Clarence."

But ultimately Debra was right about one thing: the reason I like that movie so much is not because of the sadness but because of its happy ending.

When I think of *It's a Wonderful Life* I am reminded of what I once thought was an amusing story. Francie had a high school friend named Charlie Leibrandt who went on to play professional baseball for the Cincinnati Reds, the Kansas City Royals, and finally the Atlanta Braves. He was lucky enough to have played in a number of baseball playoff and World Series games. Francie, her friends, and I followed Charlie religiously. Every time he came to play a Chicago team we went to the game. We even went to games in Cincinnati and Kansas City. When Kansas City played Detroit in the 1984 playoffs, we drove to Detroit to watch Charlie pitch in a classic three hit, 1-0 deciding game against Milt Wilcox of Detroit, who also only gave up three hits. The only run Charlie allowed was on a botched double play.

I am a big sports fan, especially baseball. Yet, I am nothing compared to my father-in-law. He is a dyed-in-the-wool Chicago Cubs fan who watched their games on TV regularly. One day while I was watching the Cubs with my brother-in-law, George, and Francie's dad, announcers Harry Caray and Steve Stone brought up Charlie Leibrandt's name during their broadcast on WGN.

My brother-in-law, upon hearing Charlie's name, turned to his dad and said, "Dad, in the movie *It's a Wonderful Life* remember the part where Clarence the angel finally brings George Bailey to see his wife Mary and she's a spinster librarian?"

"Yes. Ahh, he always strikes out with men on base," Francie's dad answered, more interested in the game than George's question.

"Well, when Ken's guardian angel shows him Francie, she's not going to be a spinster but instead married to Charlie Leibrandt and living in a big mansion on the lake."

There was a full two to five seconds of complete silence. I thought I saw my father-in-law glance upward, his expression I interpreted as him thinking, Geez, that wouldn't be so bad, free tickets, maybe meet some players. He suddenly turned to George and said, "No, no, no, we like Ken." George always teasingly—I think?—reminds me of that story.

The worst part of losing everything is not what I have done to myself, but what I did to everyone else, especially my wife and kids. It is as if a tornado came through my life, leaving behind a path of destruction. I almost wish Clarence would show me the lake house with Francie there, sipping tea, reading a book, sitting by the fireplace with Charlie. No cares, no worries. Through no fault of her own, I was about to take Francie down a road that no one deserved.

The fall of 2007 was about to change not only how I viewed the autumn season, but how I viewed life itself. It all started with a meeting I set up with the owner of my new biggest customer, Monday, October 29, 2007—at ten a.m. in Palatine, Illinois, to be precise. I was a little nervous all weekend. The previous Friday, my general manager and I spent the whole day rehearsing the information we wanted to obtain from the customer. The timing of the new order, how many units will be bought, a distribution and ship schedule, any engineering changes, anything to help us set financial goals.

MPC, at the time of the meeting, was a small manufacturing concern with about forty employees, mostly Mexican immigrants. The previous year we sold about 4.5 million dollars worth of fabricated packaging products such as baskets, containers, point of purchase displays and shelves. Most of our work was done for three industries: food service, healthcare, and point of purchase—POP. To the food service industry we sold a number of items that ended up in Burger King, McDonalds and other fast food restaurants. Our health care items were scattered throughout hospitals all over the United States. The customer I was about to meet with was in the POP industry. This was the customer that I'd recently found through Francie.

The POP industry included companies that produced in-store point of purchase displays that promote a customer's product. Almost every store you go into has a POP display. They can be as simple as a small cardboard item on a counter promoting a product. They can also be complicated and much larger, such as POP displays seen in Home Depot promoting a variety of items from paints to lawn tools. The job I was meeting about this particular morning was a large, involved display that would be sold for over a thousand dollars each. We made a thousand of these displays from the end of 2006 through the first quarter of 2007. It was the largest purchase order in MPC's thirty year history. This order and its subsequent reruns were MPC's life saver.

The initial order of a thousand display units was called 'Release I' of the total marketing roll out. Earlier in the year I was told that at least two thousand more display units called 'Release II' were scheduled for delivery for the remainder of 2007 and into 2008. Then there was a potential for an additional five hundred display units, or 'Release III', scheduled to be ordered after all of 'Release II' items were delivered. If this was true, there would be no looking back—MPC would turn the corner. My financial dreams would become a reality. I was on the verge of the American Dream. I was about to receive an almost guaranteed 3.5 million dollars in business over the course of the next three years for one product.

After analysis we felt we would at best break even on the initial thousand display units. This was not a major concern, because we also knew there would be a learning curve on making, packing, and delivering the display units. We understood and had already corrected any cost overruns. We were now set up to make a killing on the next twenty-five hundred display units. That is what my meeting was about, the next twenty-five hundred units. Initially, it was hoped by my management team, and the bank, that Release II and possibly even Release III would have happened by mid summer of 2007 and last through 2008. This would have provided a much needed infusion of cash and allowed more than enough time to find new customers. I asked my contact all summer long about the additional release orders and usually received an answer along the lines of, "Once the first thousand units of Release I ship, the next two thousand units of Release II will be ordered immediately."

Since by early October 2007 we had shipped all but two hundred of the initial thousand units of Release I, I recommended to the customer that we meet to discuss Release II. This would give us the much needed logistical time to set ourselves up to manufacture and assemble an additional two thousand units as the final Release I items were delivered. The customer agreed and the meeting date and time was arranged.

I don't recall much about the meeting except my contact Larry telling me, "Although statistics prove the effectiveness of the displays, our customer lost tens of millions of dollars last year. They have to cut costs wherever they can and, as a result, we are not getting any more display orders from them for the foreseeable future." I remember him shrugging, and finishing the devastating news with, "The downturn in the housing market—it's killing lots of ancillary businesses, also—that's the main reason for this, um … *change* of plans."

It's a funny feeling when the body goes numb. Like an out of body experience. I heard and answered questions, most of the time correctly. I shook the guy's hand goodbye. I left the meeting room, took the elevator to the first floor, walked to the parking lot and got in my car. I eventually drove away. When my composure returned, minutes after driving away, I realized all those exodus movements had been done instinctively and not consciously. It's similar to driving on a highway, and all of a sudden noticing I'm in a different lane or on a different road altogether and not being able to remember how I got there. I was in that zone. One thing I recognized for sure was that what I had just heard was going to change my life forever. While I knew the change was for the worse, I could never have guessed to what extent.

I sat in the car in our company's customer parking lot for at least fifteen minutes, trying to absorb the news. I was shaking—trying to convince myself there was a way out of this. I took a few deep breaths and said aloud, "Shit, Ken. Pull yourself together."

I had other customer orders pending. We could look to cut costs and we certainly would have to let employees go. But I knew the information I had just heard would not be well received by the bank. I understood that unless I made a compelling argument, one that I believed as well, this news would severely test everyone's patience. I realized MPC was at great risk of being closed. I left the parking lot, turned on to East Dundee Road toward Route 53, picked up my cell phone and called my general manager. I told him the news; he uncharacteristically listened patiently. He then said, "Ken, we just finished the September thirtieth quarter end inventory and it's down a half mil."

The advancement of MPC's being at great risk of closing, to the harsh reality of it being officially over, came with the inventory news. We'd already had enormous trouble with cash flow. We could not afford to lose potential revenue of over a million a year plus take a half million dollar hit in borrowing power. Essentially, I might as well have been informed, "You owe the bank a quarter of a million dollars or half of the 500 thousand dollar inventory loss that was pledged as collateral." The bank would require either additional collateral to cover the inventory loss or their money immediately. I did not have the means to get the bank either the collateral or their money. It was the equivalent of a stock margin being called.

I entered Route 53 going south back toward the Bensenville factory. In a fit of rancorous rage I yelled, "It's over, it's over, god dammit, fuck, shit, I fucking hate life, it's fucking over!"

Why, why, why? I tried to keep myself calm, but could not.

I had to call George. I wanted to notify him prior to telling the bank. George and the other family members who helped to keep MPC solvent with large loans a couple of years back deserved to know the state of affairs at once. As a part of the reorganization they were also on the hook for additional pledged sums of money. It made me sick, but as family members they were the first ones I had to be man enough to tell that I would soon be screwing them as well as a host of others. Also, as a part of the new structure, George had been asked by the bank to work with me as an advisor. For someone outside the company, he had the most intimate knowledge of MPC. I wanted to be alert for the call, so I pulled off the highway on to the shoulder and began to dial George's cell phone.

"Hey, George, it's Ken."

He almost always answered the same way, with a half shout of your name. "Ken."

"George, I was just with Larry. There's not going to be a Release II for the display units. Also, we just finished the September inventory and it's down quite a bit."

"How much?"

"Half a million."

"Shit."

"Yeah. I don't know what to do."

"Well, we have to tell Callahan." George always said we or us, never you, even though what he meant was I had to call Callahan.

The Callahan he was referring to was Bert Callahan, a tall, lanky Scotsman who was president of the bank that had lent me millions of dollars. There was an infatuation with Callahan among my brothers-in-law that I could never quite understand. I found him to be pompous, standoffish, and somewhat of a braggart. I always left meetings with him full of facts about his children or the latest manner in which he had spent money. When I first moved to the North Shore I was amazed by the number of people who let you know five minutes into a conversation that they or their spouse were a doctor. Or, how someone just redecorated a home, bought a second summer house, or came back from some exotic vacation. It was life's scorecard for people like Bert and those on the North Shore. They wanted—no, needed—people to know of their successes and business prowess. Callahan also said some things to me a year earlier that I thought were mean spirited. My brothers-in-law liked him and tried to convince me to do the same with comments like, "He's a nice guy," or "his wife volunteers for charities."

I'd reply, "He treats you guys differently than me. You're good customers and I am a bad customer." I didn't care for Bert. It made me dislike him even more that my brothers-in-law were so fond of him.

"I know. I'll call him right now," I said.

My hell had begun. That night I dreamt I was standing in a lake with water rising up to drown me. The dream revealed to me the one person who could save me.

TEN

The first time I considered suicide as an option was after my first meeting with the bank when I knew MPC was going to fail. It was Friday, November 23, 2007, the day after Thanksgiving—my favorite holiday. So much for having a favorite holiday.

Thanksgiving weekend started out in a very positive manner in spite of my situation. I was ready for the four days off. On Wednesday, our nineteen-year-old son, Bernie, who was home from Bellarmine College, was playing music with his band. Their group included Annie's son, and they were performing at Cortland's Garage —a neighborhood bar in Bucktown.

That night, Bernie's band played a variety of songs: a lot by Wilco, Van Morrison, Johnny Cash, and several songs they had written themselves. The bar was packed elbow to elbow. One advantage of a large extended family is you will always draw a crowd. All the Sabinos were there. Tony collected money at the door. Katie and Dominic, just in town from college, brought all their friends. They of course were of drinking age, so The Garage would see the advantages of having Platform 29 perform and hopefully ask them back. Even fifteen-year-old Rose and her New Trier classmates were allowed to watch the band and were right up in front of the stage dancing and singing along with the lead singer. I loved watching Bernie perform. It was another subject Annie and I talked about constantly. I did not want the night to end. I found that as the night progressed, I had too much to drink. I excused it away by saying to myself, "You need to let your hair down. It's been a tough month."

The next day the kids and I played in our annual Turkey Bowl football game, had Thanksgiving dinner at our home with only our immediate family for the first time ever, and then went over to Francie's sister's house, where we usually celebrated Thanksgiving dinner, for dessert. The dessert at the Warner's is always preceded by a Pumpkin Pie contest between Andy Warner, our brother-in-law, and Francie's sister, Eileen. The winner gets to claim a turkey hat for the year as well as bragging rights. I sat at the end of the long dining room table and took in with amusement the battle for pumpkin pie superiority. I was right, the four days off were well needed and already beginning to pay off.

As the contest continued, I felt calm for the first time in quite a while. This was despite the slight uneasiness I felt throughout the evening being with Andy and Tim. Not much had been said about the money I had borrowed from them. Words were not needed. My own sense of failure and having let them down was enough for now.

On the Friday after Thanksgiving, I decided to go to MPC to do much needed paperwork. As I got in my car and started on my way, my cell phone rang. I thought it was Francie or one of the kids. It seemed like any time I left the house I would receive a call from a family member, within ten minutes of departure. The best calls were always along the lines of, "Dad, can you give me a ride to …?" Half the time the ride they wanted was to the house that I was already halfway to.

This time the call was from one of the bankers assigned to the MPC account. He wanted to know where I was and if I could come to the bank to sign a few papers. I told him I was on my way to MPC and I would be glad to stop by. Forty-five minutes later I found myself in the lobby of Addison Trust in Bensenville waiting for Frank, one of my bankers, to bring me the papers. He arrived shortly after I announced myself at the front desk and asked to see him. As I signed the papers, Bert Callahan the bank president came out of his corner office and asked me if I had a few minutes. I was totally bummed out. There is no way an unexpected meeting with Bert Callahan could be good. I sensed they had laid a surprise attack on me and was furious, but I would not let them have the satisfaction of knowing how I felt. The only answer I could give was "Okay."

Quick, think, what could he possibly want? Then it hit me. A couple of brothers-in-law called me during the previous week and said they heard the bank might forego interest on my outstanding debt as I worked through the details on how to pay them back. I was ecstatic. I even went as far as to announce to business acquaintances that the bank probably appreciated how hard I was working at repaying their money.

Within minutes I was seated in Bert's office with Frank. Unfortunately, Nick Baron, a third banker assigned to MPC, who I considered a friend and possible ally, was not there. Bert, who is the epitome of a banker, stiff with his tie tied tightly right up to his Adam's apple, did not waste any time getting to the point. "Ken, just how are you going to pay us back the four point two million dollars that you owe us?"

So much for 'how do you do's'. I was visibly nervous because all my answers had to be based on memory. I did not have notes or documents that I could reference.

"Well, Bert, we think the building will sell for one eight, MPC has over a half million in receivables owed by customers and about eight hundred thou in inventory, a lot of which is work in process. I am also trying to sell the client accounts to another packaging company. This arrangement could generate about four hundred thousand in sales commission over the next three years. And as you know the equipment was valued at two hundred thousand and my house has four hundred thousand in equity based on its last appraisal."

The whole time Bert wrote on a piece of paper. He looked up from his notes, turned to me and said, "That still leaves you one hundred thousand short. And that's assuming that the receivables, inventory, building, house, equipment and the sales commission are all what you say they are. Do you have any other source of income or money? You know, Ken, at the end of the possible sales contract, we will run the numbers. If you still owe us money, we will come after it."

I realized my life was ruined. Starting that instant, and ... forever. I thought the meeting was over when Bert offered this final comment, "I went to the committee and we agreed to suspend interest payments if and only if you put your house up for sale immediately."

Immediately. The word banged around in my head like a raging wild boar. Our house had to go up for sale right now. It was the harbinger of certain doom—I had crossed the line from a guy who had tough times to a complete failure. All of us, my brothers-in-law and I, above all, wanted to save the house. A new job, so what? Starting over with no money, so what? Losing your house is tough to recover from, especially mentally. I left the bank; drove down the street a mile or so to a Starbucks and parked the car. I put my head into my hands feeling like I was suffocating. How was I going to tell Francie this news? I foolishly thought the bank would wait out the sales contract to see where all the chips lay before forcing me to sell my house. Like most everything I thought, I was wrong. After some deep breaths, I called George. I let him know he was right about the interest being suspended, but the cost of doing this was to sell our house immediately.

There was complete silence. Finally, George said, "Who told you that you have to sell the house?"

"Callahan and Addison Trust."

Acting surprised, he asked, "When did you meet with Callahan?"

"Ten minutes ago"

I knew that for the first time since I'd known George that he had no advice for me. So, I let him off the hook; I told him I had to go and I'd talk to him later.

I continued my drive to MPC knowing the desperation that could drive a person to consider suicide. The thought of losing the house smacked me square in the face. I was never hit harder in a football game, basketball game, or business meeting room. During the ride, I thought about ways of killing myself: pills, drowning, hanging, jumping off a building. A gun to the head seemed to be the quickest and least painful.

ELEVEN

I am sitting on a chair in an empty factory with a loaded gun lying on the floor in front of me.

It was the shortest dream I ever recorded. When I finished reading it out loud to Debra she was already looking at me. I did not have to wait for the taking off of the glasses.

She said with somber softness, "I suspected you were beginning to have these thoughts. I was planning to have this conversation with you during today's session. Ken, do you know anybody who has committed suicide?"

"No, not personally. Well, yes, I knew Joan Gordon from Winnetka. Francie and I also knew a young woman who taught our children. We think her mom killed herself. I had a high school friend and football teammate who hung and killed himself. He was one of the best players to ever play at our high school. They say drugs got to him."

Debra's jaw set, her back stiffened and she leaned forward as she pointed a stern finger my way. "Ken, it's a very selfish act. You would be hurting more people than you can imagine, especially Francie and your children."

"I know. I just can't get it out of my mind. I don't want it there. How do I get it out?"

"Ken, you have to promise me that you will call me if the urge gets too great."

I looked at her. "You know I can't make that promise."

She held her gaze on me, her eyes puffy and moist and said, "Can you at least promise that you will try to call me?"

"Yes, I will at least promise you that I will try."

Debra explained that she had for some time suspected I had been considering suicide, but wanted—was waiting—for me to bring it up. I knew that I shook Debra to her core with this one. As tough as she is, and as much as she had no doubt heard it from other clients, it set her back to see me depressed enough to mention suicide. She was not alone; I was also scared of how I was thinking.

I ran over my allotted time. Usually after fifty minutes, we were both ready to end a session. It can be an exhausting exercise. There are sessions when, mentally, I worked as hard as I could. It drained me. But tonight Debra was not going to let me leave until she was satisfied I would not do anything foolish.

Yes, I'll call you. As I'm trying to kill myself I'll stop, pick up my cell phone, and call you. 'Hi Debra, no it's just me, Ken, trying to commit suicide.' Unfortunately, that's not what I said. I let her know, "I'm frightened and wish these thoughts would go away."

She said she understood. I know she did.

As I was leaving, Debra grabbed my arm and, close to tears, said, "I'd miss you if you did anything foolish." She patted me on the back. "See you next week at six. Remember, you promised to call me if things get too rough."

It's amazing how much I thought of suicide or of running away. It wandered into my mind many times while driving home. Why don't I just continue on, wave as I pass the house? Maybe I would end up at some remote town out west. I thought of flying to Paris or Rome and becoming an English teacher. I even went on the internet and looked up teaching courses. Francie initially would cry, miss me, but then find a new Mr. Right. I would end up being a bad dinner story. But after that session, every time I thought of suicide or running away, Debra popped into my mind. I could hear her say, "Ken, it's a selfish act. Please, call me before doing anything foolish."

TWELVE

"Ken, just how are you going to pay back the four point two million dollars that you owe us?"

Callahan's words kept haranguing my ears. I ran the numbers in my head a thousand times while lying awake at night. Each time I came up short. Each time I recalled Bert saying, "We're coming after it."

He was right and I knew it. The receivables, inventory, building, my house, the equipment, and the potential sales commission would most likely be less than expected. I could fall short over a half million dollars. The most troubling number was the inventory. I did not have much control over the other items. We would collect receivables, and then put the house, building and equipment up for sale, and wait for sales commission checks to arrive. The numbers would be the numbers; they would be determined by the market.

The inventory, however, ranged from cut pieces of material lying around to fully finished parts. The inventory had no value, except to the customer that used them. All parts made by MPC were customer specific. We were known as a job shop. A customer shows up, gives us a print of the part and asks us to do a job. We may make a product one time or run the product for a number of years until it was discontinued. No one, not even the customer who ordered the part, would buy unfinished pieces—known as work in process, or WIP. To get their true value these needed to become a finished good. This was going to be difficult. We had no money and the bank was not willing to increase my debt to them. We also had vendors that, due to monies owed, would not sell us component parts needed to finish product.

It was decided that the best way to finish WIP, was to sell the MPC customers to another manufacturing company, in particular a competitor. The theory was that this new company, having an interest in customer continuity, would fund making the WIP into a finished good.

The company I found was Great Lakes Manufacturing. Much larger than MPC, Great Lakes was located about five miles directly west of our plant. The company was owned by the sons of the founding owner. Even though they were in their forties, they were old world businessmen. Both brothers attended a local Catholic High School and Thomas Aquinas College. They spent their high school and college summers sweeping, driving trucks, and doing other assorted jobs for their dad in the factory with the workers. They had a 'good' work ethic and were raised to be honest, tough, and aggressive businessmen. They were beginning to grow their enterprise through acquisitions. When I called and proposed the sale of my customer list, they were more than willing to meet. The brothers agreed to an appointment at Portillo's the next day at noon. When you watch movies or read books, deals like this are usually made in swanky restaurants or at country clubs. Not me, I was going to an old fashioned Chicago hot dog restaurant to nervously meet brothers whom I had competed against for ten years. Although the bank and George thought the talks dragged on, I was amazed at how fast we settled on a deal. I would receive a percentage of sales for a few years on the customers I turned over to Great Lakes and they would provide funds to finish WIP for these customers. With any luck, I could make and sell the eight hundred thousand dollars in inventory, as I had indicated to Bert Callahan.

THIRTEEN

After our session about suicide, my time with Debra became a series of her looking for 'the good' in my life. I know she was still worried about me and took my thoughts of suicide very seriously. We rarely, if ever, had a session where Debra did not come up with a positive that we could sit and talk about just like two old friends. She soon found the subject that I was most willing to discuss and used it on more than one occasion. Right out of the blue Debra would turn to me and say, "You like running with your friends, don't you Ken?" or, "What do you like doing, Ken?" knowing my answer would be my Saturday fun runs. It was Debra's way of making me admit there were things in my life that I still enjoyed. As hard as those days were, I still had a few isolated moments where I found myself temporarily in a state of contentment, or, maybe it was denial. I was always rudely awakened from the brief respite only to fall back into the depressed state. But I know Debra felt the more she reminded me that not all is bad, the more I might jump into these non-depressed breathers.

Outside of my family, my friends—especially the ones I run with—were at the top of my list of positives. I talked to Debra about them all the time. Going bankrupt put me in a frame of mind where it was extremely difficult to socialize. Francie and I both felt shitty about ourselves and found that we would more often refuse an invitation than accept. A social event was like a minefield. Someone might ask you where you planned on vacationing over spring break. Or, how's work? Almost every question required a lie. Whenever I had talked to someone who had gone bankrupt they always mentioned in the first couple of sentences how they got divorced or lost all their friends. I figured cutting ties with most of our social contacts was acceptable, but not with the friends we ran with. I did not want to lose them. Even though I had not let them in on my dirty secret, I needed their security blanket. There was a comfort level being with comrades even if they did not know how much I was hurting inside. Being with them helped me to keep my sanity. I foolishly worried that telling these friends about our plight might present the risk of losing them.

Every Saturday, Francie and I would meet up with a bunch of buddies for a fun run. We simply called the group our 'running club'. The club consisted of six or seven people who had been jogging together for years. We trained together for marathons and a host of other races. But mostly it was a reason to meet on Saturdays and socialize. We used the club as an excuse to have dinner parties, go out of town, or perhaps something as simple as go to a movie or a show with each other. They were my best friends—the ones I told Debra I was so afraid of losing now that I was no longer on their socioeconomic level. I would not miss the runs; it was the camaraderie and the stories I would miss most. An acquaintance once told me he lost all his friends when he went bankrupt. He became a pariah. "Ken," he'd said, his head hung and wagging back and forth, "you can't reciprocate. They take you to dinner expecting you to take them to dinner. When you can't, sadly, the friendship ends." He had looked straight at me, his eyes filling up. "People I thought were my friends would go behind my back and tell my wife that she was too good for me—why don't you divorce that loser?"

I often told Debra I feared that at some point Francie and I would have to say no to going out to dinners or vacationing with friends.

Our social circle consisted of Francie's sister, Eileen, and her husband Tim, Francie's Cousin, Todd Maroney, and our friends, Maria and Kevin. The Madigan family was always a great source of amazement to Debra. She always said, "Perhaps you're not living your life, but living what the Madigans expected of you."—or, "You haven't been true to yourself."

I wanted to believe Debra on this issue, but I always seemed to find myself doing things with Francie's family that I liked or initiated. A perfect example is getting up at six thirty a.m. on Wednesdays and Saturdays to run with Francie and her relatives.

The club was formed when Tammy, a good friend of Maria's, left Chicago for New Jersey. Maria used to jog daily with Tammy, a chatty and somewhat loud New Jerseyite. Her laugh was the type that came deep from the belly, an out loud, I mean *out loud* laugh. She was a big woman, but not in a bad way. She was tall and a little heavy, but a sexy heavy. She kept her hair close cropped, and a little uneven. She had a pointy nose. And, as I know quite well, Tammy has rather large feet for a woman. She actually borrowed my gym shoes at an out of town event because all the women there had feet that were much smaller than hers and she had forgotten her shoes. All these parts taken separately would never work for most women, but as an ensemble they gave her a quality that most men wanted to be a part of. Everything being slightly off made the whole package right. She definitely carried herself well, with a lot of confidence. She told funny stories and was always bragging about her friends. One of my first memories of Tammy is when I ran into Maria and her early one morning when they were out for their daily run. I decided it would be fun to run with them for a mile or so. As I pulled up alongside Tammy, she turned and looked at me and said, "A half hour ago I was in bed dreaming of having sex with Michael Jordan, now I'm running with you?"

Shortly after Tammy moved back East, Francie, the kids and I went to Connecticut to visit with my parents for Thanksgiving. We decided that on Friday we would go visit Tammy and her husband, Stan, in New Jersey and participate in their town's local Turkey Trot. Francie and I had run the Chicago Marathon a month earlier and, not having fully recovered from the toll a marathon takes on you, we were not in our best form. Despite this we both had a fine race and Tammy could not have been more proud of her Chicago comrades. She introduced us to a number of her neighbors, bragging about our times. Finally, we met her main running partner. Tammy enjoyed showing off her old friends, 'good' Chicago runners, to her new friend—a 'good' NJ runner. It could have easily been an uncomfortable situation except that we were all tired and happy to let Tammy talk. The whole time Tammy was telling her new friend what excellent runners we were, that we just ran a marathon.

"Wait, Ken, did I just hear them announce your name as the winner of your age category? No, sorry, someone else …." On and on she went. "Francie always wins races. Ken is forty-eight, you know."

We needed a way to stop Tammy and then it came in the form of an announcement over the loudspeaker.

"And now, ladies and gentlemen, the overall female winner is …."

Tammy's new friend said with good-natured politeness, "I'm sorry, please excuse me, they just called my name, I have to go get my trophy."

Back at home, Francie understood the void that Maria was going through with her best friend moving away. At the time I was callous and did not comprehend how losing a friend could be such a big deal. Go make another one, simple as that, I thought. I now understood, because it had become such a major worry in my life. There's a reassurance level that comes with being around people who know me and will back me regardless of my faults. So, Francie took it upon herself to call Maria, a marginal acquaintance at the time, and asked her if she would like to run with us a few times a week. She was thrilled. We decided to meet at our local Starbucks and run two and a half miles out on Sheridan road and then back—a nice, five mile jog. Our course has never varied over the years except for an occasional change in the winter. With snow or inclement weather we might take a shorter and less dangerous route through Winnetka back roads. After a while Kevin, Eileen, Tim, and Todd joined us. Of course, the morning was not complete until we spent an hour or so after the run at Starbucks making the world a much better and safer place.

For me the highlight of a run is when I'm alone with another runner. It gives me a chance to talk one on one. I have listened to work issues, children's shenanigans, and even marital problems. Other times we talked politics, or merely about recent movies or books. I always thought the best person to match up with was Maria.

Maria is the product of a big Italian Catholic working class family from the west side of Cleveland. She attended Marillac, an all girl Catholic high school. Everyone loves Maria. She is happy, upbeat, and very giving. She is the best gift giver I've ever met. I loved to watch her at Starbucks after a run when she would hand one of our friends a birthday gift. As she watched the person open the gift her face became radiant. It was as if Maria was opening the gift herself and had no idea what's inside the package. Her emotions rose with those of the recipient. She held her hands in an almost prayer like fashion directly under her chin. Since her gifts were so good, the gift receiver was always taken by surprise, somewhat flabbergasted that Maria would take the time to buy such a thoughtful present. When the recipient looked up at Maria, she would rise out of her chair, half clap her hands, give a big smile, and run over to hug the beneficiary.

She was especially most generous with her biggest talent, cooking. Maria loved to cook Italian meals. We often ended up at her home for various celebrations or for 'just no reason' dinner parties. She married her high school sweetheart, Mike Olson, a surgeon at Evanston Hospital. Francie and I had by then come to using Mike as our doctor. If we complained about an ailment during our run with Maria, she would drive home and immediately tell Mike. As soon as Francie and I walked into our house after the run we would get a call from Mike. "Ken, is it the lower or upper back? When did it first start to feel sore?"

Maria portrayed herself as an innocent and naïve person to most. We in the running club were privy to a less innocent Maria. At times she would curiously or innocuously ask a question or make a statement that would turn heads. You would think, did she really just ask that? When you looked at her, you could not tell if she was going for shock or just naively asking a question.

Maria made me read books that her all female reading group would read. She loved getting the male perspective. One of the book club books Maria suggested I read was *House of Sand and Fog*. After reading it Maria and I planned to have our own mini reading group conversation during a run. What did you like about the book? What did you think of the main characters? Etc. During our first run, after reading *House of Sand and Fog*, Maria turned to me and said that in her opinion the story seemed unrealistic and at times totally hard to believe. "I mean really, can you believe being married for nine years and not giving your husband a blow job?" At first I felt like I was about to give out a nervous snort or embarrassed laugh, but was able to control myself.

There is something that gets to men when they hear a woman say those two hypnotic words: blow job. I always felt if a woman wanted something from a man—anything at all—she had only to say those two words. Just the revered thought—*blow job*!—can send a man into a rapturous reverie. After hearing those magic words, most men would run through a wall, if asked, in order to receive.

After a few seconds of beatific day dreaming, I realized I didn't know how to respond to Maria's question. No matter how I answered, yes or no, I would reveal way too much about my relationship with Francie. So, I guess it's easy to see how a conversation like this would distract you and make you forget about, oh, I don't know ... maybe the world ending, never mind a little bankruptcy. The runs were like Novocain. I knew it would quickly wear off, but while it was working the pain was masked. I couldn't feel a thing.

FOURTEEN

November moved into December in swift fashion. According to our strategy, we had thirty-one days to make and sell the 800 thousand dollars worth of inventory. In our agreement, Great Lakes agreed to provide 25 thousand dollars to MPC on Thursday of each week for four weeks. When trying to cover payroll, and buying material and component parts, it is absolutely ridiculous how fast 25 thousand dollars disappears. I broached the subject of increasing the weekly amount with Great Lakes and was pleased to learn they were not intimidated by increasing the dollar amount. They felt strongly about ensuring that their new customers did not have an interruption in product delivery. Once a product was manufactured and sold, Great Lakes knew they would receive their funds from the amount collected by MPC. They were smart enough to know that the seamless conversion of customers from MPC to Great Lakes was the top priority and the way for them to gain the most. Therefore, while I was responsible for building product, I also introduced Great Lakes to my old customers and helped with the conversion of these customers to them. It was a busy December.

The next order of business was to make decisions on which employees to keep and which to let go. Another casualty of a company going under is the employees. Forty employees, within a month, would lose their jobs. Some had been with MPC for more than twenty years. I was letting a number of them go right before Christmas. One was a long-term welder named Juan. I tried to keep him as long as I could, but called him into my office when it was clear that we had completed our welding work. I explained to him that we no longer needed him and I was sorry that I let him down. He looked at me with sad eyes and said, "No, Mister Ken. You were a good boss and I am much worried about you. I want to thank you very much for keeping me as an employee for as long as you could." He shook my hand and left.

Juan returned a week later, with his sixteen-year-old daughter, to pick up the welding helmet he'd left behind. He was one of many of the ex-employees that would show up unannounced to talk to a friend or get something they'd left behind. It was hard for them to let go.

Juan approached me and introduced me to his daughter. Unlike her father she spoke perfect English. The daughter informed me she was a sophomore in high school. I thought she could easily be my daughter Rose's friend. I wanted her to be proud of her dad so I let her know that Juan was a great employee and I was sad that MPC had to close. Juan said something to his daughter in Spanish; she turned to me and said, "My father is very sad too." I returned to my office and, since there were still people around, closed my door. I sat behind my desk, put my elbows on my knees, and lowered my head into my hands. I rubbed my eyes and thought, my God, what have you done to forty families? It was a scene I repeated many times for a multitude of different reasons.

The Christmas holidays, usually a source of great anxiety for many, had tied Francie and me in knots. As soon as Bernie and Dominic arrived home from college, we explained to all our children that this Christmas was going to be much different than those in the past. We tried to lower expectations, hoping that Christmas morning would not be a total disappointment.

For the past ten or so years our family usually woke to a 'theme' Christmas prepared by Francie. The theme was typically centered around a family trip that began on Christmas day. One year we went to Las Vegas to visit my brother. That morning, the children came downstairs to a casino themed living room. Another time we went to Keokuk, Iowa, to look at eagles as they fed along the Mississippi River. Plastered all over our living room wall, while bird chirps played on the stereo in the background, were pictures of eagles. That year the only presents, besides the trip, that the kids received were hiking boots. Over Christmases past we traveled to San Francisco, Houston, downtown Chicago, San Antonio, Austin, Washington, DC, Atlanta, Costa Rica, Orlando and Miami.

This year Francie decided on the theme, 'We are Family'. Our gift for each child was an empty photo album. On the dining room table we placed every photo we had in the house. Their 2007 Christmas present was for the children to take pictures that they liked of themselves and other family members and put together a photo album. As Sister Sledge boomed out, 'We are Family', our kids came down the stairs to what they now tell us was their favorite Christmas of all time. Their trip was to Bensenville, Illinois, where as a family we would build inventory for MPC.

On December 26th we as a family packed into my Volvo and drove to Bensenville. Francie was going to act as receptionist for a week. Katie ran a press in the metals department. Dominic was a factory assistant and Bernie worked in shipping. Tony, since he had been working for MPC, would act as their supervisor. Their help allowed MPC to get closer to its goal of creating finished goods inventory without expending a lot of extra money. The only problem was my family would see firsthand the disaster I created. With so few employees and so many of them out of position, MPC looked like a horribly run company. The phone rarely stopped ringing with threatening calls. A number of employees had insurance or vacation pay complaints. Francie wanted to satisfy everyone and had not yet learned that it could never be done. She constantly felt bad and always looked like she was ready to cry. One day an employee came into the office and in broken English asked Francie for help with an insurance issue. Francie wanted to write him a check for two thousand dollars to cover his expenses. She could not imagine that a five million dollar company had *no* available cash flow whatsoever.

Tony, hearing the exchange, turned in his chair and, facing Francie's desk, said, "You know that in a short period of time Dad and I will be out of work. Surely you must also know that if we wrote him a check for two thousand dollars it would bounce."

It was clear to both Tony and me that Francie did not really understand the depth of the disaster. After her week at MPC the realization began to sink in. She saw for the first time how our lives were going to change in a very frightening way.

FIFTEEN

I started to understand what a person with an addiction feels like. I needed, not wanted, to see Debra on Wednesdays. The feeling seemed to be as much a physical as a mental state. Leading up to Wednesdays I felt nauseous thinking about the upcoming session, about what I needed to accomplish, and knowing that I only had an hour to air out all my thoughts and complaints. I was overly anxious to try and achieve a resolution to my condition. I wanted to come in and say a few things and walk out cured. I began to rely on her more and more to keep me sane and balanced. I delayed decisions with people until I had had a chance to discuss them with Debra. My worst day of the week was Thursday. All day I thought about the session I had the night before and recalled something I forgot to bring up. Or, why did Debra say that? Or, six more days to go before I can discuss a certain issue. As each day passed and my session got closer I became more at ease. The only exception was if I had not recorded what I considered were enough dreams for the week as Wednesday approached. Every night I put pressure on myself to remember to record the dreams.

I also did not want to miss one minute of a session. I wanted the full effect, all fifty minutes. I was totally nuts if, on my way to meet Debra, I got stuck in traffic—making me late. Once, on a near-blizzard night, traffic was horrible. I realized I was going to be over an hour late, causing me to miss the session completely. I called Debra and unloaded on her. "I hate this. I am wasting your time and mine. I left early enough to account for traffic, but not this much."

I was ranting and raving when Debra calmly said over the phone, "Ken, because of the weather my seven o'clock cancelled; you'll be fine. Things always work out." I ended up with an hour and five minute session that night. Debra, seeing that I had become unglued, suggested I come twice a week. I was worried about the money, what Francie would think, and felt all I would be doing is increasing an addict's dosage. So I declined.

SIXTEEN

Building the inventory turned out to be a much more difficult task than expected. To start out we had limited people resources. But the bigger problem was acquiring material, component parts, and other basic items needed to run the factory. MPC had to buy an enormous amount of outside parts that were customer specific and therefore for us vendor specific—the very same vendors that we had not and were not likely to ever pay. So, we had to be creative purchasers. We bought items for cash, we asked Great Lakes to buy items for us, we used variations of an item, and we searched high and low for new vendors.

During this time MPC received hundreds of calls demanding payment. I tried to take them all and explain MPC's situation. It was astonishing how many people flat out refused to believe that we were not going to pay them. I called our cleaning service and told them to stop coming to MPC because we could not pay the amount owed them, never mind any new charges they were accumulating. They replied that we had a contract so they would continue to show up and expected us to pay. I begged them, letting them know they were working for money that they would never see. Yet, every Monday I showed up and the place was clean. And every Monday I'd call and we would have the same conversation about their contract with MPC.

I called the finance company for my car five times, letting them know I wanted to voluntarily surrender my car. I explained that I no longer had the means to pay the monthly loan amount. Each time the person on the other end of the line assured me the information was entered into the computer and my car would be picked up within a few days. I stopped paying in November, yet still had the car in February.

I called and left a message with the company from which we leased our truck, pleading with them to please come pick it up because we can no longer pay the monthly lease. I got a call back a few days later, asking me to bring the truck in because it was time for the truck's free annual maintenance work. Two weeks later after another call by MPC, two men in their thirties showed up wearing black jackets cut at the waist and donning sunglasses. They came into the loading dock and looked suspiciously at our truck, like they were FBI agents. Talk about overestimating your job.

I said, "Can I help you?"

One of the two goons, appearing as though he expected a fight, said, "Yeah, we're here for the truck."

I loved his startled look when I said, "It's about time."

I began receiving calls at six a.m. at home, on the MPC phone, on my cell phone, and on Francie's cell phone. When the MPC line was disconnected and I changed my cell phone number, the real estate agent with whom we listed the building started receiving calls. I received emails from him telling me so and so from so and so called. Next came letters from lawyers and collection agencies explaining I was now being or about to be sued. The calls at home or to Francie were the toughest. I remember getting into shouting matches with collection agencies and how one threatened to garnish Francie's wages, since I was technically unemployed. I was home one particular morning, just getting out of the shower when my home phone rang. It was a collection agency that laid into me. My only response was, "Listen asshole, the bank is getting everything including my house. There's nothing left for you, so take a number and get in line, pal."

I will never forget the pit in my stomach as Rose snuck out of her bedroom and walked past me into the bathroom. I was called names, threatened, yelled at, and made to feel like the scum of the earth. I was served a summons by a detective at my house to appear in the Circuit Court of Cook County. MPC vs. Plaintiff, amount claimed nine thousand dollars. Most of the callers had nothing to gain personally; they were just doing their jobs. I was a number on a list of scofflaws; call, ask for money, threaten, hang up, and call next week. Even though I knew this, it wore me out physically and even more mentally. I began to jump whenever the phone rang. I tried to explain to callers that I did not want to be this person, that I had intentions of trying to pay everyone back. But realistically I knew it would be close to impossible to do. What most of the callers did not realize was that I did not need them to make me feel like the lowest of low. I had those feelings and regrets without their intervention.

Francie often said, "What would it take to pay all your debts?" I did not have the heart to tell her that, with the amount owed her family, the bank, vendors, and employee back wages or vacation pay, we would need millions to drop from the sky. The family and vendors were surely going to suffer financially.

A second problem with building inventory was managing the employees with regard to payroll. Each week I had to cut staff for budgetary reasons. Every Friday, I sat with my General Manager—before he left MPC—and Tony to decide what tasks had been completed, who to let go as a result, and what tasks would we do the upcoming week. The key was to lower payroll significantly each week. We did not always keep the best employee or longest tenured employee. We kept the best buy, the best employee for the hourly wage.

By the time mid January rolled around only two employees were left. One spoke very limited English, the other none at all. The only tasks left to do at this point were to assemble product, pack product, and ship product. Since the Great Lakes money ran out, I was paying the two workers out of my own pocket. Once in a while they would forgo some of their pay for a ladder or microwave. I really believed they were trying to help me. One day while I was in my office, Hector, one of the two employees, walked in with a Pepsi. The tide had turned. Hector understood that I was in a much lower place than he could ever imagine being.

Handing me a can, he said, "Mister Kin, here for you is a Pepsi."

"Thanks Hector. Where did you get this?"

"De man with de truck. He still come."

A staple of all industrial parks are the little trucks that show up full of sandwiches, sodas, coffee, and snacks. They know the break times of all the area factories and are parked outside your door as the break bell rings. The workers will pile out of the plant ready for a snack or even lunch. Once they are finished, the driver/owner will slide down the sides of the truck covering the goods and drive a couple of doors down to the next factory to try and sell more candy bars, chips, sandwiches, and drinks. Even though MPC was down to two employees the truck still showed up every morning at nine a.m.

During January, Hector had several family issues that made him miss a number of days of work. I did not mind. It saved me money. On days that Hector stayed home, I would go out back and work with Tito. It was a great excuse to get away from the phones. We both were experienced in assembling the products left to ship, so we did not have to communicate much. This was a good thing, because I don't speak Spanish and Tito does not speak English. However, standing next to a guy for eight hours and not talking is nearly impossible. So, I would give Tito instructions in English or ask how many more pieces are left to assemble today? He would answer, always in Spanish. He might have answered the question I asked or, more likely, like me didn't care what the question or answers were. We both just wanted to talk. I might tell him a story or complain about the bank. Tito would listen and then talk for a while in Spanish. I wondered from time to time what I was being told, knowing I would never find out.

Yet, there were certain situations where I really needed to communicate with Tito. Great Lakes might have a question which only Tito had the answer to, or times when I had meetings out of the building knowing I would be gone for hours at a time. I thought of calling Spanish speaking friends to translate for me, when it dawned on me, Google.com—Language tools.

I would run into the office, sit at a computer and type in I am going to a meeting at Great Lakes for one to two hours. Continue to assemble the carts all day today. My telephone number is 847-222-2222.

I'd hit enter and watch the following magically appear on the screen: *Voy a una reunión en Great Lakes durante una a dos horas. Continuar ensamblar el carritos todo el día hoy. Mi número de teléfono es 847-222-2222.*

After hitting print, I would walk out to the plant and hand the paper to Tito. He always smiled, shook his head and said, "Okay." We now had a tool with which to communicate.

While driving to one such Great Lakes meeting it occurred to me, if something happened and Tito called, I'd have no idea what he was saying. Language tools was not available in my car. I figured I'd better at least learn to say "I don't understand, but will call you back soon" in Spanish.

SEVENTEEN

During one session Debra asked me if I have broken down yet. I lied to her for the first time and said no. I always wondered if I could be completely honest with Debra. I was afraid of some of my thoughts. There are times in our lives when unwanted thoughts pop into our heads. The conscious thoughts I could control. I could force myself to dismiss them. Even if I could not push them completely out of my mind, at least I could keep them to myself. Driving home I might all of a sudden think, boy I'd love to blow the bank up. Well, I am not going to march into Debra's office and cry out, "Arrest me, I want to blow up the bank." It was a thought that I knew would never be carried out.

However, if I was true to the therapy I had to record every dream I could remember. I had no control over the dreams. What if one of my dreams was a wet dream, or if I dreamed of killing someone or, even worse, child molestation. When I went to bed at night I let go any control of my thoughts. Which was the main reason Debra had me record the dreams. It let her inside my mind without editing. It was the reason we analyzed them. They were not conscious thoughts. It was my unconscious mind at work. My no-holds-barred thoughts. Over the course of seeing Debra, people I knew as a child and had long forgotten popped up in dreams. I dreamt of events that were the happiest of my life and events that were the saddest. I had a habit of, in my dreams, mixing and matching people from all different walks of my life. I might be in an office setting working with grammar school, high school, college, and work friends who have never met each other. In the dreams they all know each other and at times I was the person with whom they were all at odds. I dreamt of my family, work, sports, drinking, jail, drugs, women, children, travels, battles, heroism, and cowardice. I dreamt of almost everything and everyone that I had known. Mostly I dreamt of conflict. After reading a dream Debra would ask, "What did this dream mean to you." I'd always give some basic response. She would take her glasses off, look up at me, and have the most amazing analysis of the dream.

I'd say, "Wow, how did you think of that?"

She'd laugh. "Shit Ken, I've been doing this for over twenty years."

One time I had a dream with Annie in it.

Annie was lying on a beach with her feet in the water. She was much younger, but I was still my same age of fifty-three. The water was an azure blue, as beautiful as can be imagined. From the beach you could see in the distance an island full of palm trees. An island that I knew I had to get to. In order to get to the island I would have to walk past Annie and swim my way over. I could not bring myself to walk past Annie, because I would have to tell her what's happening at MPC. I was too embarrassed and did not want her to think badly of me. She smiles and waves at me as I walk the long way around the beach.

It was the first dream that I was afraid to show Debra. I loved Annie as a friend. But was I unconsciously trying to express something more? I didn't think so, but Debra always saw dreams differently than me. I love Francie with all my heart and I respect Annie way too much to ever do anything inappropriate. Yet, from the moment I had this dream right up until I was running up the stairs to Debra's office for my next session I could not get it out of my mind. Something told me to rip the dream up and pretend it never happened. But I couldn't. For some reason I felt this dream was less innocent than running into Annie at the beach. It stirred an emotion in me that I knew I had to deal with.

At the time of this session, I was in the thick of going bankrupt. Debra did not concentrate on the dreams as much during this period. Instead she allowed me the chance to vent and discuss what had happened during the past week. I would spout off reports like, "Yesterday the machine auctioneer came. Can you believe the machines are worth nothing?" or, "The bank wants me to put the house on the market immediately."

Debra would say something like, "What a bunch of assholes," and then would tell me a comforting story. Toward the end of a session Debra always popped up, grabbed her copies of my dreams, and said, "What do you think about looking at the dreams? Ken, why don't you pick one?" I hesitated in a quandary, but something nagged at me. I knew I had to know, so ... I gathered my courage and picked the Annie dream.

I read the dream out loud and again watched as Debra slowly removed her glasses. I was intent on looking at her as closely as I had ever done. I did not want to miss an inflection or movement that might reveal something, but ... nothing. Debra had seen and heard far too much in this office to let a silly dream about my sister-in-law cause a stir. Debra heard of affairs, spousal beatings, drug abuse, suicide attempts, and alcoholism. She had worked with people who were connected to organized crime. How could this dream cause even a slight ripple in her?

Debra looked my way and said, "It's obvious that Annie and you have feelings for each other." She looked me dead in the eyes, tapping her glasses on the table. "Ken, have you ever had an affair with Annie? And don't try and bullshit me."

"*No.*" I matched her penetrating gaze and intensity of tone. "I love Francie too much and I value my friendship with Annie. I would never do anything to ruin that."

She appeared satisfied, nodded. "Good."

As I left Debra that night and began to drive home, something she'd said in the session came back to me with surprising force. "It's obvious that Annie and you have feelings for each other." She did not say, "It's obvious that you have feelings for Annie." I then started to remember other things that Debra had said that I know did not come from me. She mentioned during one session Ed Maroney and his fight with cancer. She talked about Dick Ryan, my brother-in-law the psychologist. I know I never mentioned Ed or Dick. Annie was still seeing Debra. Oh my God, Debra is hearing stories from both Annie and me. Does Annie tell Debra stories about me? How is Debra handling this? Does Annie know I am seeing Debra?

It was silly how such a little thing affected me. I had never felt uncomfortable with Annie until after that session. Am I in love with Annie? Does Annie love me? Now, ever since my Annie dream, I am nervous when I see her. Do people at a party see us together and think something is going on? Does Dan, her husband, worry about Annie and me? Do I now have to watch what I say to Debra? As my life was spiraling out of control, I began to distance myself from one of my best friends because of a dream. My mind was so fragile it was easily tricked. It takes a lot of strength to combat the perceived bad vibes that bombard you when you are down. Some of the tricks are self inflicted. People might ask, "Why are you worried about such n' such," or, "Don't let that bother you." I wanted to listen to them, snap my fingers, and be completely under control, no worries, but I couldn't. I was not strong enough to control how miserable I felt.

So, when Debra asked me if I had broken down yet, I said *no*. I was afraid of revealing a weakness. It turned out that the real weaknesses were the tricks I was letting my mind play on me. I was still a little spooked about having divulged the Annie dream. I felt the dream revealed way too much to Debra. I was apprehensive about throwing even more shit her way. I would be showing an emotional side that was ready to break at any moment. If I was thinking logically I would've been high up on a mountain top screaming the information down to Debra at the top of my lungs. Yet, I knowingly lied to her, even though twice I had found myself physically out of control. One time welling up and shaking, and the second time crying like a baby. I did trust Debra and desperately wanted her help, but I could not bring myself to say to my therapist that I had cried uncontrollably while driving my car to work.

I wanted to yell, "Debra, I am a complete fucking basket case, an emotional train wreck. I hate life. Please help me."

I remember clearly the date of the first incident. It was January 7, 2008. It was my eldest child Tony's first day at Great Lakes. Great Lakes, as part of the deal with MPC, agreed to hire five of my employees, Tony being one of them. Tony had worked for me since May, 2001. When I hired him he was going to College at St. Norbert's in Green Bay, Wisconsin. As Francie and I liked to say, he had a little too much fun. So we did not allow him to go back for his junior year. Instead we announced to him that he should work with me at Ideal Manufacturing, a division of MPC. We also encouraged him to take classes at Oakton Community College. He eventually went to Loyola University where he graduated with a degree in Economics.

Working there, for me, was a bad fit. It was a torturous job where it was impossible to be successful. The Ideal workforce was mostly middle-age men who lived with their moms. We had guys who did not show up to work because they or their 'old lady' were in jail. Once a worker called in and said, "I know I told you my dad died last month, but this time he really did die, so I can't come to work."

The ex-owner had a sexual harassment suit against him by the only female employee. Our best worker was an ex-con. The place literally was up for grabs. As a result, I decided to move the Ideal equipment into MPC, pretty much fire the whole Ideal workforce, and have the MPC employees take over production. The move was horrendous. All that could go wrong did.

Toward the end of the move I went back into the Ideal factory and Tony was sitting on a push cart all alone. No one was in the plant, the place was completely empty. He looked up at me and his eyes were all red. I was not sure but he may have been crying. He sadly said, "Dad I did not try to be a fuck up at college or work. I wanted things to be right." As a parent I was crushed. I knew he was struggling with this job, but I was thinking only about myself and the money I could lose. I pushed Tony as hard as anyone has ever been pushed. Earlier that year I saw an essay on his desk at home that he wrote for a class at Loyola. In it he talked about Ideal and how the job was killing him inside. How he was eating Tums like they were M&Ms. That day in the factory I sat next to him and said, "Look, you're a college graduate, you have a great girlfriend and you helped me with the hardest job imaginable. I don't think you're a fuck up," and kissed him on the forehead.

I watched Tony grow for seven years as an employee, but mostly as a person. For the first time in those seven years I, because of my fuck up, was going to work without Tony. As I drove to MPC on January 7, 2008, I began to think of Tony not only as an employee, but also as a son who brings Francie and me so much pleasure. From the second I bought MPC in 1998, I always thought of the day when I would retire and my five children would take over. I thought I would build a company that would generate enough money to get them all comfortably through life. I destroyed that dream, and now Tony was off to work as an engineer for Great Lakes. As these thoughts rolled around in my head, I began to well up. My arms began to shake. I had trouble controlling my emotions. I managed to keep from crying, but that was all, and that barely.

The second time I broke down was also in January. It was strange because I actually broke down because of a sports story I heard on the radio while driving to work. On the ride in to the job I listened to Mike and Mike in the morning on ESPN 1000. Mike Greenberg is a rabid sports fan who rarely played sports growing up. His partner, Mike Golic, was the football captain at Notre Dame University and played defensive end in the NFL. They are knowledgeable, funny and very entertaining. I love the combination, Greenberg a smallish New Yorker who is Jewish and Golic a big football playing jock who is Catholic. They provided a release from all that was going on in my life. So, it was ironic that their show caused me to disintegrate.

I was in traffic in the heart of the Chicago loop on the Kennedy Expressway when the Mikes announced that after the break the head basketball coach from IUPUI would be on the show. I was half listening so I was not sure why Ron Hunter was about to be interviewed. It caught my attention. I figured to listen to a coach from such a small program might be worth the wait. So, not to miss any of the interview, I listened to the ads instead of changing the station. When Hunter came on, Mike and Mike let the audience know that during that night's IUPUI game against Oakland, Hunter was going to coach barefooted. He was doing this in support of Samaritan's Feet. Samaritan's Feet is a program that provides shoes for children, especially in African nations. Part of the price of admission to that night's game was to bring an old pair of shoes. Hunter had set a goal of collecting forty thousand pairs of shoes that he personally was going to take to Africa for distribution. He had collected thirty thousand to date. Hunter in the interview talked about how his whole team wanted to accompany him to Africa and help deliver the shoes. Here were a bunch of eighteen to twenty-one-year-old kids wanting to do the right thing. Toward the end of the interview the Mikes had a representative from Converse come on the show. The rep donated fifteen thousand pairs of shoes to Hunter's cause in Converse's name. That put the number at forty-five thousand pairs of shoes, more than his goal of forty thousand.

I do not know what about the story hit me, but on the Kennedy Expressway in the middle of Chicago I began to cry, a cry that would last a good minute. I finally got the composure to wipe my eyes. I looked at the cars beside me to see if anyone noticed. Luckily most people looked straight ahead, unconcerned about the total nut case of a person in the car next to them. Over the remaining twenty minute drive to work I continued to well up from time to time.

At our next session, I came clean with Debra. It's like when I was younger and would fib to a parent, teacher, or friend, and my conscience would finally get to me where I couldn't take it anymore. So, right after her usual offer of a drink I blurted out to Debra that, "Yes, yes I have sort of broken down."

She looked at me like she already knew that and said, "You broke down over something good that you heard, didn't you?"

EIGHTEEN

Bucky and I first met at MPC in early January, 2008. We'd spoken on the phone many times, but I at first rejected his offers to get together. It just seemed too confusing and hard to try and sell portions of MPC to two separate buyers.

Bucky was introduced to me by one of my vendors, Albert Deerpath. Albert, an extremely large man, who is half Cherokee, owns a manufacturing company that provided secondary work for MPC. Because of his size, even in the dead of winter Albert worked up a sweat while just quietly sitting in his office. He is a rather gregarious man who you could not help but immediately like when you sat down to talk with him, especially after receiving his usual greeting of, "How's everything, brother?" Albert, like all my vendors, made a call to me one day to inquire about the money owed to his company by MPC. I explained to Albert that we were broke and that there was a great likelihood he would never see the money.

"I'm in to the bank pretty deep, Albert. They got the house, everything."

He politely said, "How much?"

"Over four mil."

Albert then related to me how he had lost everything years back and he knew what I was going through.

"Ken, I am going to have Bucky Armstrong call you. He is a friend and business associate of mine. He also went bankrupt and has since bounced back. He owns a metals company. He might be able to help you. Hang in there, brother. We'll get you through this."

I had become a member of a fraternity that, like every other constituent, I would do most anything to revoke the membership. I reluctantly set up a meeting for eleven a.m. on such and such day. From the other end of the phone Bucky said, "We would be there earlier, but it takes an hour from our hunting club."

I was out in the factory when I heard MPC's receptionist. Terry sounded nervous, her page over the machines barely audible. "Ken, you are needed up front ... ahh, right away."

When I came in from the back of MPC into the office area, two giant intimidating men dressed in bright orange hunting jackets, with green and brown camouflage Cabela hats, waited to greet me. Bucky is a bear of a man, with thin gray black hair and glasses. He has a large, almost circular face. He's not particularly tall, nor would you call him fat. He just was all around big. But he was the smaller of the two men standing in front of me. The second man, an obvious associate of Bucky's, was at least a head taller than me and weighed in at, on a good day, a mere two hundred and fifty clicks. He had a full black beard and a menacing look about him. I felt like Jeremiah Johnson himself had stopped by to take a look at MPC. Bucky introduced himself and his associate, who I would later learn was his twenty-seven-year-old ex-University of Illinois standout football playing son, Justin. From our introductory handshake up until they left, I may have said a handful of words—this was clearly Bucky's show. Bucky wanted to see the factory and he wanted to know my situation. I told him I had lost a great deal of market share and as a result the company was losing money. Therefore I needed to come up with a large amount of cash to pay back a bank.

Tony and I took Bucky and Justin on a tour of our factory. As we went from machine to machine Bucky asked what each was used for, and what type of product ran on it, and then halfway through our answer he would go off on a tangent.

"Ken, we are dinosaurs, no one appreciates manufacturers any more. But I'm proud of what I do. No one is going to take this away from me and I'm not going to let them take it away from you. What's this product?" Bucky said as he pointed to a basket I made for a food service company.

"It's a coffee basket we at one time manufactured. It's made in China now. They do it for a third of the price."

Those goddamn Chinese. We're shooting ourselves in the fucking foot. Don't those asshole politicians get it? Well, you and I are going to this fucking client and we are going to tell them that they are going to buy this product from us. Fuck going overseas."

"But they get it from China for a third of the price," I repeated.

"Fuck that. You'll see. They'll be doing business with us."

I felt like 'the Don' was going to send Justin and a couple of the boys to see this customer and 'Make him an offer he couldn't refuse.'

The whole time we walked through the factory, Justin would go over to a machine and look it over or he might ask Tony a question. I saw that he made mental notes with every answer he received. I quickly surmised that Bucky was the politician/salesman, while Justin followed in his wake picking up the pieces, enacting his orders and requests.

After we went through the factory, Bucky asked me, "How much business do you have left after the dust settles?"

"A very shaky one to two million."

"Do you know the machines that we need to run that one to two million?"

Tony answered yes for me. Bucky then made us get a can of spray paint and mark the twelve to fifteen machines that Tony identified as crucial to making the product for the customers MPC had left. Bucky abruptly ended the meeting saying he was going back to his factory in Franklin Park and would arrange to buy and pick up the inventory and identified machines. It can't be this easy, I thought.

As they were about to leave, Bucky said, "Do you and Tony hunt?"

Worried that my no answer might take him back a little, I put on my most masculine face and made up the lame excuse of having grown up outside NY City and that my dad was not a hunter and therefore I never had the opportunity. I did not want to let him know that killing a fly made me queasy.

"Justin and I are going to get you and Tony out for a hunt."

Between us, Tony and I have never seen a real gun, so obviously neither of us had held or fired a shotgun. After they left, I let Tony know we were invited to go hunting with Justin and Bucky. Tony looked at me and said, "Why would we do that, we hate hunting."

"Tony, we need to make this sale happen. If Bucky takes the machines and our remaining customers, it puts me closer to satisfying the bank. We have to do this to help insure the sale."

Salesmen are a strange breed. Most salesmen believe in the axiom, "Don't take no for an answer." As a result, salesmen will go to great lengths to make a sale. Exaggerating, outright lying, changing their view to match a customer's view, entertaining, gifts, meals, repeated phone calls or visits, spying on potential customers, mailings, knowing all about a contact including his dog's name, are a few of the tricks salesmen incorporate into their daily lives.

Of all the stories told in a company, the strangest always seem to come from salesmen. The insurance salesman giving out condoms that had printed on them, 'For your protection, buy insurance from Duke'. The bag salesman playing catch with nerf balls in his client's back yard before going to a hockey game. The one that popped into my mind as Bucky and Justin left was my brother-in-law Tim's hunting story.

A customer asked Tim, a non-hunter, to join them in Kentucky to hunt pheasant. Tim, hoping to increase his business with this customer, drove seven hours to some remote area of Kentucky. Early the next morning, at five a.m., he met his two customer contacts in the lobby of the hotel. Off they went to hunt, where Tim knew he would be sitting in a trench hole in the middle of nowhere blowing bird whistles for the next six hours. It was a cold damp morning, but Tim convinced himself to hang in there for the sake of the sale. After arriving, Tim was instructed to go wait in the trench hole, while they go get all the 'stuff'. Tim naively thought they were bringing food and perhaps magazines. As he was settling in, the two customers jumped into the bunker. First a table was set up, next a projector was placed on the table, and finally a makeshift screen was set up against one of the bunker walls. Sporting movies?

Home movies, perhaps a hunting film? Nope, porn flicks. Next, out popped the Wild Turkey Bourbon. So here was my straight laced brother-in-law, who is not a big drinker, sitting in a bunker in the middle of Kentucky at six in the morning, hunting—while watching dirty movies, and doing shots of Wild Turkey.

Tim always ended the story with, "Ken, I got the sale."

I was excited that night to go home and tell Francie that, the machines could be sold, I had a possible job offer, and the additional customers could be sold to Bucky. I then related to her about Bucky wanting to take Tony and me hunting. Growing up with a dad who owned a company, she understood and encouraged me. "You must go for the sake of the sale," she said, her eyes still on her work.

She then drifted her gaze up from her art work over to me and said, "I hope Tony doesn't accidentally shoot you," and went back to her drawing.

NINETEEN

I am terrified, running for a train. I see that I am in a big indoor railroad station, like Grand Central in New York. I'm being chased and I don't know by what or whom. I must get on the train. I jump on a railcar just as it is about to leave the station and run into a private compartment. I close and lock the door and sit alone, frightened to death, waiting for something bad to happen.

My dreams were getting darker. They revealed stories of being frightened, of conflict, and of anxiety. I knew Debra thought I was and had been extremely depressed for quite a while. She also had expressed to me she felt I had been keeping my anxiety hidden from everyone, including her. I knew that I purposely had not given Debra the whole story—that or sugar coating some of my problems. I had tried to frame stories in a way to make myself look better than reality. I rarely talked about Francie or the kids. When we talked about family it was because Debra initiated the subject. I believe two things gave her clues to my mental state: my dreams and my overall demeanor. I could not completely hide how much I hated life.

"Ken, it took me a long time to realize just how much you are keeping to yourself. How depressed you are."

It seems ridiculous, but when you are depressed and someone with authority tells you this fact, you almost take satisfaction in it. I had lost the will to control or to try to change my depression. The depression was not like a light switch that I could turn on or off. I now understood that it would take time to change. I still did not have a grasp on just how long. I began to know and appreciate how much Debra was trying to guide me through this horror show I had created. I knew Debra wanted to teach me to be happy and to enjoy what I have. She listened to complaints, let me sit and say nothing, consoled me, or admonished me with, "Ken, you have to stop being so hard on yourself," or "There you go again, your fault if something goes bad, but somebody else gets credit if things go right." All with the common purpose of steering me toward a more fulfilling state of mind. She recounted stories of hers or would listen to mine. Hers were optimistic, mine were pessimistic. The sessions never had an agenda, except to read a dream or two before I left. On occasion even that was skipped.

During one meeting I reluctantly repeated a story I was sure I had brought up before. When finished, I looked at her and she acted surprised at what she'd just heard.

"What?" I said, "I've told you that before."

"No you haven't."

"Then I wish I had not told it to you now."

She looked saddened. "Why?"

I sat saying nothing.

"You're afraid I'll pass judgment on you?"

Deaf mute dumb in a chair.

"Oh Ken, we still have work to do. I would not pass judgment on you. You should know that by now."

As I approached the second door ready to leave, Debra gave me the expected little tap on the back that I knew was another way she used to connect with me. She, as always, thanked me for coming. She liked, appreciated, or loved our session tonight.

"Have a great week, Ken. I can't wait for our next session."

Is it even possible, I mean really—who could actually leave a therapist's office more depressed than when they arrived? What a shit head I was becoming. Sorry to say, but it was one of the few times I left Debra's a little more down. This particular night I was wondering about all the work she said we had left to do. I got in the car thinking, you're such a fuck up, how can you go to therapy to get depressed. Man, wow, if that doesn't beat all.

TWENTY

I was still in a major funk when Saturday morning rolled around. I woke up again thinking about my session, but also the Annie dream. Ever since the dream about Annie I had this paranoia about losing friends. I was kind of worried and blamed the dream for being partially responsible for Annie and me drifting apart. I also felt—well, knew—that my work situation probably played a bigger role in my not seeing Annie as much, as well as a number of other acquaintances and friends. This Saturday especially I was almost tempted to stay in bed, roll over, and make some excuse to Francie about feeling sick and skip the run. I figured if I'm going to lose my friends, I might as well get started. After an internal mental struggle, I managed to convince myself to get up and go for the run. I'm glad I did. It provided me with the only laugh I had all week.

We often said things during our runs with little fear of reprisal. Our motto of what is said on the sidewalk stays on the sidewalk had never been broken. We know little tidbits about each other that our spouses may not even know. We acted as each others' therapists. Of course I was saying less now that I was seeing Debra. I do not have any regrets. I preferred to keep as much of this part of my life to myself as possible—especially with my closest friends, odd as that sounds. There were many Saturday mornings where I wondered if by keeping silent I was giving clues that something was up. Usually on the runs I had something to add. Most times I was not Mr. talk his head off, but I always added my two cents. During the runs when we discussed certain subjects like how to invest for retirement, I would go stone cold silent.

This was another area that I think Debra found curious. She never really understood why I was so afraid to open up to my friends. I think she felt there were two potential positives: I most likely would get sympathy or help, and I would have the opportunity to get things off my chest. Many times I found her encouraging me to talk to my friends. She obviously did not share my concerns of pushing friends away.

I guess it was kind of curious. I always welcomed hearing other people's stories and relished trying to help them with their problems. I never looked down at them or thought they were bad parents if they had a tough kid story. But my mind would not let me reverse the situation. I logically should have known these friends would go out of their way to help me. Yet, in some respects I worked at making sure the talk was directed away from the problems I had created. I was petrified that I would be a burden to my friends. My fear of losing people so close to me was at times overwhelming and became crippling. Plus, I did not see the potential positives out weighing the likely negative. Maybe they would listen, but I felt this was why I was seeing Debra.

I was beginning to feel like Dorothy in *The Wizard of Oz* when she and her pals the Scarecrow, Lion, and Tin Man finally meet the Great and Powerful Oz. The Wizard of Oz understands each character's problem and has a solution immediately at the ready. Out of a large bag he pulls out a diploma for the brainless Scarecrow, a medal for the Cowardly Lion, and a testimonial for the heartless Tin Man. They all get what they were seeking. Dorothy, who wants to go home, gets nothing. She turns to the Wizard and sadly says to him there is nothing in that bag for me is there? Like Dorothy, I kept looking in the bag and saw nothing in it for me.

The person who most took advantage of using the running club as a sounding board was Maria. She often asked the men in the group questions such as, do men do things a certain way, or what motivates men, or why do men not think through various subjects? After listening to the answers to her question she would tell us a story about what Mike her husband did the other night and how it had completely baffled her. It struck me as funny, maybe more ironic than funny, to be hearing these types of conversations. One of the original reasons that Annie recommended I go see Debra was because of my relationship with Francie and her family. Maria was confident and secure enough to use us as a method of self examination. Me, I needed Debra.

After a man question from Maria, I always tried to calm her down, "You're over analyzing things." I would then tell her my crazy man theory. "Men only have four basic needs that they worry about. Not in any particular order: sports, sex, eating, jobs." Maria would tell me she doesn't get it. "Not only that," I'd say, "but this rule applies to all men from the ages of sixteen to ninety. So my sons, my dad, and me, we all worry about the same thing."

In spite of my well thought out theory, every once and a while she would go into a story about how Mike was driving her crazy. For example, she wanted to talk to Mike about something and he fell asleep. I would tell her his sex and eating needs were probably satisfied, his job was settled for the time being, and there were no sports on TV. No motive, not trying to be mean, simply put, it was time for a man to sleep. Our conversation always ended the same way, Maria saying, "I don't get it." Every now and then she would turn to me during a jog and say, "Really, I mean ... sports, sex, eating, and your job—I don't get it, there has to be more."

Well, on this particular Saturday Maria was enraged at her husband Mike. She had recently traveled to Europe with three other forty-five-year-old women. They started in Paris and then went to Belgium, the south of France, and Cinque Terre in Italy. While in a Paris lingerie shop, Maria found a very sexy pair of underwear. All of the other women encouraged Maria to purchase them. Mike will love it; think of the romance ... *lingerie from Paris*. Ooh, la, la, ah, bien sur, and so on they went. Maria made the purchase. While continuing her travels throughout Europe, she was concerned about the sexy underwear, making sure it was properly handled and packed as she and the other three women went from city to city. So much so that it became a joke among them. The first night home from the trip, Maria decided to show off the lingerie to Mike. I'm sure there were fireworks, yet Maria had a great way of sometimes letting you know enough, but not all, of the sordid details. In her opinion the lingerie from Paris worked.

So, here it was a month or so later and the four women, with their husbands, were meeting for dinner to exchange photos and share stories about their European adventures. Kristin, one of Maria's fellow travelers turned to Mike and said, "So, what did you think of the underwear that Maria purchased in Paris?"

Mike looked puzzled. "What underwear?"

Maria felt this was a giant slap in the face, that Mike had purposely embarrassed her. When they got home that night Maria went to her dresser, yanked out the undies, wagged them in Mike's face and said, "This underwear." She then threw them in the garbage.

I've always wondered what Mike's initial reaction was. I imagined him sitting on the edge of his bed trying to figure out just what was happening. "I was just at a dinner party, drinking wine, looking at pictures of Paris. Now my insane wife is throwing a pair of her underwear in the garbage. How did I get to this place?"

When confronted by Maria, Mike of course probably did not remember Kristin's question or ever having seen the garments. I know that if I was in the same situation as Mike on the night my wife returned from a ten day vacation, appreciating the style of her underwear would be about a thousandth on my list of things to consider. My mind would immediately race ahead of what she was wearing—however sexy—to getting the clothes off her and out of the way. Women must be made aware of the fact that after five days of no sex a man has x-ray vision. We can and usually do look right through any article of clothing. After five days of no sex, a woman can be dressed like she is in the Arctic Circle: layers of clothes, gloves, hat, and top it off with a fur coat, and we men still can visualize you naked. It's the one and only super power men are born with, a God-given gift that we hold sacred. So of course I totally understood Mike and how he could have said, "What underwear?" Because of the intensity of the subject for Maria, our gait slowed a little as I turned to her and said, "He wasn't thinking about the underwear."

Her eyes narrowed quizzically, looking at me as if to say, *What? I really don't understand men. There has to be more.*

Debra always understood that I needed the humor, I needed my friends, and most of all I required diversions. After this run I knew for certain I did not want to lose these moments. Who would've guessed that in the middle of a bankruptcy the story of someone's obsession of carrying a sexy nightie from town to town in order to please her sex-craved, unnoticing husband would be the ever so slightest help in allowing me to move an hour further away from my problems? I never missed a Saturday run. At almost every appointment with Debra, I confessed to her how panicked I was over my biggest loss being the probability of losing these relationships.

I knew she agreed with me on the magnitude of the loss. But she would always say, "Well, shit, Ken, if they forsake you because you're having hard times, then they weren't really your friends, were they? Your true friends will stick with you." Debra always had faith that my friends would stick it out with Francie and me.

TWENTY-ONE

David Morales was the son of immigrants; his mother came to the United States from Cuba and his father from Peru. He had two brothers and one sister. Three of the four siblings were attorneys, the fourth, non-attorney, was the richest of them all according to David. Their father taught them that nobody was going to give them anything; it could only be achieved through hard work. Francie and I found David in the yellow pages under Bankruptcy Attorneys.

His office was a small, one story house located on the busiest street in Skokie, Illinois. Stuck in between stores and businesses, it would have been hard to find, except that it was so out of place on this street. Francie and I arrived in separate cars at the same time, having just left the local Starbucks. Coming from different directions, we had stopped for a cup of coffee so we could prepare the litany of questions we needed to ask Mr. Morales.

The front door of the house opened into a large room. There was not the typical reception area with the young, good looking blonde receptionist found in most law firms. I saw immediately that the room had a few desks, shelves, cabinets, bookcases, large chairs, and a working fireplace against the far wall. For being such a large room, it was cluttered—mostly with stacks of papers. There was hardly any space on the walls. They were covered with pictures, posters, framed cut out newspaper articles, and all sorts of memorabilia.

"Hello, is anybody here?" I yelled

"Yeah, I'm in the back office," came a response from an unseen person.

Francie and I came through the front door and took a left toward the voice. We weaved our way through the maze of paper piles to the end of the room. There we found a little hallway with an office on each side of the hall. In the office on the left we saw for the first time our bankruptcy lawyer. He was a handsome forty-five-year-old, with jet black hair, a deep tan, and a Romanesque face. He sprang to his feet as is customary when meeting someone for the first time. I noticed we were about the same size with the same medium build. For a work environment he had a reposed manner highlighted by his polo golf shirt and sweatpants. Looking like the epitome of being in shape, I found it a bit odd that he was using a cane to balance himself. When he came halfway around the desk, the leg cast settled my dilemma.

His office, like the front room, was cluttered with files, loose papers, books, and coffee cups. It looked to me to be highly disorganized. He had the usual bookshelves full of law books and framed degrees hanging on the wall. The office also had pictures of his family and vacation spots. One of the photos was David—and possibly his dad?—fishing. Another was a group of people on a sunny beach. I wished I was in either spot and not in an office about to discuss going bankrupt.

"Sit down, sit down," David said, motioning to chairs. "Let's start from the beginning. Why do you think that you need to go bankrupt?"

I explained, taking my time, trying to be as meticulous and precise as possible, as much as I could about the MPC situation. At the end of my narrative, he asked us, really me, a bunch of questions.

"How much do you owe the bank?"

"Do you have any personal guarantees with vendors?"

"When will the equipment be sold?"

"Who did you sell the accounts to, how much sales does this make up?"

"Is the house already on the market?"

"Who is selling the building for you?"

He then went through the bankruptcy process and what he estimated the costs would be to file. During his explanation, Francie began to cry. I think sitting in an attorney's office, discussing our life accomplishments and assets like they were play money took Francie to an emotional place where I had already been and that David had probably seen numerous times. A lot of what Francie was hearing was being told to her for the first time. David and I, both of us emotionally callused to this kind of situation by now, offered a kind word and then got back to business.

David stood and ruffled through some papers on a credenza behind his desk. Not seeing what he wanted, he started opening desk drawers, and then cabinet doors. He again turned to the credenza and found what he was looking for. He handed me the papers and said they must be filled out and returned to him with a check.

His advice, however, was to wait a month or two before filing.

"Ken, right now you are selling a house, equipment, accounts, and a building. There will be UCC filings, an assortment of other state and possibly government filings, and contracts provisions that a bankruptcy filing would totally confuse and most likely cause problems. It's best that you let all these things come to completion prior to filing. Come back in March."

I left David's office shoulders slumped and a little down with the thought swirling in my head, Perfect—just perfect. Only I could have trouble even trying to file for bankruptcy.

TWENTY-TWO

Winding down MPC, like the weather, continued to drag on. When we got into the beginning of February, 2008, it was already the fourth largest snow fall in Chicago's history. Having been in Chicago for thirty years, I know that is saying a lot. Sensing that I was being worn down, Francie called me when I was on my way to work one day and said, "Ken, you do know the snow melts. Pretty soon it will be spring and then summer. You'll look around and there will be no snow. You will have forgotten all about the snow. You'll be in the present swimming in the lake, sitting on a porch reading, going to a barbeque, whatever. The point is the snow melts and goes away, so will your torture. Trust in yourself, you're doing a great job."

Francie was absolutely great during this stressful time. She often said, "We are going to handle this like my mom and dad would. We're going to keep our heads up and look for the good."

Debra, like Francie, never veered from looking for positives. At times I almost found myself being half annoyed with her because of this. I wanted to scream out, "How the fuck can I look for something good when all the walls are caving in on me?" I often wondered but never bothered to ask or find out if she believed in God or not. But her spirituality and goodness could never be questioned.

We might be in a session and she would ask me, "Did anything upbeat happen this week?" When I was forced to think about it I could always come up with at least one yes answer. I told her how Tim Kelly called me one day. After some pleasantries he said due to blah, blah, blah he had to buy a new car by December 31, before the year end close. Would I like his old one? He basically saved me a four hundred dollar a month car payment. I told her how business associates like Bucky, his son Justin, and Albert came to MPC and helped me clean up the factory. How ex-employees welded and packed for free, about Tony showing up to help me organize, how the Great Lakes owners unannounced came over with lunch for my employees and me, or how Francie and all my children showed up during Christmas vacation to work. Debra made me tell the whole story and would with interest ask questions. She loved talking about the goodness in people. I know she wanted me to see this and embrace it. The problem was, being in the middle of a shit storm, made it difficult for me to see any good. I was too mentally worn out. Sitting with Debra I often found myself bringing up a sad or depressing story I just heard about or experienced.

I would say, "I guess I don't have it as bad as the Maroney's. Ed always had tough luck and now he's dead from prostate cancer at the age of forty-nine."

Debra would look at me and say, "Ken, that does not make your situation any better." Immediately she would change the focus back to the positive.

When February started, I was prone to mood swings, especially when I was with Debra. I might lash out at someone or something. Most of the time that someone was me. "I hate myself and what I have done. I was weak. I should have demanded more from my employees or Tony. I let the bank push me around. I deserve what I am getting."

Debra, ever the calm one in the face of my storms, would say, "No one deserves this. It's horrible."

With Debra's help and guidance I tried to look for things or situations that could help get me through a week, day, or hour. I had what I thought was a pretty good distraction. In the past this distraction always made the end of January, or in this case the start of February, for a winter month, half tolerable. It was the end of the season National Football League championship game—the Super Bowl. This year because of my brutal work situation the game really had its work cut out. I am not a particularly enormous football fan, but I definitely love the pomp and circumstance of the big game. I love the two-week buildup of Super crap. I liked to read and absorb all I could about the game and bring the discussion to our family dinner table. I might challenge everyone to name a player on each of the two teams in the Super Bowl. This year I tried to convince myself that the game had an added importance for me. I needed, and with Debra's help looked for, diversions such as this to take my mind of off the impending MPC disaster. What better way than sports.

The NY Giants, my team growing up, were playing a team from Boston, the New England Patriots, New York's hated rival. The Giants surprisingly were in the Super Bowl against the highly favored undefeated team from Boston, led by their gruff coach Bill Belichick and the GQ quarterback Tom Brady—who had on his elbow his super-model girlfriend, Gisele. Francie and I were invited to a Super Bowl party at a bar called Champs. The host of the party, Ted Solensky, had a daughter who went through grammar school with Rose. The party was being thrown in honor of Ted's wife, Sophia, who passed away years earlier. Francie, who had some preparation work for an art class she was teaching, encouraged me to go to the party with Rose.

On the ride over I told Rose that I may not even last the first quarter, so be ready to leave. Partly, I had trouble being with people. I was always afraid that someone would ask me, "Hey, Ken, how's it going?" I would have to lie and say fine. The other reason was I actually preferred and enjoyed watching the game alone or with a few friends. Analyzing the game or getting a feel for the game always seemed better with fewer people. I always bragged to Francie that I'd seen every Super Bowl but one. In 1977 Francie and I both played basketball for Manhattanville College. While we were in Florida on a three-game road trip, I was in a car traveling to my next game site while the Super Bowl was being played. I did get to listen on the radio as the Oakland Raiders destroyed the Minnesota Vikings while a Manhattanville teammate and I sped across Alligator Alley.

I was a little noncommittal about who I was going to root for. I had been in Chicago long enough to have switched my alliance to the Chicago Bears. The only NY team that I continued to follow and cheer for was the NY Yankees. A little part of me wanted the Giants, but I think a bigger part did not mind seeing perfection. New England entered the game 18-0. The only other undefeated team in modern NFL history was the 1972 Miami Dolphins; they were 17-0 having played two fewer games than the current Patriots. I was lucky enough to be in Florida at the time of the Dolphin's famous run. I became a Dolphin fanatic, watched every game and knew every player. I knew firsthand the excitement of a perfect season.

A few years after their undefeated season, while Francie and I were at Manhattanville, we went to see the NY Giants play the Dolphins at the Meadowlands. Toward the end of the game Francie half-assed said to me, "I know Tim Foley." Tim was a defensive back on the Dolphins and played on the 1972 team. Being a defensive back on my high school team, I idolized Tim Foley and Jake Scott.

"How well do you know him?"

"A little."

"I am not going to wait outside the locker room door for an hour if you only know him a little."

Immediately after walking into Champs, Rose left me for her friends. Alone, I walked up to the bar and grabbed a stool in front of one of the many TVs displaying the game. As I ordered a beer I heard one of the announcers mention the 1972 Miami Dolphins.

I chuckled to myself thinking of one of my first visits to the Madigan house. Shortly after arriving from the east coast, I accidentally walked in on my father-in-law having a conversation with a good looking thirty-five-year-old. They both politely stood up and the young man extended his hand and said, "Hi, I'm Tim Foley."

After talking a few minutes to deal with my 'man confusion', I ran out of the room, found Francie: remembering she said, "She knew Tim a little." I yelled, "That's more than a little." Once again I was getting the 'what an idiot look' from a woman. Turns out Tim grew up a couple of doors down from the Madigans and went all through grammar and high school with my brother-in-law Mark and Francie's older sister Millie.

Early on during the first quarter of the game, I texted Rose that I was ready to leave Champs. She came running over just as Mike and Maria walked into the bar. Francie also had a change of heart and showed up with her sister Eileen. We ended up watching the whole game, sitting at the bar, on a large screen TV. The Giants upset the Patriots and won Super Bowl XLII on last minute heroics by their much maligned quarterback, Eli Manning. I did not care. We walked out of the bar into another Chicago snowstorm and went home. Beer and the Super Bowl got me through another day. Tomorrow I would be back at MPC, my small break from the shit storm over. I got in the car half drunk and hating life. I hated the party. I hated socializing. Fuck it; I decided I was through with going to parties that made me feel uncomfortable. It's also when I decided that, besides the running club, fuck friends.

On the Monday evening after the Super Bowl I came home to find Francie preparing dinner. She barely lifted her head as she was cutting an onion for the salad, when she asked about my friend obsession. She wanted to know why I thought we were going to lose all our friends. I told her how almost everyone I talked to who had a company failure always seems to mention very early on in the conversation how their friends abandoned them.

She looked up from her chopping. "Why, is it a money thing, a shame thing or what?"

I didn't really know the answer. I could tell that Francie already felt hurt about the thought of losing our close friends.

I tried to soften the blow by saying, "We really don't have any friends. Besides Kevin, who moved away to Denver, and Maria, the rest of our friends are relatives."

We occasionally went to dinner at low key, affordable restaurants with Francie's high school friend Rebecca and her husband Steve. High school chums tend to stick with you through thick and thin. That's about it. Now my in-laws, Eileen and Dan, would be devastated. They both have tons of friends and have social events going on all the time. In the past few years Francie and I had circled the wagons, closing our social contacts to mostly family and the few mentioned friends. We sort of liked it that way; it allowed us more time to hang with our kids.

Annie once told me a story about her dad that I loved to repeat when we joked about having no friends. Mr. Sullivan, Annie's dad, died of cancer. The last days of his life he was bed ridden in horrible pain. The cancer attacked his body relentlessly. Annie visited her dad daily and always came away with some great golf story or little life philosophy. One day while Annie was visiting, Greg Thompson showed up unannounced at the Sullivan house. Mrs. Sullivan was beside herself with joy—finally a visitor for her husband. She ran into the bedroom and told Mr. Sullivan that his friend Greg stopped by to visit. Mr. Sullivan, with his back to his wife, stated with abrupt, curt firmness that he did not want to see Greg and please to tell him to go home. Mrs. Sullivan lowered her head, looked at her husband, and very demurely said, "Gene, he's the only friend you have left." Mr. Sullivan turned toward his wife, groaning with pain in the effort. "I know, and I'm trying to lose him too." I think Mr. Sullivan died two days later.

TWENTY-THREE

On February 6, 2008, the Illinois primary took place. I knew leading up to it that I had to take a sincere interest in all the candidates and their positions. I became, especially at the dinner table, animated and opinionated about our elected officials and their part in US manufacturing's demise. I wanted to make sure my voice was heard loud and clear. It needed to be heard on terrorism, education, health care, yes—but most of all on the goddamn economy. I also wanted to make sure my children participated in the political process and understood the importance of speaking up to these out of touch politicians. Do your job, Mr. or Mrs. Politician, or get your ass voted out. In the course of my admonitions I might challenge a child to name a presidential candidate and to tell me generally what he or she stands for. I was proudest when a child might blurt out an obscure candidate like Dennis Kucinich and tell me his policy.

Like most Catholics my age, I grew up in a Democratic household. I'm pretty sure that my mom does not to this day waste her time reading the ballot. She goes in to the voting booth and checks the box that indicates a straight democratic ticket. Dad fakes a little bit, but I know the majority of his votes are for Democratic candidates. Catholics at one time were not held in as high esteem as they are today. We heard our parents talk of Italian, Irish, and Polish immigrants who came to America at the turn of the century, all having to endure prejudices. Those immigrants worked hard and integrated their children into the American way of life. Their children became America's police officers, postal workers, fire fighters, carpenters and, like my dad, electricians. They in turn wanted an even better life for their children. My generation, their children, were to become lawyers, doctors, educators, and businessmen. I remember how important the 1960 election was to my parents. How they and all their friends would stay up late into the night talking about Kennedy, as my brother and I secretly sat on our beds in the next room listening. They smoked their Tareyton cigarettes, drank gin and tonics, and talked of the importance of a Catholic being president. I remember the women saying, "Not only that, he's cute." I also remember my mom crying when he was elected. Dad said with pride to me, "Now, someday you can be president," and I could tell he finally believed it. A Catholic in the White House. Four years earlier, no ... *one month* earlier, it was unthinkable. But here he was, John Fitzgerald Kennedy with his stunning wife Jackie leading the other members of Camelot down Pennsylvania Avenue on Inauguration day. I was too young to understand the true importance of this event, but not too young to know that my parents understood.

When I was in high school I lived next to a good friend, Claude Hoyne. He lived in an apartment above a store on Greenwich Avenue in Greenwich, Connecticut. His parents were both from Ireland and moved to the US in their late teens. They both had brogues; I couldn't understand his dad and just barely his mom, I always paid close attention when she talked. I remember she sometimes used half Gaelic and half English when she was mad at Claude and wanted to make sure he 'got the message'. Once in the early seventies I was over at Claude's and the neighbors were making noise. Mrs. Hoyne took a broom and rapped it a couple of times against the wall and yelled in Gaelic, "pog mo thoin." I think the translation means, "Kiss my arse." She turned to me and in her lovely, beautiful-to-listen-to Irish accent said, "Those goddam Italians—uh, well, sorry, Ken. You're half Irish, though, aren't ya?"

What I really remember about Claude's apartment were the two pictures hanging on the wall as you entered. One was of the Pope, the other John F. Kennedy. Almost ten years after his death, Kennedy still held a place of honor in Catholic homes.

We barely understood why our parents talked of the hard times that our grandparents endured. We started to live on the right side of the tracks. We started to go to the right schools and join the right country clubs. We also started to become Republicans. I was one of the new Catholic Republicans, owning a company and living in Wilmette, Illinois, in my five-bedroom house. I, with all the other North Shore Catholics, talked about how Reagan will lower taxes and Bush will be hard on our enemies. We became enamored with the Reagan Revolution.

My College friend Murph had a different adult life than me. He was a Christian brother for ten years, taught in Catholic high schools and ran soup kitchens. He worked with and felt the pain of the homeless and less fortunate. He never left his Bronx roots. He would call me and tell me why I should be voting for this Democratic candidate or that Green Party candidate. He mailed my children literature about candidates or other important issues. When he came to our house he would lecture the Kellys and my children on Wal-Mart and Nike. "Don't you want your planet to be environmentally clean?" he'd say, and in unison the kids would shout, "Yes!" He was like the pied piper, only I imagined him in a Scottish kilt playing the bagpipes as the children followed him out of the room chanting green slogans. He once told me that he had an acquaintance in San Francisco who was not liberal, he was radical. Murph said he wished he could be radical. I loved that he gave my kids the other side. I asked him once if he ever voted for a Republican. He said, "Yes, and I still regret it. He turned out to be a liar." When he was living in upstate NY, I think he voted Republican for the dog catcher or something like that.

Murph would call me and say, "Ken, they're stodgy old white men with their underpants up their asses. They are the guys our parents hated when we were growing up." He was right, I remember the dislike my parents had for Nixon and Ford for no other reason than they were Republicans and they did not truly understand the poor. On this February 6th, the day Rose, my daughter, got her driver's license, I felt it was more important than ever that I cast a vote. With my work life in shambles I had to be heard. After passing her test Rose and I left the DMV and headed toward my polling place. I knew I would return to my roots and ask for the Democratic ballot and not my usual Republican one. I walked into the voting booth and promptly selected a woman, Hillary Clinton, over the African American candidate Barak Obama, walked out, returned to the car, turned to Rose, and said, "Maybe someday you can be president," and believed it.

TWENTY-FOUR

After Tony had left to go work at Great Lakes, I woke up most mornings completely depressed. The worst days were the ones where I knew I would be going to the factory and would be there all day all by myself. No deliveries, no real estate guys, no equipment salesman, just me, alone for eight hours. I rarely turned on the lights while at the factory, except for the one in my office. I made sure that all the blinds were drawn. The paranoia was real. I was afraid of a vendor, creditor, or old customer showing up. Nothing good would come out of it. Almost every person I came in contact with was demanding something of me, mostly money.

"Mister Sabino your company owes us two thousand dollars, how do you plan on paying us? You understand that you signed personally."

"Mister Sabino, on January 6th your water will be shut off if you don't pay us ...."

It was unnerving to be in a 50 thousand square foot facility alone. All day long I imagined hearing things or at times thought I saw someone in the factory. On a few occasions when I went in the plant, I'd hear something and shout out, "Hello, *hello*, who's there? Is there any one there?"

I would scamper back into the office like an unnerved rabbit and lock the door leading to the front office area. I wondered if this is what it's like to be driven to madness. I remembered all the babysitter stories about someone else being in the house who wants to kill them. Most people live hectic lives and pray for the day when they can sit with no one around and get their work done or clear their mind. For me it was the opposite. All I seemed to do was sit and think of all the shoulda, woulda, coulda's. All types of bad thoughts popped into my head; Rose will fail in school, Bernie is going to get hurt playing lacrosse, Francie is going to leave me, I've taught my children how to accept and be a failure. A lot of times sitting in my office alone, I would suddenly start to breakdown, my eyes filling up and spilling over.

***

On February 10th, I heard on the radio that Chicago Mayor Richard Daley declared the winter of 2007-2008 the year of the pothole. It snowed again last night. The fucking snow will melt! It will be Wednesday again soon.

TWENTY-FIVE

At this point in my sessions with Debra it seemed as if I talked most of the time. During the hour I might catch myself and say, "I'm sorry, I am not letting you talk."

Debra would look at me and say, "I think at this time in your life it's important for you to have your say." She let me bitch, complain, praise, or talk about Francie, or the kids. It did not matter. The one thing that bugged her was when I beat myself up. Debra always found an excuse for me, "Ken, there is nothing you could have done about that."

She once said to me, "You have a habit of criticizing yourself and I don't know why yet." It revealed to me that she was working hard at trying to uncover what made me act the way I do.

It was also at this time that I seriously considered quitting therapy. Since December 31, 2007, I was unable to pay myself due to the fact that the bank no longer honored MPC checks. As a result, the little money I had saved during the past few years was dwindling at an alarming rate. The pressure of running out was enormous. The fact of me spending a hundred and fifty dollars a week to run into a bathroom and record dreams would become increasingly more difficult to hide from Francie, and, if found out, to justify. I was already doing my best trying to keep from Francie at all times just how much money we had left. I really did this for what I believed was her own good. It allowed her to have at least one less worry.

Coincidentally, as I was thinking of leaving therapy, Debra intimated to me that she was a student at the Jung Institute working toward a degree in Jung Psychology. She was proud of the fact that she would be one of a very small number of people in the world who would be so qualified. As part of this program she had to have a patient who she could openly discuss and basically use as her class project. One of the criteria was to submit as a case study one of the person's dreams. Debra wanted me to be that patient. My identity would be well camouflaged. "No one would ever know who I was," she assured me.

Debra let me know that I would be doing her an enormous favor. And, because I was doing her a favor, she could not charge me for my sessions. "Ken, I think that you really have to continue with therapy." A little disheartened I asked her if I'm really that bad off. She expressed that she was worried about me, but kept returning to the fact that I really was the ideal patient model for Jung Psychology. Besides, I would be doing her an incredible act of kindness if I agreed to be her model. I knew, because of my financial situation, that I had to accept her offer if I desired to continue with therapy. I did not want to stop seeing Debra. I felt like she read my mind, figured I was probably close to having depleted any savings I might have had by now, and found a way to give me a graceful and acceptable out on the money.

"So, that's settled then. You know, you really are doing me a favor."

"What dream are you picking?"

She handed me a paper, and I read it.

I walk up to an isolated house and go around to the backyard. It is very dark and misty. Through the mist, I barely see a bunch of vampires swirling around. They turn as one, see me, and are startled. I'm scared to death! A couple of the vampires rapidly fly over my head. I turn and run to my car out front. Up ahead, as I am driving away, I see a jet black carriage with six of the blackest horses flying low to the ground as they hastily travel down the road. The vampires are crowded in the carriage. There is one vampire on top of the carriage holding reins while he is whipping the horses into a wild frenzy.

"Why that one? I would have picked a different one," I said, thinking of my dream in the lake and meeting Debra at the building.

"The longest dream isn't necessarily the best. I love the imagery in this dream, don't you? It really does reveal a lot about your state of mind."

I wanted to ask if there was more to the dream than just the imagery, but was more interested in hearing about Debra's program than my state of mind. I do remember that the night I had the vampire dream I woke up terrified and sweating.

Shortly after that session Debra quit the Jung Institute. She said she was tired of being around those people and didn't need another degree to justify her knowledge of Jung Psychology. Besides, the process was too long. As she explained all this, I shook my head and almost unknowingly and certainly unintentionally let out a sigh.

"Are you disappointed in me for quitting," she was quick to ask.

"I could never be disappointed in you, but we agreed I didn't have to pay because I was the patient you're using in class. Now that you quit the program, I'd feel horrible about not paying."

"Oh, Ken, don't be silly, I have three open spaces each week that I use for pro bono work. You're one of the three. We are not going to talk about that anymore."

And we never did.

***

I applied online for unemployment on February 13, 2008, feeling ashamed. It's another thing I will keep from Francie and my friends. I will receive a check every other week that is a far cry from what Francie and I had become accustomed to.

TWENTY-SIX

It's amazing how irrational we can be at times. Francie's Boston College educated friend, Cheryl, whose mother died of lung cancer, smoking cigarettes and excusing it away. Annie's great fear of flying, no matter how many times you prove how statistically safe it is, will not go away. Or, Francie waking me up at 11:10 p.m. to ask me if our daughter Katie, who was supposed to be home at eleven, is all right, "You don't think she's dead, do you?"

I'd say, "Relax," knowing she was being a typical teenager disobeying her curfew.

Nothing can compare to how irrational you can be when the stress level is turned up to the nth degree. Debra addressed this issue with me on a number of occasions. She explained it's normal for stress to either make a person regress or act irrationally. She then related a story of how one time she was so mad at her mother's boyfriend that she unconsciously went back to eating chocolate chip ice cream. Something she had not done since her childhood.

There were times when I thought the bank wanted to investigate financial improprieties and perhaps send me to jail. I believed when I walked into social events that everyone was looking at and talking about me. I was sure that around every corner there was evil, darkness, or another bad thing looming. As I got closer to the building close date, I could not control my nerves. It was by far the largest source of money that would be used to pay back the bank. I was certain that failing to sell the building would be catastrophic. Each month about eleven thousand dollars of real estate taxes accrued and the monthly interest amount was close to another eleven thousand dollars. Plus, utilities would have to continue to be paid. The building sitting for a year could cost up to a quarter of a million dollars. The phrase 'adding fuel to the fire' kept shadowing my consciousness.

Immediately after we put our plan together on paying back the bank, I called Brian Fagan, a family friend who worked for BFA Realty and asked that he take responsibility for selling our facility. Brian was a tall, well-built, balding man, with a half grin that usually occupied his face. In spite of his intimidating size he was a gentle man who had a tranquil demeanor. This served him well with his clientele of mostly small, pushy, bossy, business owners. Brian, like me, grew up in a modest lower middle class environment and because of marriage had moved to the North Shore. He found his niche in buying and selling commercial real estate properties, enough so to be a member of a country club and own a nice house in the Chicago suburb of Lake Forest.

Brian was familiar with our property. A year earlier, I thought of either selling the building and moving to a smaller, tax friendlier spot in the western suburbs, or of leasing out half our space. Brian was brought in to help. The project was immediately cancelled when we miraculously received our million dollar purchase order.

Brian's call came surprisingly soon. It was as if his workers had not long ago gotten back from the job of placing the for sale sign in the ground in front of our building when my phone rang.

"Ken, I think we have a serious buyer."

"Who?"

"Your next door neighbor, the one to the west of you."

It was as good a feeling as if I'd won the lottery. I even received calls from Tim, George, and the bank congratulating me. "Can you believe how lucky you are?" And I thought, Yeah, I'm one helluva fucking lucky guy!

Manny Lee owned the company directly west of MPC. When he first walked into MPC to look the building over I was taken aback. Daily, for four years, I watched his trucks going up and down Commerce Way, big blue trucks with the name ML Food Supply written on their sides in Greek like letters. It was a company that supplied meat to Greek restaurants throughout the Chicago metropolitan area. So I was pretty surprised when a forty-year-old Asian male walked into MPC instead of a tall dark Greek guy.

Manufacturing concerns are owned by people of every nationality, gender, religious beliefs, and race. Somehow or other we all landed in a building that made products for the American people. We made pen tops, screws, plastic bags, mop handles, concrete piping, and sausages for grocery stores. We made big items in big concerns like cars and we made small items like toothpicks. We were at one time America's economy. We believed in the statement supposedly declared by then General Motors President Charles Wilson, toward the middle of the 20th century, "What's good for GM is good for the country." We all had a story on how we became manufacturers. My dad started the company in 1958. I sent out resumes after college and ended up in manufacturing. I bought this company in 1998 after a long search. We were proud that we supplied America's goods and could talk about our companies for as long as anyone would listen. We knew the raw materials that went into our product right up to the boxes they were packed in. But, sadly, as Bucky used to say to me, "Ken, we are becoming dinosaurs."

Manny, soon after his first visit, made an offer on the building. We finally agreed on a price of 1.7 million dollars. It was time for me to come clean on the pending lawsuit against the building.

MPC's General Manager had always wanted to implement a safety program at MPC as a means of controlling escalating out of control workmen compensation insurance costs. So, in 2004 we hired a consultant and on his directions began putting in safety measures. One of the first initiatives that we undertook was to paint yellow lines on the factory floor indicating storage, work, shipping, or walking areas. We also painted all our machines green. When completed, the factory looked like a different place. MPC had arrived. We had the feeling you get when you buy a new car. We invited customers in and had them walk between the newly painted yellow lines as we talked about our capabilities and our new safety program.

After painting the lines, our production manager had the empty paint cans and barrels properly stored on a skid in our parking lot waiting for a paint removal company to take it away. The skid was placed close to our eastern neighbor's property. Months later we received notice from the Illinois pollution board that this same neighbor was suing us for releasing toxic waste onto his land, causing his building to sell for thousands of dollars less than expected. I was to be prepared for a phone conference call to discuss this serious matter a week or so after receipt of the notice.

To prepare for the conference I talked a great deal to Todd Maroney, an attorney, during our Saturday run. His advice was to settle fast. "Ken, environmental issues can be tricky. You could actually have protestors with signs outside your plant. You have to be real careful with these types of issues. We are in a very environmentally conscious world."

The funny thing about this is if we had acted improperly I would not be in the mess I was in. Typically, the empty paint cans would have been thrown in the giant general dumpster sitting in one of our unused docks. They would have been hauled away with all the other garbage in the dumpster and no one would have been the wiser.

Our neighbor was angry because when he went to sell his building a Phase I environmental study revealed slight traces of some form of toxic substance on his property. This caused the buyer to lower his offer by a hundred thousand. Having seen the empty paint cans stored close to his property my neighbor told his staff attorneys to sue MPC for the lost money.

In preparing for the conference call, I called the owner of the paint company that hauled away the empty cans. He said the paint was water based and in his opinion basically harmless, going so far as to say, "You could practically drink the paint and it wouldn't kill you."

I inquired about the Phase I results and learned that the amount of substance found on the property was negligible. It's a very common substance and almost always found on industrial sites. Car emissions cause the type of results that were found. The substance has never warranted a monetary fine and rarely would affect the price of a sale.

I felt ready to do battle. My notes and arguments were ready. I sat in my office, door closed, waiting, when Terry my receptionist announced on my speaker box that Judge Blah Blah is on line two.

This first of many phone conferences concerning this issue was to be my last. The judge, after introducing himself, asked that the two parties—my neighbor's representative and me—do the same.

"Hi, I'm so and so and I represent the such and such Trust."

"I'm Ken Sabino and I'm President of MPC."

The Judge then asked me if I was an attorney. I said I was not. No sooner had I got the words out of my mouth, he declared the conference was over and will be rescheduled for next month.

"At which time Mister Sabino, you must have an attorney available to participate."

"Why can't I represent myself? I know everything there is to know concerning this subject."

"Mister Sabino this is not allowed. Please find representation between now and next month."

When I tell attorneys this story, they laugh and say, "How do you think we make our money?"

Almost monthly for two years, I received notices that the suit had been postponed until next month while one of the two lawyers gathers info to be provided … so that … whatever.

During November 2007 my attorney, Wiley Granderson, called and said, "Ken, after heavy negotiations and some haggling we have agreed that MPC will pay the trust twenty thousand dollars," which, incidentally, was the same amount I owed him for his services.

Two fucking years and basically I was paying my next door neighbor enough money to cover his attorney fees. The neighbor essentially received nothing. Wiley got twenty thousand dollars and the neighbor's attorney would be paid twenty thousand dollars. MPC was out forty thousand dollars. What the fuck! And they wonder why people tell lawyer jokes.

There was one major problem. In November, 2007, MPC did not have twenty thousand dollars lying around. So at the time of Manny's offer for the building, MPC had not paid either the court ordered debt to our neighbor's trust, or the fee to the attorney who was now going to help draft a contract for the building sale. Technically, the suit was not settled. Not only that, it could expose the only thing that could potentially stop the sale—a report indicating there was toxic waste on the MPC property. In Wiley and Brian's opinion this would surely spook Manny. At a minimum he would most likely ask for a price reduction.

While this was going on, I confessed to Debra that I could not control my nerves and how shot they were. Everything made me nervous, not only with work, but away from work. As far as decisions go, I became incapacitated. My decision making was so bad I often had trouble deciding what to eat for lunch—causing me to skip it half the time. I was worried about being worried.

One session I said, "I'm afraid my nervousness will blow the building deal. I will send out bad vibes, scaring the buyer away."

Debra laughed. "Ken, first of all, why does this concern you? All you're talking about is the degree of the disaster. Do you owe the bank this or do you owe the bank that? Besides, don't flatter yourself, your vibes are not that powerful."

***

On February 15, 2008, I woke up to the tragic, impossible to understand news that a gunman on Valentine's day had entered a crowded lecture hall at NIU in DeKalb, Illinois, and shot and killed at least five students before taking his own life. The night before my youngest, Rose, had gone to a Chicago Bulls basketball game with a friend. She wore a NIU sweatshirt that Dominic her brother gave her for Christmas. My children, trying to make light of our situation, all teased Rose that she would be the only Sabino who, because of financial reasons, would have to attend a state school, instead of a Catholic college. I again welled up going to work, this time it was over something incredibly sad.

***

Spike O'Dell on WGN radio announced that already that winter there had been fifty-five days of visible snow on the ground in the Chicago area. I was beginning to worry that it would never melt.

Debra was right again; neither story, especially the first, made me feel better or improved my situation.

TWENTY-SEVEN

I began to reveal more and more to Debra. I told her my fears and what made me anxious, I let her in on things about Francie and me, about my children, things that bothered me about in-laws, friends, or growing up. I had reached a level of depression I could not control. To keep from losing friends, family, and a wife, I used Debra as my crying wall. I would sometimes angrily tell her a story and look up to see the compassion in her eyes. It would not make me lose my anger for the person or situation, but I did appreciate her feeling for me. It kept me from taking my problems to Francie or friends. I was scared and she knew it. I was afraid of failing my children, of failing Francie, and of failing myself. I was fearful that I would not be able to bounce back, to ever live a fulfilling life. The downward spiral of depression was continuing, taking me to a place I knew I had to be prevented from reaching. I was afraid of never coming back, whether I succumbed to alcohol, drugs, bitterness, apathy, or pure hatred of all things.

Early on in our sessions, before October 29, 2007, I had told Debra how I had planned on living in France for a year or two after graduating from college. One of my big life regrets was not following through on this plan. We had not spoken of this in quite a while. Our discussion subjects had become moodier and more intense.

Out of the blue during one February appointment, Debra said to me toward the end of our hour, "Ken, I know someday you will complete your plan and live in France."

After Debra's France comment, when I felt especially down, I would ask her, "Do you really believe I will get to France?"

She would always with enthusiasm respond, "Yes, I'm positive you'll get to France."

A little monotone, I'd say, "I'm psyched that you say that. You really believe it, right?"

"Ken, you will get to France."

"Are you usually right with your predictions?"

"I'm always right. I have confidence in you. I know you and Francie will one day live in France."

"Wow, I believe you," I said, shaking my head not knowing if I really did.

It almost became an inside joke. We had the same banter on a few occasions, "Really, so you think I'll get to France?" I was acting like my friend Maria when she asks during a run, "Really, men only have four needs? I don't get it." I think Debra believed giving me hope was the only way to keep me from sliding completely off the cliff of coherence. She had to get me to believe in myself again.

One thing I felt sure about was Debra did have confidence in me. I loved knowing this. I figured she had seen a number of North Shore high powered people with various problems. She had seen success, failure, depression, and all types of maladies. In her opinion she felt I would land on my feet. It's hard not to like a person who, in spite of all she knew about me—being a miserable failure and having destroyed a life—still had confidence in me. I did not know it at the time but I needed Debra to have confidence in me. I believe she understood that I would respond to this confidence.

In spite of her confidence in me, I was more depressed, more anxious, and overall in a much more dreary stage. I felt myself drifting away from sanity's shore. I looked forward to getting home to have a drink. On a number of drives home I'd stop at a Bensenville liquor store and buy a beer or two and a pack of gum for the ride home. I started to feel like some of the dads I remembered when growing up. The dads who would wild-eyed nervously pace up and down their living room floors all morning long waiting for twelve noon to arrive. As soon as the clock struck twelve they ran to the liquor store or their local bar and began to drink. This way they could proudly announce to their family and friends that they never had a drop to drink before noon.

I also felt less religious and had less faith in mankind. I was harsher with my criticisms of others when I was with Debra. But I was the most punitive with myself. I began to hate myself, what I stood for, and how I acted. I did not feel sorry for myself. I began to think I deserved what I was getting. God had it out for me, so, I was mad at God too. I would miss mass and not have my usual guilt.

It was as if I would look to Him and say, "What, go ahead and try. You think there's more you can do to me?" When I was at mass I did not pray. I sat and became upset with my situation. I really did not fault anyone except myself. I hid these feelings from everyone, including Francie, except Debra. She saw my inner hate. She heard my inner hate.

"I could have prevented this. I could have made decisions that would have stopped this disaster. I buried my head in the sand." I did want to run away. I was not prepared for this. I no longer cared if I lived or died. Dying was no longer terrifying to me. I looked death in the face and thought, "I'm not fucking afraid of you. You can't be any worse than this hell."

Debra saw me slipping and led me through this miserable month. It was as though she was riding a kayak traveling down the rapids on the Shenandoah River in West Virginia, steering me through the worst month of my life. I had given her quite a challenge. At times I sat and did not respond to questions.

If Debra would say, "Ken, you can't be this hard on yourself," I would look at her with my eyes partially closed, squinting in a sort of anger and simply respond, "Why not?"

There were times when I felt, no knew, that I was being an ass on purpose. Not once did Debra ever appear upset. Like the kayak she rolled with the rapids. "Well, because it was not your fault business left the US for China." She would act as though she was making an important announcement to imaginary listeners, with, "Hold on everybody, Ken made business move to China." Debra knew she could say things like this without fear of reprisal. She knew I liked and respected her too much to ever truly be mean to her. During sessions I might go into moods of anger, depression, or guilt. I would then suddenly jump up in the middle of all this and tell a funny story and would immediately get one back from Debra. I found myself constantly rubbing my eyes, holding back emotions. I promised myself to never ever break down even slightly in front of Debra. Sometimes I would stop mid-sentence so that I would not say something mean or emotional and immediately get challenged.

"Ken, what were you going to say," she'd ask.

"Nothing."

"That's not true. What is on your mind, what's bothering you?"

"Nothing, I am not going to tell you."

"Are you sure? This is the one place you can say whatever you feel."

"No, I really don't want to tell you."

"Okay, but if you do, let me know."

She would listen if I was willing to tell and let it go if I was not. Never, however, without a challenge.

We were not as funny with each other during this period. I would still get a Debra story almost every session and she was still Debra acting like Holly Golightly, but I had changed, and it takes two to tango. Debra was going to stay firm and lead me back. I knew it was her strategy. She had to make me see the good. She had to stay strong. She never wavered in her faith that I would make a comeback. She constantly told me that good things were going to happen to me. It was the only month in which I had trouble believing her. The depression at times was overwhelming. I tried to hide it from everyone. If I went to a social event I would prop myself up, tell jokes, laugh. But inside I was dying. Hiding the rage made me doubly depressed when we left the event. I was living a lie. So each Wednesday when I entered office number four on Greenwood Avenue I had a lot of backed up, stored up shit that might come out. But, even with Debra, I managed to hold in some of my feelings.

Looking back, I marvel at how she led me through this period. How she put up with me. I knew it was her job, but she did not deserve some of the shit I was throwing her way.

TWENTY-EIGHT

On the last Sunday of February, Francie and I went to an Oscar party thrown by Jimmy Warner, one of our nephews. As we entered the fete I heard Jon Stewart's voice blaring out of the 24" TV warming the crowd up. Francie's sister, Millie, came over to me and said I looked tired, but that it was understandable. It's amazing how many people made similar comments to me around that time. I could hardly look in the mirror. My eyes began to have bags under them and my face looked old, sad, and haggard. I gained ten to fifteen pounds. I felt like I ate a lot less, but drank a lot more. I felt like my whole diet was coffee, coke, beer, and junk food. I'd wake up to two cups of coffee and immediately switch over to my three or so cans of coke throughout the day. When I got home I usually drank three beers to calm me down. Breakfast and lunch were usually missed. Dinner, prepared by Francie, was my only good meal and seconds were no longer par for the course. To keep some semblance of countenance I forced myself to shave every day, but considered it may be something else I'd soon drop. The walls at MPC do not care if I shave.

Even Debra said to me when I walked into my last session of the month, "Ken, you look beat up."

She constantly admonished me, "You're still keeping too much inside you. You can at least let me know how bad things are. I am here to help you."

By the way, the winner of the best picture Oscar for 2008 was *No Country for Old Men*. I laughed at the irony. I had not seen the movie yet. But the title jumped right out at me. I felt old and more and more like the deranged loner the TV clips were portraying. Like the character in the movie, I was afraid that, if tempted, I would make the decision to keep a stumbled upon two million. I certainly could use it.

At the party I felt awkward. I had lost my company and for eight hours a day I sat in an office wondering how this will all end. I snuck and chugged three beers and left my nephew's at nine, well before the best picture was announced while Francie and I listened in our bed at home.

I knew Francie was worrying about how much I had been drinking, my eating habits, and my exercise regimen—or rather lack thereof. Because the stress wore me down so tremendously during this period, I would have been much better off if I had done the complete opposite of what I did with regard to the three. But I had absolutely convinced myself I would not be able to sleep unless I had at least three beers before going to bed—which did nothing to help my weight control. I never felt overly hungry and I totally rationalized that exercising in the dark on cold snowy roads was dangerous. Tomorrow or the day after, I'd often convince myself, the snow and ice will melt making it safer and more enjoyable to be out for a run.

My four times a week runs were cut to three days, then two, and finally to Saturdays only. I blamed it on the weather or being too busy. I showed up on Saturdays more to socialize than run.

Murph called one night and asked me how I was feeling physically, and I couldn't help but think Francie had put him up to it. He told me how he gave up drinking for Lent and he had been doing this for the past twenty-five years. "It's good to clean out the body," he said.

He also said how his brother does two hundred push-ups on his way to the shower each day. He takes off his shirt does twenty-five push-ups, takes off his shoes and does twenty-five additional push-ups, takes off his socks, twenty-five more push-ups, etc. "Ken, you should try this." I almost laughed, but ... out of respect didn't.

I wanted to say, if I'm lucky maybe I'll see if I can do five push-ups after I take off each article of clothing. After I hung up, I went to the fridge for a beer.

I once told someone at a social event how Francie quit drinking on her thirtieth birthday and hasn't had a drop, besides communion wine, since.

The person politely said, "Why would she do that?"

"Well, she confided in me there is alcoholism in her family and she's afraid of becoming an alcoholic."

The person said, "So am I, but it hasn't made me quit." Yup, I'd say that just about sums up how I felt about the whole subject.

I was mostly eating fast food—when I did eat. The will to eat, drink, and exercise right left me early on. I just did not have the discipline to do these three appropriately. Logically, I knew that if I drank less, exercised, and ate properly I would have felt much better and had more energy. Debra reminded me exercise is the first line of defense against depression. She always asked me during sessions if I ran during the week. Although I could tell she was disappointed with my response of, "No," she usually let me off the hook.

"Oh, you'll be back to running soon," or, "It's hard to run in the snow, when it warms up you will start running again," she'd say.

It's not easy to get motivated to exercise when you feel like your whole world has caved in. When I did run, my chest burned with pain. It's one of the many ailments that I had since Christmas.

Looking back it was incredible how much the stress and depression broke me down physically. I constantly had back pains. I felt nauseous. For most of February when I went to the bathroom the pee burned. I would get migraine headaches. I had a loud cough that always seemed to pop up at inappropriate times. The most frightening ailment was the chest pains I felt during jogs or times of enormous stress. During one Saturday jog, I told Maria and Tim that I felt a slight chest pain mostly while running. I wanted to gauge their reaction without being overly dramatic. Both suggested that I go see a doctor, have the proper tests. I did not dare tell them that our health insurance had been dropped as of sometime in November and that Francie, Dominic, Bernie, Rose, and I had no medical coverage. I did not need or want a lecture on how important health insurance is for a family. Those types of situations always remind me of the time when one of our friends, while we were in the city, saw a person with a severely dented car door. The door and window were held together by duct tape. The friend turned to Francie and rhetorically said, "Why doesn't he just fix the door." It was easy for us to fix the door. We would drive to our local mechanic and, without inquiring as to the cost, ask the mechanic to fix the door. We would come by later, hand over the company credit card, and drive home with a door looking like new. This is a much harder task to accomplish without money or insurance.

I did not know how to apply for health insurance coverage. I'd always had an employer—most recently my own company—that provided health coverage for no or very little cost. I feared that when I did discover how to apply, I would most likely need a physical—concerned that one of my ailments would be serious enough to prevent coverage. I was also worried about the expense of insurance, plus I justified that the lack of insurance was just temporary. I would be working for Bucky or someone else soon and the problem would be resolved. I did, however, wake at night sweating at the thought of an injury or disease that could attack any one of us.

It was a call from my son Bernie that finally made me look into getting coverage. Bernie phoned us to talk about school and how lacrosse practice was starting since the regular season was fast approaching. He mentioned that he had a chance to start, because one of last year's starters broke his leg. He also mentioned that another teammate recently had hip surgery. The conversation stopped me dead in my tracks. I had a son playing a contact sport at the college level and he was not covered by a health insurance plan.

The next day I called a friend who worked in the insurance field and told him my dilemma. He recommended a company web site on the internet that provided health insurance the same day you applied. The insurance could be for a month at a time or longer. A health exam was not required and the cost was reasonable.

The ailments did not go away. But now I didn't have to worry, for Francie's sake, if they brought me to the hospital and found something wrong with me. At least the hospital bills would be paid.

TWENTY-NINE

I am inside an arena. Both sides of the court are filled with spectators. There are no seats behind the goal areas, only on the sides. I am with my daughter Rose and we are watching a game that is a combination of hockey, soccer, and volleyball. It is an exciting game with tons of action and cheering. During the contest one of the players receives a penalty for unsportsmanlike conduct. His penalty is to sit in a tub of butterscotch pudding. During this break in the action, two characters dressed up as superheroes appear high above the court. We are unsure if they are flying around for our entertainment, when three menacing evil figures appear. We now understand that this is not entertainment, but for real. Unflummoxed, the two superheroes magically flick their wrists at the evil ones and poof, *they disappear. As the last one fades away, out of his ashes the word 'love' appears.*

It was toward the middle to the end of February when I read this dream to Debra. As I lifted my head ready to be asked if I had any thoughts about this dream, Debra jumped up from her chair. She looked at me and said, "I have to go to the bathroom."

She skipped through the outer office into the bathroom. I loved it. This, I thought, is something you don't see in the movies or on TV. Would the movie *Good Will Hunting* have been as successful if Psychiatrist Sean—Robin Williams—announced to patient Will—Matt Damon—right before he broke down and cried, "Excuse me Will, hold your thought on that for a second will you? I have to go pee." In looking back at prior sessions, I believed that some of the subtle, and at times not so subtle, things that Debra said or did had a purpose. I couldn't help but think that she might again have something up her sleeve. I heard the toilet flush. She returned, sat down, and started talking about the dream.

"Ken, what a hopeful dream."

"Why?"

"You are at a sporting event with one of your children. It's fun, though I'm not quite sure I get the combination of different sports. But mostly it's good triumphing over evil and the word *love* coming out of the evil one's ashes can't be bad."

"Yes, yes, I think I agree." It was one of the first dreams I had with a positive slant to it. I couldn't speak for Debra, but I was desperate for anything positive.

"Your unconscious thoughts might be ahead of your conscious thoughts. Unconsciously, you see things moving in a positive direction. Ken, this is a good, constructive dream."

I left her office that night feeling slightly positive for the first time in at least five months. I figured it may not last, but at least for one night I could watch a *Scrubs* rerun, drink a beer, and relax without negative thoughts constantly rolling around my head.

And the more I thought about it, I ... I think she just had to go to the bathroom.

THIRTY

Logically, I should have felt a lot better than I did. I had set in motion the five legs of the plan that was laid out almost five months earlier. I was reaching the end of the 'horror show' part of going broke. The building was set to close in March, our house was on the market, the inventory had been built and sold, Bucky had offered me a job, and arrangements were being made to move the equipment out of our building. The reason I felt like shit was every day I got reminded of what a failure I was by vendor calls for money, the bank, and an empty building. Another major reason for having meltdowns was that, although my plan was set in motion, until I signed papers and shook hands there was still a chance that something could go wrong.

At this point, my days consisted of making myself available to whoever wanted questions answered or access to MPC in any way.

As far as the building went, Manny Lee was going to have it demolished and use the property as a parking lot for his semi-trucks. I foolishly thought this meant very little work on my part, figuring, "Why inspect a building being torn down?" Yet, I had various people clambering all over the building. First there was an environmental Phase I that had to take place to ensure our property was toxic waste free. Then the environmental Phase II to make sure that the Phase I was okay. The water department and gas company marked in paint on the ground where their lines were so they would not get ruined during demolition. Roofers came by to remove Freon from the air conditioners. We had a company come by to check for asbestos. Scrap guys stopped by to see if they could make a buck. It seemed like every day there was a new company or person checking on something or other. I had to worry about waste removal, electricity into the building, fire inspectors, insurance adjusters, reports coming back, reports being analyzed, and complying with report suggestions.

I received calls from Bucky or Great Lakes asking about certain customers or how MPC made a product. At times even the easiest request about a certain product could put me in a tizzy. Three months earlier I had forty employees who each had a specific role in making and shipping a product. That whole employee base was now spread throughout the Chicago area. Tony was great, but now he had his own job, making me feel guilty every time I called to see if he could stop by and help. My job had been to steer a ship, and leave the details to my crew. Well, now I was captain and crew.

I began to feel like a boxer. During the first couple of rounds of October, November, and December, I was in the ring dancing around feeling everything out. See where the bank stood, making calls to see if someone would buy inventory, and calling realtors to get a sense of the housing and building markets. As we got into the middle rounds of January and February, I was getting tired and the opponent was starting to land a lot of body blows. I felt more and more pressure from the bank and vendors. My personal money was getting low. Now, I was coming into the later rounds as March approached. Each punch started to hurt a little more. Punches upon punches start to take their toll on even the most conditioned fighter. My body and mind were both worn down. I was trying to do all I could to make it to the final round. Each call I received was on top of hundreds of previous calls. I felt like I would be knocked out at any moment. I would try to be positive and then a right hook would land on my chin. Any one incident could totally depress me for hours or even days at a time.

My body started to ache all over, especially the arms. They felt extremely heavy—like I was carrying around hundred pound weights. I tried to sleep more, thinking it would make my arms feel better. It never worked. Life was a large mine-filled obstacle course. Every time I managed to get by one obstacle another would be waiting that needed to be jumped over, climbed under, or maneuvered around. There were times when I was totally paralyzed. I might sit and stare for hours accomplishing nothing, except for fantasizing or daydreaming motionless in my chair, trying to escape from the reality I had made.

One day when I arrived at MPC, after a one and half hour drive caused by more snow, an attorney for Chicago Manufacturing, an old vendor, called. During our conversation he let it be known that a personal guarantee had been signed by me and his client was very interested in discussing how they would be getting their due monies. By signing the agreement I put Chicago Manufacturing in a better position to go after their money. Therefore, Mr. Attorney told me, although he hated doing this, a lien will be put on our house. Just hearing those words put me in a funk all day long. Toward the end of the day, I was finally able to send the bank an email explaining what happened. They were entitled to know that a lien was about to be put on the house that they had laid claim to. It was, I thought, a courtesy call. Their email reply was that 'their only suggestion' was for me to contact an attorney. I wanted to say, "While I'm at it, I just might as well spend some money on new clothes and shoes."

Of course in the middle of all this Debra went on vacation for two weeks. I'm not a big fan of the movie *What About Bob?* with Bill Murray. But now I understood why a patient would follow his therapist on vacation. Many Wednesdays I did not take the opportunity to express to Debra my frustrations or anxieties. But it's an amazing feeling to know that for one hour each week, the outside world will stop for me. And, during that hour I had the full attention of Debra to disclose my most intimate secrets. There are 168 hours in a week, about forty-nine I spend in bed, out of the remaining 119 there is only one hour where I'm able to sit, hope, dream, complain, laugh, to do as I pleased with my fragile mind without any fear of repercussions. And sitting across from me, separated only by a table with a candle on it, is the person whose responsibility it is to teach this old, depressed, beat up man how to enjoy life. Knowing that I had that hour was the key. Whether I used it correctly or not was irrelevant.

I began to rely on Debra for more than analysis. She became my advisor on most everything, including business. When I first learned in October, 2007, that MPC was in ruins, I could draw on a number of resources and received quite a few supportive calls.

"Ken, if you need anything let me know."

"If I can be of any help ...."

Toward the end of February, I was basically alone. There were very few people calling to see how I was doing, no one helping, and no advice being offered. I was Daniel Defoe's Robinson Crusoe on an island by myself. The will to quit was constantly staring me down. Why continue? I would walk back into the factory and yell at the top of my lungs, "Fuck you," not even knowing who or what it was directed at. No one was there to hear or commiserate with me. I had made the conscious decision to not let anyone know just how bad my situation had become.

Debra was the only person who heard the loneliness, the sense of despair, the complete feeling of failure, of running away, of disappearing, or the thoughts of suicide. Not even Francie knew how desperate I had become. I thought I knew what it was like to be a prisoner of war subjected to daily torture—with no information at my disposal to give my torturers to get them to stop. I welcomed the thought of a nice, safe, secure county jail.

I started to feel bad about things or events that happened many years ago. How I might have acted toward a person or situations in the past. Most of my thoughts on foregone events were triggered by, and had relevance to, my current situation. Can you believe I started to feel shitty about how I acted some twenty or thirty years ago? I wanted to call people up and apologize for something I may have done or said that in all likelihood the person had long forgotten. I recalled acting without sympathy in a number of situations in the past. One day while wallowing in the loneliness of MPC I remembered spurning my high school romance. When I first went off to college, I had a home town girlfriend who I wrote almost every day. After a few days at college, I made some friends, got involved in my classes, and as a result slowed my letter writing down to one time a week. In these letters, I would tell my high school romance that I loved her and couldn't wait until Thanksgiving to be able to hold her again. Then the fraternity parties started. I was in awe of the mature, sexy, beautiful coeds who came up to me at these events and asked me, "Where are you from?" or "What classes are you taking?" I fell in love a thousand times.

I would go back to my college roommate Paul and say, "Do you think, Molly, that good looking junior from Sarasota could ever like me?"

He'd cluck his tongue and say, "What about Nancy, your high school romance, isn't she waiting back home?" After the Thanksgiving break I never again wrote my ex-girlfriend a letter. I forgot all about her. I was an ass. I didn't give a shit about her.

Sitting in my office I started to feel like the spurned girlfriend. No calls, no letters. I only hope that Nancy eventually found her true love and doesn't give a shit about me.

Part of the exodus of help and calls was my fault. I fought hard to mask the disaster going on around me. It's like when you ask someone, "How are you feeling?" I believe most people only want to hear the answer 'fine' and not some long winded explanation about every disease or cold the person had over the past year. When someone asked me how I was, I always answered, "Fine." Any time I felt like writing or calling someone to even broach the subject of needing help I talked myself out of it. I was always sure I would be greeted with disappointment. Most people have their own problems. We are all self absorbed. Whether it's a child, work, marriage, in-laws, or money, it does not matter. My father-in-law imparted his wisdom on the matter to me, "Ken, if they put all the problems in the world in a big bowl and asked everyone to pick out the worst ones, we would all pick our own."

If I was about to tell someone my story I would catch myself and immediately stop. I'd just imagine them on the other end of the line. "What? Oh, right, right bankrupt, bank, no money. Can you believe the coach only let little Johnny pitch for one inning?" And to them that was a much bigger problem.

Debra was the only person I could turn to not only for sympathy but also to help me in matters of business. She knew my story and so this provided me with a comfort level. I did not have to fake around or put up walls to hide the MPC fiasco. Another good thing about Debra was she always had advice.

"Ken, I really think you should contact an attorney about going bankrupt."

"It's time you really start to look for a job."

"Ken, you do know you need to get your taxes done."

"Have you found someone to clean the factory? What about …."

The problem was I did not always take her advice. A number of times I'd make some flimsy excuse to Debra about how I was working on so and so and planned on contacting the tax accountant, but had not got around to it. I would get to MPC with this or that intention, but always had trouble following through. The simplest tasks seemed overwhelming. It was like I was looking at a completely cluttered basement and saying, "Well, I'll get to that tomorrow." My work ethic, like a muscle not used, had atrophied.

I was afraid of being one of Debra's failures. "Yes, I once had this patient who I could not help. He never opened up. Kept everything and I mean everything trapped deep inside. Shit, I tried and tried, yet nothing really worked. I wonder whatever became of him."

THIRTY-ONE

I needed March to arrive. I needed for the waiting to end. I needed Debra to unmask what it is that can help me survive this hell-on-earth I had created. As February was coming to an end, I often sat in my office alone or on the drive to and from work and fantasized way more than usual. It was an escape I had used in many different forms at many different times in my life. While growing up I could easily sit in a classroom or in my bedroom and transport myself into a fantasy world. I believed I was going to be a great man, a man who made a difference. People would clamor to get a glimpse of me as I walked down streets, red carpets, or athletic stadiums. I always could mentally put myself into the shoes of someone greater.

Here I was a middle-aged man, in utter ruins, dreaming like a schoolboy. I visualized being a hero, like Robert Langdon in *The DaVinci Code*, or being cool like Robert DiNero. I welcomed danger like James Bond and Jason Bourne. I sang lots of songs on many stages with Mick Jagger, Van Morrison, and the Grateful Dead. I played guitar in stadiums with the Red Hot Chili Peppers while Anthony Kiedis soulfully belted out Aeroplane. Presidents, both Republicans and Democrats, sought my sage advice. In my imaginary worlds I had married Nicole Kidman, Meg Ryan, Kiera Knightly, and Uma Thurman. I imagined the setting where we would meet and how I would win each of these starlets over. They all loved me unconditionally. After all I was their hero. I danced the twist with Uma Thurman countless times to Chuck Berry's 'You Never Can Tell'. I told Kiera Knightly on a number of occasions that she had "bewitched me body and soul." I believed there was a Hogswarts full of witches and wizards. That good always triumphs over evil. That Lord Voldemort never really had a chance. Reading a book or watching a movie at times became exhausting because I became the main character. I could feel the main character's pain or success; the story was happening to me. Books were always better. In a book the hero always looked like me. He had my mannerisms. I just borrowed his heroism.

I not only did this with movies and books, but made up situations in which I imagined my life turning out differently. What if I went to Yale University and met a different woman? Would I then have become a movie star, a famous athlete, a statesman, or an inventor? Would I live on Avenue Foch in Paris' high society Arrondissement? I saw myself at social gatherings in high-ceilinged, perfectly decorated rooms. Drinking champagne, I would speak fluent French and entertain the whole party with my tales of adventure. "Oui, j'etais dans le desart du Sahara quand ...." There were times that I did not want to leave my car when I arrived at MPC or home for the night. It only ended the fantasy. I would be back to the phone calls, head and heartaches.

When I told Debra that I 'occasionally' fantasize, she said fantasies were good for me. They would help relieve the enormous stress I was experiencing. I never went into the details. I often suspected Debra would not comprehend just how deep rooted my fantasias were or how much I mind-tripped. Once when Francie and I were at a party, during the MPC ordeal, we ran into the mother of one of her pre-school students. Francie and the woman must have been talking for ten to fifteen minutes, when I heard Francie say, "Ken, Ken, Misses Moore just asked you a question." I apologized and explained that I was thinking about the words to the song 'The Chimes of Freedom' by Bob Dylan. Ms. Moore was a little taken back. Francie turned to the woman and said, "It's not you. He does that a lot."

I had wandered back to the sixties when the song was written. I was marveling at the words and how they recently touched a nerve. I felt like I was the aching one in the song who could not be nursed.

I thought what if I had written that song? Would I have been able to get it published? Maybe my son Bernie and his band could have made it famous and I would be introduced at their shows. "All right, we have a special treat tonight. Before our next song we'd like to introduce the great song writer, Ken Sabino."

I also wanted to know what made the people in my fantasies successful. What common trait did they share? The trait that I needed and wanted, but was obviously missing. Were they lucky, in the right place at the right time? Was it their tenacity, their brains, or purely their incredible skill? Is there something I could have done to prevent the disaster I found myself in? I always wondered if my depression somehow was responsible for what happened to me or is what happened the reason I'm depressed.

When I would let Francie know how different it would be if I had been a success at my job, she always responded, "A person with a depressed personality could win the lotto and still be depressed. A person who is generally happy will always be happy."

When I related Francie's words to Debra, she agreed, and added that I have been depressed for quite some time. She wanted to explore this through my childhood and my relationship with my parents and siblings. She tried to get me to talk about events that centered on growing up in Connecticut. I rarely had something to share. When I did it was juvenile, offering things like, "I remember senior year in high school when we played Blessed Sacrament of New Rochelle in football and I tackled their great wide receiver Bob McMillian. I remember the feeling of being proud, satisfied and happy. They put my picture in the Greenwich

Times." Or I might say, "I liked pretending to be a musical group, my friends Paul and Claude, my brother Marty and I would lip sync while a Crosby, Stills, Nash and Young record played, scratches and all, in the background."

When I talked about sad events they mostly centered on death: a good friend being shot in a bar, how my friend's mom passed away, or how sad I was when my grandfather died suddenly on Christmas Eve. I related the story about a buddy's car accident on the way home from school. And yes, of course, when my friend Sonny picked me up at O'Hare airport to drive me to Evanston Hospital to see my son for the last time. I know Debra wanted more and she also knew it would be hard to get it from me. I had trained myself to live in a fake world.

If Debra had asked me, "What would you fantasize as your best or worst memories," I could have talked all session. I could have gone on and on with all my great escapades where I heroically saved the day. For those limited bad stories, I'd tell how I overcame anxiety before I whisked away the girl or brought the diabolic evil one to justice. But I would never fail ... *never*. The story always ended the same, with the hero, Ken Sabino, in his golden years sitting with his faithful spouse Francie in a villa in Tuscany, Provence, or Florida. The sun is magnificently setting behind the rolling hills as the great man takes a sip of his aged red Bordeaux wine. The hero and his wife are comfortably surrounded by family members, their children, and grandchildren. The grandchildren are all demanding, "Please, Pops, tell us the story again about how you saved the day."

THIRTY-TWO

Since there was not much for me to do at MPC as we entered March, I intensified the last and, according to Francie and Debra, most important item to be addressed, looking for a new job. Bucky had already approached me and asked me to work for his company. The problem was that as we neared March, I had not been paid one single penny by Bucky. As luck had it, bad luck naturally, Bucky ran into medical problems during the middle of February requiring stays in the hospital. This not only slowed down our negotiations, but also moving equipment, signing contracts, and my employment agreement. My hunch was that once we started our negotiations Bucky would want to pay me a percentage of sales. My fear was that the customers I was bringing over to Bucky from MPC had already found alternate routes for packaging products.

A new world of job search awaited me. I thought the initial step in looking for a job would be to prepare a resume—a task I last completed twenty plus years earlier. I figured after I did the minimal work needed to update it, I would immediately contact head hunters and be on my way.

Kevin, my running buddy, had moved to Denver, Colorado, a year earlier to take a job that was the result of an extensive job search. I reasoned he would be the best place to start for advice. Kevin, being a doctor's son, grew up living a privileged life, only three houses—yet still a full half mile—from Francie in Wilmette. He had a slight air of entitlement and was of the opinion I should too. Kevin was a loyal and reliable man. Kevin and I had developed a tight friendship during the past few years as a result of our running club and playing golf together. I knew he would take the task seriously and go the extra mile for me.

When Kevin moved west our club lost its social chairman. He had an amazing quality of being able to get us to do things as a group, go out to dinner, watch a movie, or bike along the lake. Kevin, like Maria, originally joined the running club because of a problem he was experiencing. Needing a way to vent the issues, he figured—correctly—that he would have both a physical outlet and support group with our runs.

Accounting for the hour time difference, I figured eleven a.m. Chicago time would be a good time to call. After some pleasantries, I got down to business.

"Hey, Kevin, calling to see if you can give me some clues on finding a job. I have a deal with the company that bought the MPC accounts, but ... not so sure it's going to pan out well. I may have to find something better."

Hiding the fact of MPC's real failure, I made some flimsy excuse for my job search. "You know how ex and new owners eventually have a falling out. I prepared a resume I'd like you to look at. When it's ready I'll send it along to head hunters. Do you still have the names of the head hunters you used?"

After a little chuckle Kevin said, "Dude, it's the twenty-first century. No head hunters, you'll use the computer. It's all done on the Internet nowadays." He chortled again. "Where the hell've *you* been?"

You have to have a certain type of personality to say 'Dude' when you're over forty years old. Kevin has that personality. Now, a Dick Chaney type ... he would have trouble throwing a *dude* out at someone.

Kevin turned me on to the world of Careerbuilders.com, Execunet.com, Monster.com, and Craigslist.com. He led me through the maze of searching for jobs on the internet. He instructed me to look at postings on manufacturing trade organizations' web sites. He said I should contact people in my industry via email. He gave me a pep talk on not underselling myself. He also warned me to be prepared for a long and extensive search. It was then that I recognized he, like a number of others, assumed I had sold MPC for a profit and therefore had the time to properly search for a high paying, exciting position. I did not have the heart to tell one of my closest friends that Francie and I would most likely be living with a relative in April if I did not find a job very soon.

Kevin was not the only person who made assumptions about my situation. I received calls from family members, old friends, even business associates congratulating me on retiring or asking me what's going on? My old high school friend and college roommate Paul called to let me know he was happy for me and proud of me. I wanted to stop him a number of times but didn't. I let him go on and falsely praise me.

By not coming clean on the MPC disaster, I had left it up to everyone to make up their own interpretation. Generally, most people did not want to assume the worst. I never corrected them. I was amazed at the assumptions people made about the amount of money I made on the sale. I had to white lie constantly about my retirement plans.

On rare occasions, I received a call expressing concern. There was one instance I recall where the caller did not assume a good situation. It was a call I received from Murph.

"Ken, I am calling to ask you one question. Once you answer I'll not ask or bother you again on this subject, unless you bring it up. Is everything okay with MPC?"

A little stunned, I lied, "Yes, Yes. It's been tough though. Losing market share to Asia, and gas and raw materials prices sky rocketing hasn't helped. But all I can do is fight it out. It's the life I chose."

"Good, Finley had me worried. He said he's been trying to call you and email you at MPC. The phone is disconnected and the emails bounce back to him. He's been in business a long time and according to him, those are signs of a company going belly up. He didn't have your home phone so he called me."

"Tell Finley not to worry. Here is a number he can reach me at."

I hastened to change the subject. I asked him what he thought of Ralph Nader joining the Presidential election. I figured this would get him worked up enough to forget about MPC and me.

Keeping it all trapped inside my head was excruciating. My mind was screaming to let it all out, but I resisted. I wanted to scream—shout out to everyone who I came in contact with—*look at me I'm dying inside,* help *me!* But I was afraid, afraid of the reaction, afraid of losing a friendship, afraid of how I might act. It was a subject that Debra and I discussed constantly. Was I ashamed, worried what family and friends would think, or was I embarrassed to ask for help? I expressed to Debra that I believed if I asked for help I might be hopelessly let down by the answer—I would rather not take the risk. Debra often responded that she knows asking for help is extremely humiliating. "Ken, I know you feel ashamed asking for help, but you must." She informed me of how the First Methodist Church often gives money to parishioners to help pay a mortgage. "You'd be surprised at how many people on the North Shore need help. Have you talked to Paul or Murph about your situation?"

I had not. I dared not. They thought highly of me and I did not want to let them down. I lied to Murph and I purposely let Paul believe I was a success. Paul and Murph of all people had seen me at my worst. They had seen the high school and college Ken Sabino. I know they would be concerned and nonjudgmental. Yet, I could never bring myself to tell them how much I was now suffering.

I'd say to Debra, "Why am I like this? I don't know how to express myself. I come off as whiney."

"It's something we are exploring. When we have the answer, we'll work on correcting it."

I jotted down a note at the time of the Paul and Murph calls to remind myself to give Debra my exact feelings on this subject during our next session. God, I felt like her vacation would never end. I needed to hear, "Fuck, Ken, stop worrying about Paul and Murph. You'll tell them when you're ready. Now, how did everything else go these past two weeks? Tell me about the bank."

***

Toward the end of February there were a few people who were beginning to understand just how bad my problems were at MPC. The facts of the house about to be gone and the money loss were now known to my children, George, Dan, Annie, Eileen, and Tim. They, along with Debra and Francie, began helping me to build the raft to get off Defoe's deserted island. Almost every day Katie, my eldest daughter, called to ask me how I was doing. Was there anything she could be doing to help? Ironically, Katie was working for Catholic Charities in their newly formed Homeless Prevention Center. Rose, my youngest child, always had a positive attitude. She would constantly go up to Francie and say things like, "Don't worry about Dad; he is smart and will figure it out." Dominic and Bernie never asked for money even though I know it was much needed at college. Tony told me he would not do anything for Bucky unless he agreed to hire me. Recently Annie had again started to frequently text me with words of encouragement. Tim Kelly called about once a week to see if there was any way he could help.

THIRTY-THREE

On Saturday, the first day of March, 2008, I drove out to Skokie to meet with David Morales for the second time. The moment to officially go bankrupt was just about upon me. On the 15th of March the building would be sold, the MPC client accounts had been sold, inventory had been built and sold, and the equipment was sold. So, according to David, I was ready to file for Chapter 7 and wipe the slate clean as of the 16th of March. I showed up at his office at about eleven a.m., directly from my Saturday run. I again walked into the large cluttered room. This time I noticed there was a heavy-set older man sitting in the middle of the room. He was dark skinned and a little hard to see with the fire blazing next to him. He had on a herring bone suit jacket and sat stoically in a large armchair, legs crossed, looking at no one or anything in particular. He looked well groomed in spite of his clothes being as old he was. I felt like I had walked into an old time private eye's office. It was like something out of a Sam Spade novel. I sort of waved at him and did not get a response. Behind the old man a TV had on a basketball game. He may have been listening, but, I know, unless he had eyes in the back of his head he was not watching. I was about to say something to the man when David came out of the back office. "Hey Ken, how is everything? Are you hanging in there? Come on back." I walked back to his office thinking it was pretty strange not to be introduced to the gentleman.

David asked to be updated concerning the equipment, house, building, and account sales. I tried to fill him in as precisely as he would let me. I could tell that sometimes details were not necessary. He then gave me the information I needed to prepare in order to go bankrupt. I had to list all creditors, addresses, contacts, and amount owed. I had to fill out forms detailing how much I was paid in the past two years. I needed tax returns for the past three years for MPC and myself. I had to list all properties I owned. I had to identify all my bank accounts including those that had been closed during the past year. All numbers had to be precise. I needed to show who had been paid what. Once all the information was gathered, David would file the necessary forms, and then all assets would be controlled by a trust. The members of the trust would, within forty-five days, call me to come before them to be questioned about the amounts owed. David put a little fear into me when he said, "With an amount this large they will have extensive questions. Also, the trust will take control of your house immediately after filing."

The biggest fear that people like the bank, trust members, and vendors have is something illegal is going to or may have already taken place. The bank, the day after I called informing them of MPC's problems, sent an auditor out to MPC to look at all financial information. Almost immediately after the MPC situation was known, the bank also sent out two representatives to take an inventory of all the equipment in the factory. Their worry was that I could sell a piece of equipment to a friend, vendor, or competitor and get paid under the table. So, theoretically I could sell equipment, product, steel, computers, or almost any item in the factory for cash. Another item that concerned the trust and vendors is when exactly I knew my company was going under and did I continue buying goods and services knowing the severity of the situation. In other words did I buy items with the knowledge they would not be paid for?

Another form I had to complete for David was called a Transfer Statement. On the report I had to list all monies over six hundred dollars that had been transferred out of my personal accounts and the MPC accounts within the past ninety days. The sole purpose of the report was to follow the money. They wanted to make sure I did not foresee financial problems and just happen to move millions of dollars to an account in Switzerland. I understood the concern and laughed to myself when I filled out the report and listed my February mortgage payment and the six hundred and ten dollar Visa payment I made electronically in February as the only transfers out of my account within the past ninety days. I wanted to put an asterisk on the report.

* I was not smart enough to put the house in Francie's name; I did not move money to my children. I have a ton of college loans that I cannot include in the bankruptcy. There are no offshore accounts. Sorry guys, wish I could help, but you're going to be amazed at how dumb I was. There is no money to follow. All I have is a 401(k) account that is about to run out of money.

Toward the end of our half hour meeting I wrote a check to David for a portion of the amount I owed him for his services. Since it was getting down to my last dime, I hoped it was money well spent. We said our goodbyes and David walked me to the door. As I was leaving, I noticed the old gentleman was gone.

Driving home, I realized I was into another intense moment where I was about to expose my whole MPC work life to a committee that would make judgments and decisions determining what my life would be like until the day I died. I was worried about how this would affect my in-laws, the accountants I worked with for the past ten years, Francie, and the kids. The seriousness of going bankrupt, believe it or not, was becoming real to me for the first time.

"On work applications, some employers ask if you have ever gone bankrupt."

"You may not be able to get a loan for a house or otherwise for quite a while."

"You may have to get out of the house sooner, depending on what route the trustees go."

There was more, but I stopped listening and comprehending. I went to work on Monday at MPC for perhaps my last week and began to gather the information David had listed. I kept thinking about the old man. Was he real, did he notice me and how did he disappear? David never gave any indication there was another person in the room. I wanted to be the mysterious 'private eye', sitting cross legged listening to a basketball game in front of a fire, just watching the world go by unaffected by all its troubles waiting for my next case. And then, like magic, poof, disappear at will. No bank, no trustees, no lawyers, no new job, no stigma, no Ken Sabino.

I knew all I had to do was to hold out for a few more days. I would then take my familiar seat across from Debra and we would discuss all these issues. It's weird but I know I was also thinking I must remember to ask her about her vacation in Mexico. It was important to me to know about Debra.

THIRTY-FOUR

Debra's vacation was over and I was once again driving north on the Edens Expressway toward Greenwood on a Wednesday afternoon. The only person more relieved than me was Francie. She saw my anxiety and sullenness, and watched as three beers a night became four. During the drive I realized I had too much to talk about. I had jotted down numerous notes and recorded way too many dreams over the two week period. I was also aware the depression was physically and mentally taking ever-increasing control over me. My money was running out and I was about to sell the building—leaving me truly unemployed. Within forty-five days I would be sitting in front of a bankruptcy board of trustees defending my financial life, and our house would soon be gone. At our family dinners Francie, the kids, and I began to openly discuss the probability of us staying with Francie's mom, "While your dad and I figure things out."

This junkie needed his fix. I had to get into the sanctuary and shoot up. I realized that my greatest anxiety was that with so much on my mind I would blow the hour. So to ensure a great session I kept running all the topics over in my mind I considered most needing resolution. Prior to leaving MPC I reread my dreams for the umpteenth time and tried to think of their meaning or what Debra would interpret as the meaning.

I was almost happy in a pathetic way. I would be able to openly discuss all that had bothered me for the past two weeks without restrictions. Not only that, I would be able to get the answer as to why they should or should not be bothering me. If I was lucky, I would get an entertaining Mexican vacation story thrown in for free. I had become a person who went from being openly afraid to see a therapist to one who was obsessed with his next session.

There is a TV show on the USA channel called *Monk* that Francie and I had been watching regularly. Adrian Monk, played by Tony Shalhoub, is a private detective who cannot help but pay attention to even the smallest details in his daily life. In addition, he is a meticulous neat freak—to the point of having an obsessive compulsive personality disorder. As a homicide detective he brings these traits to crime scenes. He will notice a minor detail about the crime scene that all the other detectives missed. Always there will be doubts by someone concerning Monk's abilities, even though for the previous hundred weeks in a row he's solved the case. On the show, because of all his phobias, his wife's tragic death, and his constant state of unhappiness, Monk sees a psychiatrist. It is some of the best interaction on the show. Stanley Kamel, the person who plays psychiatrist Dr. Kroger, does a marvelous job of working with Monk. He helps him through his problems, he offers suggestions, and he tells Monk when he is wrong about an issue. On one show Dr. Kroger decides to retire and has recommendations for Monk as to who he can see. Monk cannot get comfortable with any of the other recommended therapists. He needs to sit in his same seat with Kroger in his same chair seated to Monk's right. The session must be on the same day each week and at the time that Monk has become accustomed to. The show exaggerates some of the points for comedic effect. But it is still about as good an interpretation of the relationship between a therapist and patient that I've seen on TV.

Monk is right about the relationship in a number of ways. I know that if Debra asked me to switch seats with her, I would not be able to concentrate all session. Like Monk, I am used to the regularity. Debra, even though I have never accepted, must ask me before we start a session if I would like something to drink. I would be thrown off if she didn't. She needs to end each session in the same way. I need to hear, "What a great session. See you next Wednesday at six." Debra and I have invested well over a year together. For the first six months that I saw Debra I hardly spoke or opened up. Like Monk, I would not be able to sit in a new office, in a new chair, with different books on the shelf, and continue on with a new person right where I left off with Debra. I would definitely have to go back to square one. I may or may not talk. I may or may not hit it off with the person. Debra and I have established a trust.

The relationship would be hard to explain for a number of reasons. I could not tell friends that I sometimes picture Debra slightly hovering above looking down at me when I feel anxiety. I imagine her telling me to calm down and then taking the deep breath she takes when I start to get worked up during a session. I rely on Wednesdays as a means to get me through difficult times. Debra rarely says, "And how do you feel about that?" like the joke you often see with psychiatrists on TV or in the movies. She engages me, reprimands me, advises me, tells me when I'm wrong or right, and she feels my pain and sadness. On many occasions I tell myself when confronted with an issue, "I'll ask Debra about that," and immediately jot down a note on the moleskine I keep in my back pocket. The moleskine that I worry I'll accidentally leave at a party exposing what a wreck I am. I always believed that it was the therapist who kept the patient coming back so they can make more in fees. I now know it's the patient who has trouble cutting the cord. I feel like I will be going to Debra for years to come. Why would I quit? Each session seems like a date. I prepare the questions I will ask. I want Debra to know all about me. I want her approval. I am like a schoolboy. I cannot imagine having a male therapist.

The week off from therapy made me edgy. It seemed as if I had tried to quit smoking or drinking. I felt weird physically and mentally, but at the time could not really pin down why. I reread the notes I had jotted down during the previous two weeks. I realized some of my issues either worked themselves out or they did not seem as big anymore. I should have seen this as a good sign, but did not.

I arrived way too early for the session. Since it was getting dark I did not mind waiting in my car in front of Debra's office. But I still slumped down in the driver's seat just in case someone was around that I might know. As I sat there I once again tried to recount in my head all the issues I needed to discuss. I silently gave myself a pep talk to tell her, "The fears I have, the anxiety, how tied up in a knot I am."

At ten to six I exited my car, crossed the street, and opened the door to Debra's downstairs foyer. As usual I ran up the stairs as silently as I could until I reached room number four. I entered the outer office and immediately ran into the bathroom. After an hour drive I always had to go. I washed my face and was now ready to sit under harmony and tranquility, and have my pathetic life straightened out. I left the bathroom and took a seat on the couch in the outer office. In recent months the door between the two offices had been closed. Debra had obviously filled the time slot directly in front of me. So upon my arrivals I tried to listen to see if I could hear voices coming from the inner office. If I heard muted voices I knew I had a little wait before the door would swing open. Occasionally, the five o'clock would not show, and I would get to enjoy—ha, ha—an extra five to ten minutes with Debra. This night I heard muffled goodbyes and a door shutting. The person before me was probably as anxious as me to come tonight. A few minutes later I heard the turn of the knob and the door separating the two rooms opened. "Ken, how great to see you. Can I get you something to drink?" I wanted to jump into her arms and tell her it was already the best I'd felt in two weeks.

We talked a little about Mexico. I did not forget to ask her about the trip. She went with three other couples and they all had two meals a day together for ten days and never argued. "Can you believe it?" She did get sunburned. "God, not so good for a girl from LA."

Once we finished with small talk I went straight into the status of the building, my job, my money, and the equipment sale. I was a loose cannon, jumping from subject to subject. I could not get all the issues out fast enough. I had been reviewing in my mind each issue on a daily basis for two weeks. The faucet was open and out flowed issue after issue. The whole session was—sorry, not the session, me—I was *nuts*. I did not wait for questions or follow ups. I watched Debra in amazement as she listened patiently.

Finally Debra interjected, a little surprised, "You're still going to MPC in Bensenville?"

"Yes."

"Fuck, Ken, that's crazy. You have to get this over with. You can't continue to go to MPC. You have to stop."

"Well, the building is scheduled to be torn down next Thursday, so that has to be my last day. Sorry, I have been talking, complaining, and bitching the whole session."

"Ken, of all the people I see, you complain the least. And you have the most right, considering that your issue is probably the biggest right now."

In a somewhat goofy, relieved manner I felt some sort of satisfaction with that statement. I always worried that I was wasting everyone's time, especially Debra's. I was taught that if I had a problem, I should go solve it. I felt like I was being pushed to my mental and physical limits. The problem is I did not know how my situation compared to normalcy. What is my pain threshold? Had I started to crack way before what was normal? Was my problem, comparatively speaking, small? I felt like Debra had just confirmed that I did have a big problem and my mental and physical states should be worn out to the max.

I had shot all my bullets, I was physically drained. Debra filled the void. I think she sensed I was ready to share intimate details with her.

"Are you bitter," she asked.

"About what?"

"Living here in Chicago. The jobs you've had. Toward Francie, your in-laws, the bank, anything, or one?"

"If I am bitter, it's directed inward at me. I never took the initiative to put myself in a situation that would make me happy. It's not Francie's fault that I live in Chicago. I should have presented a better case for either moving or taking jobs I would be happy with."

"Ken, what bothers you most?"

"A few things; everything going on in my life right now I feel is out of my control. I am awfully unhappy and I made a ton of bad decisions that led to this disaster. This has made me a little gun shy on making new decisions. And, I am a complete nervous wreck."

After each of my answers, I noticed Debra madly taking notes. She was trying to comprehend everything that I was saying. I knew she was trying to find out what will work for me.

Does she pour over her notes before I arrive? Had she, like me, prepared for this session and as a result had a ton of questions to ask me. What goes on when I leave? Are notes recorded? Does Debra talk about me into a tape recorder like I've seen on TV or read about in books? Maybe someday I'll ask Debra these questions.

She looked up from her notes. "Ken, are you ready to lash out at anyone or anything?"

"No, I've learned to contain myself."

Debra then suddenly moved to the front of her seat and half laughing belted out, "Do you remember when George Costanza goes to rageaholics on *Seinfeld*?"

We both laughed. It was our perfect segue into my dreams. Debra had me read two of the dreams that I recorded. One of the dreams started with Debra as a moderator. I picked it as a compliment, even though I had instructed myself not to reveal to her how much I'd thought about and missed her during the past two weeks. I almost wanted to reprimand her. Debra, you're not allowed to leave me this long ever again. How would you feel if I had jumped off a cliff? Huh?

Debra was leading a seminar in which I was a participant. I noticed I was late for another appointment. I excused myself and left the seminar room. I needed to get to another place. It was extremely difficult for me to decide on the best mode of transportation. My brother Marty showed up, saw my dilemma and said, "Take the El. The place where you're going is only two stops away. You will be there in ten minutes."

We had already talked about my decision making, so we put the dream down. She did mention as an aside that my brother represents someone I consider successful and it is why he appeared in a lot of my dreams. Marty, unlike me, did it by taking the conservative route. He lived within himself. I did consider him a success and I admired him for both this success and his pride in it.

Marty Sabino left home in 1979, like me, to follow his girlfriend, now wife Sally, to California where she was finishing up at USC. He spent most of his then saved up money on the 105 dollar one-way plane ticket to LA and the 125 dollars toward his first month rent. He was down to thirty dollars when he began applying for jobs. He was quickly accepted and hired as a sales rep for Anheiser-Busch. Because Sally and Marty had very little money and were just starting out, they lived in South Central LA, a notoriously bad crime ridden section of the city. To help with their situation Marty tried to get his neighbors to like him. Every Friday he would drive to a gang infested street corner, open his car door and, without leaving the car, drop off a case of Budweiser beer on the ground next to the lads and then drive away. Never did he offer a salutation; never did he utter a word. When the Rodney King riots took place in this section of LA, white-owned stores, houses, cars, and people were terrorized. Not one rioter dared touch an article owned by Marty and Sally. He once told me he could have walked right down the middle of the riots and would have been untouched. All because once a week he dropped off a case of Budweiser beer on a street corner.

Almost thirty years later, he still works for Anheiser-Busch. He owns a house and a condo in Orlando, Florida. All his houses have always had a pool. He travels freely. He never worries about money. He often tells me, “Ken, I consider myself to be living the American Dream.” He went from our childhood apartment with US Route 95 as its back yard, to his first adult apartment in South Central LA, to a house with a pool.

It was approaching seven p.m. I was about to get up when Debra told me that I should try to worry less. She then said, “Every day, when you get to work, write down all your worries on a piece of paper and throw them in a box. The box now owns the worries and not you. Go about the day as if you have given all your worries away.”

As I was leaving I said, “I’m glad you’re back.” I know I said it in a way that was as close to flirting as I had ever been with Debra. I hope she didn’t take it wrong. She told me as I was getting my pat on the back, “I’ll see you next week at six p.m. Thanks for a great session.” Ahhhh, normalcy!

I left the building into the cool winter air. I tried to convince myself the weather was getting ready to change. There was a different crispness in the air. As I walked across the wide snow-filled median to my car, I made sure I balanced myself to keep from falling. When I got to the car, I half chuckled to myself and thought, you knucklehead, the snow will never melt. Global warming missed Chicago.

***

My son Bernie called on March 6, 2008, from Bellarmine University. Bernie, who had never been hurt his whole life, tore his ACL at lacrosse practice that day. He would be out for the season. At midnight that night the health insurance that I signed up for on the internet expired. Only I would consider it lucky that a son tore his ACL just in the nick of time. The next day would have been a day too late and another Sabino tragedy.

***

At MPC the next day, I wrote down my worries—a new job, my money situation, the bank, health insurance, and cleaning the building—on a lined yellow piece of paper. I walked out into the factory and picked out one of the hundreds of half empty boxes lying around. I threw the yellow paper in the selected box. I looked up toward the twenty-four foot high ceiling and, half praying, said out loud, “Hopefully, Debra is right. These are your worries now.” I thought I knew one thing for sure: with any luck, in a week the yellow paper with the box would be under a few tons of rubble. I walked back into the office to sit in the dark and hoped my phone did not ring.

THIRTY-FIVE

Irritability: that was the word of the month for March. I hated the fucking bank, the fucking bank hated me. Wiley Granderson, my attorney, and Brian Fagan, my realtor, both hated the fucking bank, Bucky and, most likely, me. Bucky fucking hated the bank. The bank was fucking frustrated with Bucky. The bank fucking hated Fagan and Wiley. George—ah, shit for some fucking reason—tried to be the voice of reason, but had trouble. I probably heard the word 'fuck' or a derivative over a thousand times in the first couple of weeks of March. "The fucking bank, why did they do that?" "I'm not going to the fucking buyer and asking for a fucking extension," "Who the fuck is going to pay for that?"

Like the old proverb says, too bad I didn't get a dollar every time I heard the word fuck. The bank would have been fucking financially satisfied already.

The building, once bought, was going to be torn down and made into a parking lot. And, yes, I had been constantly humming the lyrics to 'Big Yellow Taxi' by Joni Mitchell. The buyer supposedly had demolition crews scheduled for the day after the closing. Lee owned numerous trucks that shipped meats all over the Midwest. Up until the building tear down, he had been renting space to park his trucks at night and on weekends. It made economic sense for Manny to buy a 1.7 million dollar building, spend money tearing it down, and pave a new sixty thousand plus square foot parking lot. The absolute bonus for Manny was the space was next door.

Coming up to the building sale we had a major predicament: we had fifty thousand square feet of junk, equipment, product, paperwork, furniture, computers, forklifts, and tools. It all had to be gone by the closing. The closing was scheduled for Wednesday, March 12, 2008. On the previous Tuesday and Wednesday there had been plenty of calls amongst the bank, realtor, attorney, George, and me. Yet not one item had been removed from MPC. The biggest concern was the equipment. Really, the only item in the building that had any value to the bank, and therefore me, was the 171 thousand dollars worth of machinery and equipment.

Bucky, in January, had agreed to buy all the MPC equipment and any customer accounts not taken by Great Lakes for 171 thousand dollars. One problem, he did not have his financing in order, so Bucky was not prepared to immediately drop "one seventy-one large," into Addison's lap. The bank would not let Bucky move the machines until after he had paid or showed the manner in which he was going to pay the bank. The Bank went as far as to say that I had to drop Bucky and use an alternate equipment purchaser. When we went to the market and looked at other possibilities we realized Bucky had the best deal for all involved. He was willing to pay for and move the machines, he had offered me a job, and he had volunteered to help clean up the factory. So, in March the bank reconsidered Bucky and asked me to see if I could get him back involved. When I contacted Bucky, he was still enthusiastic about the opportunity and agreed to jump back in. Two problems: we wasted about a month of valuable time and Bucky had stopped the process of getting financing. The bank, although approving of and petitioning for Bucky, again would not let the equipment be moved unless Bucky paid, showed his method of financing, or provided financial information to them. The staring contest was on; who would blink first? Bucky was insulted that the bank did not trust him. Also, he did not understand their position. He felt that if he did not come up with the money, the bank still had liens on all the equipment. All that would have been done is the equipment would be moved out of the Bensenville facility and into the Franklin Park facility. Bucky reasoned that the bank, regardless of his financial situation, needed the equipment moved. He said, “Shit, I’d be doing them a favor even if I don’t pay.”

As we fast forwarded to the Wednesday before the building close was scheduled neither party had blinked and the fuck fest was on. I was not much help. I personally saw Bucky’s point, but wished he would pay the bank and move the equipment. So, I sat on the fence, took calls, and offered no strong opinion. One thing I did believe: the bank had the weaker stand. They needed Bucky, more than Bucky needed them. The equipment had to be moved or we would forfeit any possible funds they would command in a sale. Finally, toward the end of the day on Wednesday the bank caved. They called Bucky and consented; they would allow him to move the equipment if he signed a few documents promising to pay. Basically, all the bank wanted was an IOU. Bucky agreed. A truce was on.

Bucky was at MPC with a machine mover on Thursday, the day after the bank agreed to let the equipment be moved. Bucky, the mover, and I, all paraded around the factory deciding the best method of moving or selling the excess machines Bucky did not need. Bucky had a call into a second rigger—machine mover—that was to help with some of the bigger machines. It was a big job and we only had four working days. But, wow, it might happen, the equipment moved and the place reasonably cleaned up prior to the following Wednesday close.

As I was in my momentary state of satisfaction, I heard Bucky say to the second rigger, “Are you sure next Friday is the best date you can give me?” My heart sank. When Bucky got off the phone and reiterated the news I had just overheard, I emailed Wiley, Brian, and Frank at the bank at once. I knew Friday, since it was after the scheduled close, was not going to be well received or acceptable. I felt the sooner we closed the better. I simply thought we had two choices: clean up before the close or get the buyer to agree to move the close date out so we had more time to move machines and clean up. Bucky did have one ace up his sleeve that could keep the close date as planned but still have the equipment moved out before the Wednesday close. All we had to do was pay an expedite charge to the rigger. He would then send a crew over and have the machines moved in time. I was gullible enough to think we were all reasonable businessmen with three choices, how hard could it be to come to a sound and sane conclusion? Like a broken truce during war time, the moments immediately following the open fire were the most savage. The silence or down time allowed the combatants to build up and store energy that would be released with a fury when the time comes. Oh, yeah, the time had come. Wiley, Brian, and George did not want to move the close date and blow the deal over a few thousand dollars expedite fee; neither the bank nor Bucky wanted to be responsible for paying the expedite fee, so both suggested the close date get moved out a week. The bank especially dug their heels in the sand. They did not want to pay an expedite fee. They felt the buyer should be approached and asked if we could change the close date to a week later. I felt sick about the thought of moving the close date out. I wanted closure. We were in a buyers' market. So, like George, Brian, and Wiley, I was worried that Manny might either walk from the deal or more likely want to lower his 1.7 million dollar bid. So the battle lines were drawn and the volleys were again ready to begin.

Bucky left MPC that day at about two thirty. Immediately after he left I received a call from Brian, an email from Brian, then Wiley, Wiley, Brian, Wiley, a call from Bucky, a call from Frank, a call from George, sent an email to Wiley, Brian, and Frank, a call from George, a call from Frank on the way home, on the way to work calls from George, Brian, Frank, Nick, Bucky, and George. Let me see, a thousand fucks times a dollar made me an additional thousand dollars. The bank finally agreed to pay the expedite fee; they all along had no choice. As soon as he heard from the bank, Bucky called and scheduled the movers for Saturday, Monday, and Tuesday. I barely gave a fuck—one dollar.

THIRTY-SIX

When I arrived at MPC at nine a.m. on the Saturday before the building sale, I was greeted by twenty or so workers, including Tony, Bucky, and Justin. There were two equipment moving companies already hard at work with their forklifts, cranes, and assorted other equipment. There was a bustle of commotion that had been missing in this building for the past two months. In a sad sort of way it was refreshing to once again see activity. The lights were on, there was noise, and people were running around shouting out instructions. I quickly learned that my job was to slow down the vandalism and looting. Anything not pinned down was fair game. Shortly after settling in Tony and I went into the office to see what in there needed to be moved. Upon entering we noticed a worker poking around the office. I asked him what he was doing and he very straight faced said, "I'm looking for a chair."

I informed him the office furniture was not for the taking, to which he responded, "Carlos said I could have one." I asked him to tell me who Carlos was. He brought me into the factory and pointed out another worker.

Carlos Lupino was one of the two equipment movers Bucky had hired. Bucky and Carlos on a number of occasions had worked jobs together. Bucky generally would bring in his friend Carlos as a factory handyman. He moved equipment, cleaned, fixed, basically he could do it all. He definitely was one crazy Mexican, or so I was told. He had a barrel chest for sure, but was on the short side, definitely old, and a little more than worn out looking. He had kind of a punched in nose, like he had been in a fight and lost. His dark-skinned face had pock marks and he had dark circles under his eyes. Carlos was hardly the type of person who would instill fear in anyone—never mind giants like Bucky and Justin.

Yet here was Bucky telling me I better not mess with that wild fuck. Then he yelled to Carlos, "Hey Carlos, come here a second. Tell Ken the drug dealer story."

"Oh, yeah, man, what a fucking story. When I first came to the US, I moved into the Humboldt Park section of Chicago. Tons of Mexicans, so it was easy. It was much different than today. Lots of gangs, drugs everywhere. You didn't go out after dark. There was this one asshole drug dealer. He hated my guts. He didn't think I gave him the proper respect or some shit. Fuck him. He would always tell me, 'Bro you better watch your back, someday I'm going to kill you.' So at nights when I got home to my apartment, I'd put a chair in our front room, get my shotgun, lay it on my lap, and fall asleep facing the front door. One night I was woken up by a noise on the front stoop of my apartment. Suddenly one of the door's window panes was smashed in. A hand reached through and unlocked the door. The door flew open and there he is, the asshole dealer. I said to him, 'Hey asshole you don't know who you dealing with.' He laughed because he was high on that elephant tranquilizer shit, PCP. So he didn't understand I was ready to fuck him up. He says, 'Fuck you,' to me and took a step toward my chair. So, I shot the fucker. It was like goddamn terminator. He looked at his shoulder, which was half blown off, turned back to me and started to growl like a bear. Grrrrrrrrrrrrrrrr, Grrrrrrrrrrrrrrr. I said like fuck this shit, and shot the fucker again, right in the chest. He lunged at me like a wounded animal; blood was flying all over the place. I was thinking how in the fuck is this asshole not dead. My wife came running in from the bedroom with her pistol. I yelled as I'm wrestling with the fucking bear, 'Honey, don't shoot.' I was afraid she'd kill me. I somehow grabbed the gun from her and shot the fucker one more time, he finally dies. Can you believe the pigs arrested me for murder? There's some crazy rule that if you shoot someone more than two times it's not considered self defense. I tried to tell them the creep wouldn't die. They think I'm bull shitting them so they dragged me to the station house and gave me this mousy lawyer. So, while I am in the room with this lawyer, he turned cautiously toward me and whispered that if I gave him thirty thousand dollars he would get me off the murder charge, no questions asked. So, I like say shit man okay. I figured anything else would get me sent back to Mexico. So I went to everyone I know, rounded up thirty thou and gave it to the lawyer. The next day we went to court, the judge no questions asked dismissed the charges and told me I was free to go. I'm thinking, hey, man, this is a much gooder legal system to Mexico."

Bucky unnecessarily interrupted, "Go on tell him the rest."

"O, yeah, so like two to three months later I read in the paper that US Federal agents had a mole uncover a bunch of crooked judges and lawyers. Something called Operation Greylord. So there was this payoff scheme or some shit where you could buy yourself out of trouble. They listed all the going rates. Manslaughter was twenty thousand dollars, ten for the Judge and ten for the lawyer. Can you believe that shit? That little weasel charged me thirty thousand."

Sometimes when I am in a crowd, a concert, or baseball game type of crowd, my mind might wander. I'd look around and speculate who is the most famous person in this crowd? Is there a famous dignitary, athlete, or entertainment star in the crowd? It would than digress from there, usually weird stuff. Are there porn stars in the crowd? Where are they sitting? What's the average SAT or IQ of the crowd? But, for me, the one that always pops up is is there a murderer in the crowd? How close am I to a murderer—right now? Here I was standing two feet from a person who just told me the story of shooting another man, deliberately, point blank, and with no regrets, none. I am not sure what bothered me most ... that the story did not awe me? Carlos could have just as well told me a whopper of a fishing story. Or, was it that my first thought was to try and formulate if I had it better or worse knowing that I was relying on Carlos? One thing I was absolutely certain of is I was not intimidated by the story. When you've lost everything there is not much that scares you.

As the day continued it became more and more of an absolute mad house. Although I have never been shopping on the Friday after Thanksgiving, it had the same atmosphere I imagined. Workers were trying to take tools, steel, aluminum, wire, copper. I later told Bucky, if the workers were at MPC long enough I'm sure they would have taken home the garbage and told their spouses, "Hey honey, look at this and it didn't cost a dime." It's something to watch people when they think something is for free; they would have taken the rat shit, I'm positive. At some point I did not give the rat's shit what they took, except for product. It was something that I could recycle and for which I would receive some money—not much, but perhaps enough to get Francie and me through another week.

Other than the looting, the day went well. In fact, it turned out to be a very productive day, from the standpoint of moving machines. At least four to five large trucks moved out a number of sizeable fabricating machines. It is amazing to watch a forklift pickup a machine as big as a small garage and plop it on a gigantic truck. Three to four workers would climb up on a machine and wrap chains all around it. Then a forklift comes along and lifts a twenty thousand pound machine right off the ground like it weighed nothing.

Bucky and I at one point found ourselves in the middle of the mayhem sitting alone on a stack of neatly piled up skids. We both had on winter jackets with our hands in our pockets. Bucky's was a bright orange hunting jacket. Due to the size of the trucks, all three dock doors were left wide open throughout the day. It felt as if we were working outside. Bucky broke the silence between us when he turned to me and said, "This must be hard on you, watching the tear down of your company."

It's funny because during my previous session, Debra had advised me to stay away when the building was torn down. But, for some reason, I did not feel bad about the physical destruction. I sat and watched as twenty workers rummaged through my life's work. I felt no ill will, no bitterness, nothing. Mentally, I was exhausted and anything that got me to the end was acceptable. I no longer cared.

I changed the subject and asked Bucky, "What made you go broke?"

"A big customer stuck me with over a half million dollar receivable. I couldn't handle the cash flow loss. I stopped paying vendors and as a result could not get material in. It all caved in on me."

Like getting in, we all had stories of how we got out. Some sell their businesses for a profit, some are sold for losses, some are merged, some are passed down to children, and some go bankrupt.

I've always conjectured that people looked at me and thought I was handed a silver spoon by Francie's family. "Here, Ken, here's a company. Go be a millionaire." No risks, just wake up every morning and count my money. No China, no competitors, expenses will never rise, what an easy life this manufacturing gig is.

Bucky broke my concentration. "Ken, we are manufacturers. That's what we do. I love building things. I love watching product coming off the line. So do you, you'll bounce back."

We continued to sit in quietude on the skids and watched as gradually the factory was emptied out. Hard men were doing a hard, dirty job. Dust was everywhere, as was paper, wood, and tons of other assorted garbage.

I guess it was sad in a way. Not just for me but for all manufacturers. Watching my destruction made Bucky think of his own manufacturing failings. It is almost like a death of a family member, a loved one, someone close. We all share in the sadness of death and when we are at someone's funeral we think of loved ones who passed away or our own mortality.

The last of the trucks left MPC at four p.m. for Franklin Park. They would be back early Monday morning to hopefully take the remaining machines out. I stayed for an additional hour throwing old obsolete product into the recycle bins scattered throughout MPC. When I left for home at five, I was shaking. My nerves were shot. The end of the toughest part of this torture test was four days from being over. I could not control myself. I imagined any disaster that could take place. I was even worried Manny Lee would get hit by a truck over the weekend. I suspected I was about to have a nervous breakdown. All I could think of was my next session with Debra. Get to the next session. There and then I will—should?—be done with the worst part.

I imagined walking into the session and hearing Debra say, "Ken, how did it go this week?"

I'd gleefully say, "The building sale went through. They begin demolition tomorrow."

"What are you going to do now?"

"I don't know."

As I left for home all I thought was, please God make the sale and demolition come true. Get me through the next four days. I was weak, had lost all my will to care about getting things completed, and had no authority even if I did care. When I instructed anyone to do anything I could tell I had lost all respect. "Hey, that steel is not yours. Put it back," was greeted with a smirk. I was the moronic asshole who went broke. Even the people hired to move my equipment held me in low esteem. Shit, why wouldn't they? I, above everyone else, fucking knew why they felt the way they did. Please, Wednesday get here without anything going wrong. I needed help but it was nowhere to be found. Many times I wished I had decided to see Debra twice a week, at least during the latter part of February through the building close in March. She was a comfort and gave me strength in a number of ways. "Ken, you have to see a bankruptcy attorney," or "Ken, you have to make sure they don't garnish your wages," or "Why haven't you done your taxes yet?" I know she would tell me how to handle the equipment move.

THIRTY-SEVEN

It was during the equipment move when I had an anxiety attack in Debra's office. We had just finished reading a dream that involved my friend Murph.

Murph called and said he will be in Chicago for a teacher's convention. Francie and I are completely upset about this news because of our situation.

Debra looked at me and said, "Have you told Murph yet? How about Francie's mom or your family?"

When she finished the questions, I began, without realizing it, to almost violently start rubbing my forehead as I answered, "No."

"When or will you ever tell them?"

"I don't want them to know what a failure I am. I'm not supposed to be this guy. I've always had success. I am not a mope or loser. You know the guy who when he tells you that he lost his job or he's getting divorced, you're not surprised."

Sitting up straighter, Debra said, "Ken, it's good that you see yourself this way."

A little louder, not a yell, but still louder I continued, "I have always been successful. I'd bet I was in the top ten of my class on who was most likely to succeed."

It was then it started to hit me. My heart was trying to beat its way out of my chest. I thought for a second I was having a heart attack.

"Debra, can I stand up?"

"Yes, yes, of course you can, what's the matter?"

"I don't feel right."

"Ken, tell me what's the matter?"

"My chest is killing me."

Debra did not panic; she stood up, looked me directly in the eyes and said, "I want you to breathe exactly like I do." She took a deep-in-the-belly breath, held it for a second, and slowly let it out. She said, "And please, don't look at my tummy while I do the breathing?"

If I didn't feel so shitty, I would have laughed at her slight vanity. Here I am having a heart attack and Debra's worried about looking fat.

She went to do the breathing method for a second time when I said in my nervousness, "I should have gotten the tape Annie offered me. She told me she has a tape that helps you to relax."

With an edge of harshness, Debra said, "Dammit, Ken, forget about Annie's tape and do what I'm telling you."

The seriousness of her voice made me wonder if she thought I had lost my fucking buttons. That the knucklehead might be having a heart attack and he's worried about a tape. But Debra did not feel that way; she knew I was having an anxiety attack. She coached me and helped me to continue with her method of breathing as I settled down.

Once we were seated again Debra said, "So I guess telling people is not something you're quite ready to deal with."

THIRTY-EIGHT

When I showed up on Monday the factory was again abuzz. I quickly surmised that the machines would all be gone by day's end. There was not much for me to do so I took my seat by Bucky; we watched and told more stories. I was beginning to believe it would all work out. Bucky received a phone call about the same time I saw Manny Lee walking into the factory by way of the dock door. I got up and went over to greet him.

"Hi, Manny, I'm Ken."

Barely paying attention to me, while looking around the factory he almost by rote responded,

"Oh, yeah, yeah. Hi, Ken. Yeah, I remember our meeting. Do you think the building will be cleared out by closing?"

"Most, but not everything. You're tearing it down right?"

"Yeah, yeah."

Brian Fagan called me an hour later to say, "Ken, Manny wants the building completely cleaned out prior to the close. How long do you think it will take and how much to clean the factory?"

My heart sank. I knew it would take at a minimum a week if all went well and cost at least five thousand dollars.

We were not foolish when it came to the clean up. It was an issue I had been pushing pretty hard all through February. Our strategy all along had primarily been to get the machines out of the building prior to the close. We would try to clean a little, but mostly take the risk that untidiness would not hold up the sale of the building. If during the close Manny mentioned something about the mess we would offer him a refund of five or ten thousand dollars. We assumed since the building was about to be demolished, Manny did not care about the excess wood and paper lying around. I had witnessed eighty to ninety machines moved out of MPC over a four-day period. Moving these machines had exposed a mountain of trash left behind by forty workers over a five year period. There was unimaginable garbage, chairs, tables, nuts, bolts, gloves, microwaves, clocks, tools, money, hats, clothes, wire, steel, wood, paper, plastic, curtains, pictures, and numerous other items. Almost anything you could reasonably think of was in the factory somewhere. Manny simply stated his position on the excess trash: "I do not want to inherit your mess." He felt so strongly that he made it part of the condition to close. He flat out refused to close until the place was clean, period.

Manny's comment set in motion a mini-panic. I felt there were at least ten dumpsters worth of junk. I called Fagan and asked him to stop by the plant and take a look to see what he thought. Wiley, also worried, called and asked me what I thought it would it take to get the place cleaned up. While on the phone with Wiley, the bank called me and left an angry message. They were still mad that Wiley and Brian had not extended the closing of the building. Now it appeared the close would have to be moved out. So the eighty-five hundred dollars paid to move the machines was a waste. The bank always seemed to worry about money; Brian and Wiley, rightfully so in my opinion, were worried about selling the building. While on the cell with Wiley, I waved Carlos over to see if he cleaned factories. He said he did and would charge two thousand for labor, plus an additional three thousand for dumpsters and cleaning materials. He thought he could have the place cleaned up by Monday or maybe Tuesday of next week, resulting in delaying the building close one week to March 18, 2008. I left Carlos, walked out of his hearing distance and said to Wiley, "I think he is underestimating the enormity of the job."

The bank called a second time and left another message complaining more and giving me the unrealistic ultimatum of getting the place completely cleaned up by Friday for two thousand dollars. "And, by the way, since you can't control your broker and attorney, we're charging back the eighty-five hundred dollars expedite fee plus the two thousand cleanup bill to you."

I guess in looking back I can say the bank's message gave me personal insight into understanding temporary insanity. I cannot even begin to describe the state my mind was going into. I felt the rage simmering, then boiling. I tried to stop and control it, but it's like a surge of energy that starts at your feet and crawls up your body. It had to be noticeable, so much so that Bucky and Carlos saw it and eased back away from me. These were big men, with generally no fear, who decided in favor of caution to get some distance between them and a volcano about to explode. Maybe they would return after the eruption, but for now reason said it was to go. I wanted to scream, throw something or hit someone. I was like a caged and enraged beast of the jungle ready to pounce. No one in the factory wanted to give me the opportunity. Everywhere I turned to unload was the same. No outlet—everyone was smart enough to hide until the storm passed. So I called George.

"What the fuck, two days to clean up for only two thousand dollars—are they fucking nuts? They fucking sit in their fucking well-furnished offices and have no idea what's going on. Those fucking pencil neck pricks, two fucking days. It will take that long to get the people and dumpsters in here. Tell them to go clean their basements and see how long it takes. It would take all of two fucking days with friends helping. Tell those jackasses this place is bigger than a hundred basements. Fuck them. I'm not doing it. Now they're being fuckin' unfair. Charge back, fuck Callahan."

George let me go off for a good five uninterrupted minutes without saying a word. He knew four months of built up shit was spewing out. Finally he said, "You're right. It is unfair. It's too much to ask of a person. You've been sitting around for four months without a job doing this dirty work."

George knew I needed reassurance. He gave it to me and patiently let me calm down. Once my voice lowered, he in a very straight forward and composed manner said, "Ken, you know it's better for everyone, especially for you, if you can get the building sold. Now, you of all people know better than anybody else what it's gonna take to clean the place up. Let's start there. How much will it really cost and how long will it really take?"

"Five thousand and it will take at least through Monday."

Having mellowed a bit thanks to George, I purposely decided not to call the bank back. I did not need their shit at this moment. But part of me did not mind that I was in all likelihood aggravating them. I was hoping they knew I was deliberately not calling them back. I wanted them to sense that I no longer cared about them or what they thought. I'll give the bank credit; they were persistent and I guess wanted a confrontation. Unbelievable, those numbskulls—calling me up like innocent fools to calmly discuss the clean up. I knew they were pissed about spending eighty-five hundred and felt completely misled about being told that calling Manny might put the building sale in jeopardy. When I saw the caller ID on my cell phone I knew I was just the guy to give the bank what they apparently wanted: a fight.

It was Frank. "Ken, did you get our message?"

"Yeah, I got it."

"Weren't you going to call back?"

"No."

"Well, like I said in the earlier message, the eighty-five hundred and the clean up expense will be charged back to you."

I consciously paused for effect. Not long, just five or so seconds.

"Frank?"

"Yes"

"Do me a favor and go fuck yourself. I am not signing or agreeing to pay an expedite fee or any clean up expense. And, I want you to do me a favor. Walk into that big fucking corner office, make sure he fully understands that it's coming from me, and then tell Mister Callahan to go fuck himself too. Maybe you two can fuck each other, make it easier—I don't give a shit. But you're done fucking me. Got it?"

Complete silence. The quiet lasted almost a minute, neither one of us saying a word until Frank finally broke the impasse with, "Well," and hung up.

I called George to warn him that his buddy Callahan might take exception to being told to go fuck himself, especially coming from me. I was nervous, but, don't get me wrong, my feelings about the bank and their treatment of me had not lessened; I was still enraged. Deep down I just did not want to hurt my brothers-in-law and their relationship with the bank. So I was relieved when George laughed and said, "You'll have to call the bank back. You left Nick out of your fuck you's."

George called later that day, still amused, and asked if I had received any other calls. With a worn down voice I told him no. He laughed again, "Not bad, see, the craziness should hold them off for at least a day. Who the fuck wants to deal with you now? Great strategy."

As I was on the phone going off on the bank, Paul's dad passed away. He was ninety-eight years old. The military burial and memorial service for Mr. Costella was set for Friday, two days after the original building close date. The service would be right in the middle of what was without question the most stressful time in my life. I of course had to go. Paul was my high school friend, college roommate, and Godfather of my son, Bernie. I had worked three summers for his mom and dad at their small grocery store. He was so close to our family that my brother Marty was also going to the service and my parents had considered flying in from Connecticut. When I hung up with Paul, I said a prayer to Mr. Costella. "Thank you for your timing. You're a great friend, I am now forced to leave Chicago for three days," and promptly made a reservation for Fort Lauderdale, Florida, where I would be with Marty, Paul, and Paul's family.

When someone passes away I always think of what Annie told me one time when we sat next to each other at a funeral.

Sitting in the pew, Annie leaned over and in a whisper said, "Ken, now he knows."

"Who knows and what does he knows?"

"The dead. Now he's in heaven and knows what asses we are. There are no secrets from the dead."

Jeez, sorry, Mr. Costella, but now you know what an ass I am. That I am a big broke, out of work fucking fake of an ass. Well, one good thing: at least you can't tell anyone.

THIRTY-NINE

I was more up than usual for seeing Debra this week—if that's imaginable. I was starting to become in her words 'a real prick'. I mean imagine telling George and the bank, "What do I give a fuck if the building sells. You already have all that I own." I yelled, fought, and didn't answer phone calls—all very uncharacteristic of my non-confrontational personality. It was a week where I had acted completely different than what had become expected of me. So, I was ready to enter the sanctuary and act sort of boastful with Debra.

As soon as I sat, after our mandatory greeting, I relayed all that had happen concerning the building sale. "Fuck, Ken are you okay? Are you upset?"

"Debra, I just don't give an F anymore." In front of Debra I always said F instead of fuck. I don't think to this day that Debra has ever heard me say the word fuck. I told her I went nuts on the bankers and with George. I told her I said the F word at least thirty times. Any depression and anger that I may have had soon began to turn toward glee. It was great; Debra was cheering me on like it was a sporting event.

"Great, wow, fantastic, really? No, you *didn't* say that! Great! What was their reaction? The one you told to go fuck himself, he's the one we don't like right?" I loved her reaction. It was what I was hoping to get out of Debra. My bragging worked.

The best was when I described the silent treatment and outlasting Frank. "Imagine trying to outlast me with no talking."

Debra laughed for a good couple of minutes. She, more than anyone, had seen me go silent and not talk. It was more of a celebration than a therapy session. It was as if I was sitting with Paul, Marty, or Kevin and shooting the shit. I keep wondering if this was a breakthrough or just part of what someone goes through when seeing a therapist. Debra said my dreams this week were hopeful. Was it a ploy or were things actually turning around? This was the second or third time in the past few weeks where Debra had said my dreams were encouraging and reflected a positive attitude.

"Ken, I want you to think about what I am about to say. I know money is tight. But you may want to take advantage of people you know and take a few days off when this settles down. I know you have a brother and your good friend Paul in Florida, why don't you consider visiting with them for a few days, play some golf and unwind."

I was utterly stunned. I'm sure the look on my face must have revealed something. I could not completely hide my shock. It is as if she knew my plans. Did a dream expose something? I'm not sure if Francie even knew my Florida itinerary. Paul, Marty, and I had set up golf dates for the days before and after Paul's dad's service. We surely would go to sports bars at night and watch all the college basketball tournaments being played. We would tell the same high school and college stories we had been telling for years. It definitely was going to be a major unwinding trip for me. How could she possibly know or have guessed my plans?

After Debra made her statement I know I should have divulged my plans right away. But something held me back from letting her know I would in fact be in Florida the very next morning at ten a.m. I'm not sure if I'll ever let her know I went to Florida. All I thought about on the ride home from my session that night was you are afraid I will pass judgment on you? And I knew we still had work to do.

Debra was right; I was frightened and still had trouble being completely open with her. But it was not for the reason she suspected. She would always say to me, "Ken, you know I am bound by law. I cannot repeat to anyone anything that is said inside this room." What Debra didn't know was that my fear was not about the people outside the room. I cared more about her than I could ever show and even more so I cared about how she felt about me. I did not want her to even have a slightly bad opinion about me. I wanted and badly needed her approval. It was like I was young and dating again. I wanted Debra to like, even as much as love me. I was guarded in some of my words and actions so I wouldn't show anything to Debra that might in the smallest way diminish any good feelings she had toward me. In one session I said I voted for Hillary Clinton and immediately regretted it for months afterward. I was nervous she would think I am too liberal or not like me because of my candidate choice. We did have work to do. I was tentative with my therapist whom I respected, liked and loved, and for whom I would run through a steel wall. But I was terribly afraid and it was because of these exact feelings that I would always keep some secrets from her.

FORTY

I felt a tinge of guilt when I looked out of the small window as the 737 made its descent into Fort Lauderdale Airport. I was spending money that was becoming scarcer by the minute. The guilt quickly left me. The palm trees, bright sun, and cloudless light blue sky put me in the best mood I had been in for at least five months. It was odd thinking that no one in frosty Chicago except Francie knew I would be spending three days in Florida. I was hardly missed. Francie also knew our money was running low, but she suspected I was about to have a nervous breakdown, or worse yet heart problems. So ... she made me go.

We had two rounds of golf scheduled, a memorial service, and the after party at Paul's house. Shortly after landing Marty promptly picked me up and we were on our way to Paul's work office in Boca Raton.

It was eleven in the morning when we showed up at Paul's. Paul had originally planned to work the whole day, but, upon seeing Marty and me, he decided to take the rest of the day off. After Marty and Paul had their typical arguments over where best to eat, we decided on Budzinski's for lunch. I really have begun to think they argue because they know how entertained I am by these, um ... *discussions.* I do not believe for a second that either of them really gave two shits where we ate shitty food and drank Buds. Budzinski's turned out to be perfect. It's a manly man's bar, a sports bar that specializes in chicken wings and beer. At eleven-thirty in the morning, ten-thirty for me, we had ten chicken wings and two Budweisers each in front of us. The juke box was playing seventies songs and, as I was about to eat my first wing, I noticed 'Wooden Ships' by Crosby, Stills and Nash was playing. God, how appropriate, it was like we were back in my house on Meade Avenue in Greenwich. I sat there remembering how I had expressed to Debra it was one of my fonder happier memories, lip syncing songs with Paul, Marty, and Claude. I wanted to call and ask her if she had arranged for the song to play. It hit me as the song continued that I didn't have the balls to tell her I was going to Florida. Now, CSN without Young harmonized in the background as the three of us without Claude ate wings. We were so young thirty years ago. Now we were three middle-aged men coming to bury one of our parents, knowing soon it would be Paul's mom, and then my mom and dad—not necessarily in that order, but harsh nevertheless in its *mortality-is*-real, *all right* inevitability. Marty lifted his beer, hoisted it high in the air, and toasted Mr. Costella as we began to talk about his legacy. Paul said he was going to make a small speech at the service tomorrow. I grew silent thinking about my legacy and the burden I would now probably be to my children as I grew older without any means to support myself. God, I hope I go before Francie. I can hear Tony saying, "Yeah, my dad really fucked up, but ... he was a nice guy."

The following morning, with a round of golf behind us, Marty and I drove north up Route 441 toward the South Florida VA Cemetery. During the ride I wanted to tell Marty my true story, but instead just looked out the window and made the comment, "Florida has a lot of unused land."

Marty replied, "Yeah, you and Francie should buy a house down here. You'd be next to Paul and me." I chuckled to myself over Marty thinking I had enough money to buy a second house. While we were in the car talking, Francie was most likely on her way to work, having walked past the 'for sale' sign in the lawn out in front of our house.

Since Marty and I were a little early for the service we stopped at a roadside mini-mart. We had gone far enough out of the Miami/Fort Lauderdale area to be in rural Florida. The mini-mart was about the only sign of life in the area. We were surrounded by large orange groves and, according to Marty, sugar plantations. Hardly any cars passed along the road as we pulled into the small parking lot. It felt refreshing to step out of the car and have the heat hit me from all sides and mostly the ground. The air smelled and tasted different. I began to reach back and think how people in Chicago would react if I stayed in Florida. Start over, work on a farm, and hang out on the beach on weekends. I could save my money until I was able to invest or buy into the concern that would help me become the great man I always envisioned. As we entered the mini-mart it struck me that it was strangely full of life, mostly with immigrant farm workers. It was hard to reconcile the lack of traffic with a fully loaded mini-mart. I chalked it up to the slight hangover Marty and Paul helped to create.

Marty and I looked hopelessly out of place entering the store, dressed in slacks and golf shirts, Marty with sunglasses on. Marty weighs over two hundred pounds, lifts weights religiously, and has an air of confidence that makes me envious. The workers, being much smaller than Marty and me, all had their eyes on us as we walked through the mart looking for drinks and a snack before enduring a memorial service. Marty, much bolder than me, shouted across aisles, "Hey, Ken, do you want some peanuts? Get me a Gatorade, will ya?" causing heads to turn.

As we walked toward the back, I noticed a large row of shelves filled with pants and shirts for five-ninety-nine each. Marty saw me staring, walked up behind me, and said, "Those are clothes for the farm hands. Not bad, five-ninety-nine and they're half decent clothes." I wondered how he would react if I reached up and grabbed a few pairs of pants.

The VA cemetery was large but unelaborated. We were greeted by a large African American man with a graying beard at the entry gate. He was not in military garb, but rather a plain short white sleeve dress shirt with black pants and black spit-shined shoes. I noticed two American Flags on two tall flag poles rising up into the blue sky directly behind the entrance where he stood. We informed the greeter we had come for the Costella service. After checking his clipboard, he directed us to a row of cars lined up beside a small temporary administrative building. As we approached, I could see Paul and a slightly smaller version of the Paul I remembered from high school talking among a group of people. Smaller Paul, I recognized, was his son who I had not seen since Paul's divorce—when the boy was much younger. Now he was fifteen.

Marty and I parked, got out of the car, and traipsed toward the group. For me, there is always a slight discomfort in being greeted or greeting someone at a funeral or wake. Paul ran up to Marty, hugged him, and pulled him close, which Marty totally accepted. He then did the same to me. He took us to each of the ten to fifteen people in the group and introduced us. It made me think of countless scenes in movies where brothers are together. We were for a few seconds the stars of the show as Paul rapid fire announced, "Everybody, I want you to meet my best friends, the Sabinos. I grew up in their house. Their mom and dad are my second parents."

Since there are so many veterans, especially World War II veterans, dying, the service was strictly timed, one half hour. Paul's time was twelve thirty to one. No over runs, just like the Oscars. We were led by two officials dressed in suits to an open pavilion in the middle of a spacious field of grass. Around the pavilion were little patches of flowers. The pavilion was not much bigger than a large living room. It had a concrete floor area of about thirty by thirty feet, covered only by a roof supported by four corner poles. A table sat at one end of the pavilion. In front of the table were three rows of stone benches. The benches just barely fit the Costella party. I wondered what it would be like if I had a service here and the eighty Madigans showed up breaking all the time rules and military decorum.

We sat in complete silence while Paul and his church minister stood behind the table. The table had two Bibles flanking a larger than I expected canister containing Mr. Costella's ashes sitting on it. I mentioned to Marty the size of the canister and he said, "Oh, yeah. Humans are big. Imagine how many ashes one log makes in your fire place. We're much bigger than a log." He continued, "When Sally's mom was cremated, she wanted her ashes spread out on the ocean outside of Hyannis Port. Believe me, it was painful, out on a boat, all the kids taking turns dumping her ashes in the water. It's windy and bumpy. They finally gave the canister to Sally, she's the youngest. She dumps some out, then some more, then some more. I was like, holy shit, is she ever gonna be done. Yeah, a lot of ashes."

I said, "Paul told me Mister C requested that the canister with his ashes be buried."

"Good," was all Marty replied.

I looked around and noticed the large number of dragonflies hovering, and then darting in and about the small patches of flowers. The colors were so much more pronounced and the animals and flies way more noticeable than they were in gray, dark, and dreary Chicago. I saw iguanas, parakeets, gators, and all sorts of strange birds over the course of my three days in Florida. In the distance I observed large trees bordering the cemetery. It was as if they were standing guard, watching over the soldiers and sailors who had fought gallantly for our country. My daydreams were suddenly broken by the playing of taps by a sailor standing some ten feet behind me. We all stood and watched as the buglers and two other sailors marched in sync toward the table where Paul stood. The sailors performed the ceremony of unfolding and then refolding the American flag into a triangle. They solemnly bent over and handed the folded flag to Paul's mom. One of the sailors said a few words to Mrs. Costella and then in unison the three marched away from the pavilion and completely out of sight. While Paul talked a bit about his dad, Marty and I argued in whispers over who would give the speeches at our parents' funerals.

"You're the oldest'" he said

"Yeah, but you're a better speaker than me."

As we were fighting, one of the two official men said to no one in general that "You have five more minutes." Paul yielded the floor to his minister who closed with a few words and a prayer.

***

Back at Paul's house we dined on food from the Olive Garden and drank Buds. While the SEC basketball tournament played on the TV in the background, Paul asked for everyone's attention. "Since there are only fifteen of us, I'd like it if each person said something about my dad."

Barry Samuel, a college friend, went first. Barry is not quite my height yet he looks as if he weighs twice as much as me. Barry is Jewish, so the Costellas were his baptism into the 'unorthodox' Italian way of life. He related to everyone about a trip to the Costella's apartment and how Mrs. Costella cooked him a five-course meal. In Italian families the mother always cooks for at least ten—regardless if fewer people are there. If only three people show up, it's their obligation to try and eat everything. The worst nightmare for an Italian mom, he explained to a group who already knew, is to run out of food. But they are also aggrieved if you do not make a good effort to eat all the food put in front of you. "It's kind of a no win situation," Barry said with expressive hand gesturing—to the laughter of all of us in accompaniment. Barry continued.

"So me, Paul, and Mister Costella ate course after course of antipasto, salad, pasta, meat dishes. We were about to explode Monty Python style. But, knowing our obligation, we continued to eat as much as we could. We finally finished dessert and left the table to waddle in slow, stuffed-stomach anguish into the living room to retire and watch the NY Mets on WOR channel nine. The three of us sat like beached whales, thinking Mrs. Costella was in the kitchen cleaning up when she yelled out, 'Barry, I am making you a meatball sandwich.'

"'No thanks Mrs. Costella,' I yelled back. Turning to Mister Costella looking for sympathy, I said, 'We just finished eating for a hundred people, how could she possibly think I want more to eat?'

"Mister Costella glanced sideways at me and looked me up and down paying particular attention to my wide girth. Again Paul's mom called out, 'Barry, I've already made the sandwich, you have to eat more.'"

By this time I was laughing aloud with all the others at Barry's plight recounting. Usually with Italian mom's you get the customary follow up of, 'Look at him, he's so thin.' But with Barry this was intentionally left out. Barry shook his head in a sigh and went on.

"Again, I looked to Mister Costella for support. He shrugged and said, 'Barry, you're the type of guy who looks like he's always hungry.' In other words, Barry said with a good-natured chuckle, he was letting me know I was fat. I realized I was sunk, so I took and ate the sandwich—and braced myself for whatever else might be thrown my way."

We told story after story. In the Navy, how Mr. Costella fell asleep while on guard duty and got thrown in the brig. Mr. Costella while serving during WWII thought he heard a Japanese attack, so he ran on deck and began firing a machine gun into the night sky at imaginary enemy planes and again got thrown in the brig. How Mr. Costella taught Marty and me, prior to the lotto, to bet the numbers with the neighborhood bookies. Marty shared the story of how Mr. Costella lost his fake teeth while skinny dipping in the Atlantic Ocean when our families went on vacation together to Myrtle Beach. Marty ended by saying, "Just imagine that white ass Mr. Costella was so proud of popping in and out of the water."

We learned that he chased his daughter-in-law around the house telling her how cute she was. We heard from his nephew how the man never had a worry in his life. He never was mad, felt cheated, or complained. He felt that he lived a perfect life.

The Costellas, like my friend Claude, lived above a store-front in a small two-bedroom apartment on Greenwich Avenue. They never knew where their next dime was coming from. Yet, this man felt that he lived the perfect life. He rode his bike up and down the streets of Boca Raton, Florida, until he was ninety-six. Two of those years he could not walk, but he managed to, with a walker, get to his bike, climb aboard, and ride around saying hi to all the neighbors. When he couldn't ride any more he gave the bike to Paul's fifteen-year-old stepson. Mr. Costella's grand-stepson, who when it was his turn to say something, was visibly shaking and nervous. He said everyone's stories were too enjoyable and funny. His story, he was afraid was not as good as everyone else's. We encouraged him to say anything. He turned in his chair and looked out the back glass sliding door toward the old dilapidated bike sitting on the patio and in near tears said, "He gave me his bike." It was the only time the whole weekend that I felt sad. Not for Mr. Costella, but for his grand-stepson who had lost a pal.

We woke the next morning and began anew with the teasing of each other as we got ready for another round of golf. "Look at that body; I thought you said you exercised? Hey, do you have to use Viagra yet?" Only high school or grammar school friends can get away with saying some of the things we said to each other that weekend. The golf was beyond enjoyable for three men shooting in the nineties. We laughed, told jokes, talked about our families, and our lives. Not once did I mention MPC. They both knew I was selling the company and the building was scheduled to sell the following Wednesday. They both allowed me to walk away without talking about work.

After playing our round of golf we went to the course bar and grill for more Buds, a quick burger, and more basketball games. We stayed until the last possible moment before I was at risk of missing my plane. All three of us are family men and love our wives dearly, but I had been through this with Marty and Paul on a number of occasions. We always have trouble leaving each other. Marty, Paul, and I had played golf together uncountable times. We had been on family vacations together all during high school and college. We all know every girlfriend that each of us had ever had. We played basketball and football at St. Mary's high and in recreation leagues throughout the Greenwich area together. I know that, like me, when we see each other, we recall when a more innocent time touched our souls. It was a time when we developed a lot of the traits and habits we would use in our adult lives. Marty and Paul were a big part of my development as a person. I feel refreshed and content when I am with them like no other two people in the world. It is like being at the baths of Lourdes, France, where the Virgin Mary appeared to the child Bernadette. Mary revealed to Bernadette the healing spring water of Lourdes. The healing waters that help a person cure either a physical, spiritual, or mental malady. Like the faithful 'Malades', I had traveled far and wide to be cured. I had made a pilgrimage. I was being immersed in the cold purifying bath waters. Like being dipped into the 'picines', I felt the holy water surrounding my body and cleansing me of all my worldly sins and mistakes, trying to take my problems away. The waters will bring me back to a wholeness, a renewal to begin again free of sin. Marty and Paul were the water for me this weekend without their knowing it.

Thank you, Mr. Costella. I love you.

FORTY-ONE

On the Sunday after returning from Florida, Francie and I drove to Bensenville to see the progress made in cleaning the building. I tried the front door and could not get in. I tried all the side doors with the same result. I wondered if the locks had been changed. It was somewhat confusing. Luckily, I had Carlos's number. I called and Carlos informed me that a lot people had been coming by trying to get money from me. Like sharks, people were sensing that the end was near and they were all trying desperately to recover any money possible prior to the final MPC shut down. The kicker as far as Carlos was concerned, was the cleaning service people came by and would not surrender their keys. Carlos was worried they would do something crazy, so he 'fixed' the doors. I really wish I could've seen their faces when they showed up to clean the office and found a giant parking lot where a building used to be.

As a result of my Sunday experience, I was anxious to get to MPC early Monday morning. I needed to ensure that the place would be clean enough for Manny to approve the Wednesday close. I felt with the brewing troubles of people showing up it was doubly important to close on time. In reflection, it would have been a better decision to stay away and therefore avoid all confrontation with old vendors and employees who felt they had been cheated out of money. I arrived at eight and there was one employee in the building—who did not speak English. I could not get an answer on how much more work had to be done. I noticed the offices were completely cleaned out and a great deal of progress had been made in the factory. I still worried that to have an absolutely spic and span, barren factory by Wednesday was at risk. I again called Carlos who said he was on his way to MPC. He was not reassuring, when he said, "I will have to go into Wednesday morning to finish up with the cleaning. Much bigger job than I thought. There's garbage everywhere."

I noticed there were no tables or chairs in the building, so I had nowhere to plant myself. The cleanup had now become increasingly frustrating to watch. It was like watching paint dry. Since there was nothing for me to do, I decided to drop off some product samples to a customer that I sold to Bucky. The customer was about an hour away from MPC. I reasoned the two plus hours out of the building would do me good. Upon returning I could judge the progress.

On the way back to the plant from the customer's office, Brian Fagan called to tell me that Manny had stopped by and was not pleased with the progress. He was thinking of postponing the closing until after he returned from a vacation he was leaving for on Thursday.

I could not control myself once again. I was mad at the bank for not letting me clean up earlier. I was mad that everyone but me would get money at the close. I was mad that I may have to sit at MPC for another week, delaying the job search. I was angered with myself for being a fuck up.

Brian was at the receiving end of my anger. "What the fuck. I'm not the bank's indentured servant. It doesn't do anyone any fucking good to have me not working. I don't have two fucking nickels to rub together and now I have to sit at MPC for another week. What if it doesn't sell? Do I have to fucking sit there for one, two, three fucking years? I've had it with this shit. I'm driving to the bank right now and I'm going to go fucking ballistic on their fucking asses. Fuck, fuck, fuck, fuck, fuck, fuck, fuck, fuck, fuck, fuck."

I tried to say fuck twenty-five times. I was counting off the fucks in my head; I don't know what made me choose twenty-five. I do remember wanting it to be a large number. I only got to ten of them before I stopped. Ten was fucking good enough I fucking well decided.

"Ken, calm down. I'm on my way to the building. I'll stay there for the next two days. You need to do what is right for you and your family. There is no reason for you to be here. Don't worry, Wiley and I will get the building sold."

Brian proposed to Carlos a sliding scale of pay for services rendered. Carlos would receive nine thousand dollars if the job was finished Tuesday by five p.m., eight thousand if the job was finished by Tuesday by ten p.m., and five thousand if the job was finished by Wednesday by ten a.m. Further, if the job was *not* finish Wednesday by ten a.m. there would be *no* pay.

You guessed it, on Tuesday by five p.m. we had one spotless, eat-off-the-floor clean factory. Manny approved.

I have only teared up a few times since October 29th for joyful reasons. But on Wednesday, March 19, 2008, when Brian Fagan called me at 1:04 p.m. to give me the news of the building being sold, I felt my eyes water up. The bank would receive, minus expenses; close to 1.7 million dollars in cash toward the debt owed them by MPC and Ken Sabino. I did not attend the building close. I was at home in sweat pants and a tee shirt looking for job openings on the computer. In fact, I had not been to MPC during the fifty hours prior to the close, since my blow up with Brian Fagan. I never saw the building completely clean.

FORTY-TWO

When I walked into the inner office Debra was standing, wearing jeans and a white turtle neck. It was the most informal I had ever seen her. Since I had begun to show up in more casual attire, Debra said her dressing down was in honor of me.

I was walking on cloud nine. I saw the proverbial light at the end of the tunnel. When my foot hit the sanctuary floor Debra started howling. It was an almost uncontrollable laughter. A bend over, slap your knee type of laugh.

"What?" I said.

"Ken, I have been laughing all week. Someone trying to out silence you. I mean really. God, telling the prick, what was it, to fuck off?"

"Oh man. No, I didn't tell him to F off, I told him to go F himself—and his partner."

"How great, I say fuck and you say F. My husband asked me if I swear with clients. I said fuck, yeah, I swear. I told him this is not some shitty stuffy old business transaction. Wow, you look younger. My swearing doesn't bother you, does it, Ken?"

"I love the swearing. The building sold today."

"Shit, Ken, great news. This is why I love my job; it makes it worth it to hear someone tell me news like that. See, I was right, you do look younger. What's next?"

"Well, I need to get a job and fast."

"You will. What are you looking for?"

"Hmm, I have a few things in mind. Bucky, of course, is an option. Believe it or not, I'm looking at companies that do business overseas, maybe give me an opportunity to travel, possibly a white collar job downtown." I paused and then said, "Debra, I could not have gotten through the past few months without you. I want to thank you."

I had to control myself. It was like I had had too much to drink. You know, the drinking where you get mushy and say things like, "I love you, man, blah, blah, blah," and almost start crying. I had emotionally been put through the ringer for months. It's still hard to believe my mood and feelings during those days immediately following the building sale. It really was as if I was a giddy drunk.

Debra, sort of, refused my thanks, "Ken, you're a great client. This is what I do. I know that when we're done things will have worked out for you. I have the greatest job in the world. I love helping people through problems. I am positive you will be a great story. You read I suppose about Bear Sterns and their problems?"

"Yes."

"See Ken, everyone is having a tough time. It's not just you. Hey, maybe screaming at the bank helped get the job done."

I couldn't help myself, so as if I took another shot of Wild Turkey, I leaned over my bar stool, and slurringly told Debra her enthusiasm is infectious. It was, at least on this night. Although I pathetically managed it once or twice, it was nearly impossible to walk out of Debra's office and not feel good about myself. I had created a colossal disaster and here she was telling me, "Shit, Ken, stop beating yourself up. You're acting like it was your fault."

I wanted to cry, a joyous cry of happiness. I was nearing the end of the toughest part of living the nightmare of a company going broke. I was a middle-aged man sitting in an office with my therapist, laughing about situations that only six hours earlier seemed horrendous. It was a blissful cry in spite of knowing and understanding my life would never be the same. That I probably forfeited any hope of ever being rich, hell, of just being middle class. The possibility of never going to a nice restaurant, unless invited, was very real. I had not committed a crime, but I was in the process of going bankrupt, a stigma that would never go away. I had put myself in a position where even modest goals would be very difficult to meet.

I usually strolled to my car after a session, today I ran. It was the first time I believed that I could be taught, that I was being taught to control myself, to have balance in my life, and to be happy. It was the first time I believed there was a method to her madness. I sat in the car for ten minutes wanting to cry the whole time. I called George and told him the building sold. I hung up and called Tony and gave him the news. Almost coincidently, Marty called me and said he was in Miami on business and had dinner plans with Paul. They both wanted to know, "Did the building sell?"

"Hell, yeah, the fucking building sold."

"How great, Ken. See, I told you it would all work out!"

FORTY-THREE

I always wondered if Debra consciously made a decision to subtly change the direction of my therapy once the building sold or if it just sort of happened. I almost immediately recognized the change in the tone of our meetings after the middle of March. We began to concentrate on the decision-making process. Why did I make some of my past decisions? What inputs did I use in making decisions? I had been devastated by the MPC failure for a number of reasons. Among the biggest were the decisions that put me in a position to fail. We used the past to look at some of the choices that were now in front of me, like future employment and housing? We were looking at the decision-making process in a much different manner than I was used to. What we were really beginning to focus on was my future happiness. Now that I was about to finish off the hardest part of the MPC debacle, it was the theme that Debra had begun to pay attention to. She wanted to help me make judgments that would please me and not others. When I questioned her on the new direction, she said it was not her, but my dreams that led us down this path.

Another change was Debra began to ask me much earlier in the sessions if I had a good week of dreams. It's as if she knew the dreams would be more upbeat. I began to look forward to analyzing and discussing my dreams. They usually took us down un-chartered paths. Paths could lead to danger or to beautiful wide open fields with opportunities. They were avenues I could not control, but I was not as intimidated as before by where we might end up. I also suspected the dreams were showing more to Debra than I could ever express verbally. During one of my late March sessions two of the four dreams I had recorded during the week were about other women and me, beautiful women whom I did not know. They were not sexual dreams, but rather romantic dreams.

Debra concluded my dreams, in particular the ones with beautiful women, indicated a willingness to approach future decisions with less of a linear and more of an intuitive slant or, as Debra always expressed to me, "You're beginning to use the right side of your brain. See Ken, you would have gone to Paris after college if your decision making was in touch with the right side of your brain." All I know was, my dreams at this juncture made Debra feel positive, so it made me feel good. I saw that she was trying to guide me into a more fulfilling state of mind. I was the clay and Debra was the artist trying to shape me. Each session she would form a little more of the sculpture.

I am walking in a quaint Paris quartier with a good looking French woman. As we pass small Parisian shops and parks, I hand her a Monet and two other pieces of art as a present. It starts to drizzle so we duck into a small store to protect the art. We are both at complete ease and satisfied that the art will not get wet.

During earlier sessions these types of dreams sent a slight shiver up my body. I felt they meant I wanted to be unfaithful or in a strange way it made me feel like I was cheating on Francie. I learned over the course of my time with Debra that they had a different meaning. I was trying to get in touch with my feminine side. To Debra this was a tremendously good sign. It was a subject she began to focus on during our times together. Having guided me through the grueling month of February, it was time to prepare my psyche for a more fulfilling life.

I would never tell anyone, particularly a male friend, that my female therapist told me, "You're trying to get in touch with your feminine side."

Debra absolutely loved these types of dreams. It showed her a side of me that I had trouble comprehending. I still don't know if I fully understand the significance of the feminine side. I remember when Debra first discussed the subject, I worried that it had something to do with sexual orientation. Jesus, don't tell me I secretly like men. I could not even bring the issue up with Debra. I wondered if bringing up the subject meant I had gay tendencies. Luckily for me, and I guess Francie, I have learned it has more to do with decision making and how I act, how I approach life and its difficulties. Men tend to see decisions as black or white. They are much more linear than women. Women tend to act more on intuition. According to Debra most women lack the male qualities that would help them in decision making and life situations, and the same goes for men in reverse. Men in her opinion need to have a feminine side to help them cope with life struggles.

During late March sessions, I'd look at Debra and think, am I really to believe you are going to teach me to be happy, to enjoy life? Please, God, as crazy as it seems, make Annie right. God dammit, Debra, make me happy; please put balance and harmony back into my fucked up life.

FORTY-FOUR

My mind had been temporarily fooled. Selling the building was like taking an opium-based drug. It was an enormous step indeed but, like a drug, the building sale allowed me to conceal numerous other problems. I willingly let myself fall into the trap. I wanted and allowed the drug-induced euphoria to win, to last forever. I believed I was the king of the hill. I was on top of the world after the building sold. The bank, George, Wiley, Brian, and I all collectively let out a sigh of relief. It was three days before Francie's birthday and four days before Easter. I anticipated correctly that my contact with all the parties involved with MPC would be minimal from the building sale until at least the Monday after Easter. I was free to sit, put my head back, and hallucinate. Luckily it turned out that this year, 2008, was the earliest Easter could be according to the Christian liturgical calendar. The next time Easter falls on March 23, everyone alive on the planet will be dead, since it's in another hundred and twenty years or something like that. It turned out to be a perfect time to have sold the building. For at least a few days I had the distraction of Easter week to keep my mind off MPC and, more importantly, everyone else's mind off of me. Thursday, Holy Thursday, Bernie and Dominic came home from college and the house was lively again.

Like an idiot, but a happy one, I drove to the bank through another snowstorm on Good Friday. A storm that left six inches of snow on the ground. A snowstorm in which the wind was strong enough to make the snow blow sideways as it struggled to get to the ground. I did not care. In fact I thought it was wild watching the snowflakes manically dance to the ground. It was like they were falling to music as the windshield wipers helped keep the beat. I was high at a concert, the world had order. Eddie Vedder's voice with Pearl Jam blaring on the radio guided the snowflakes harmlessly to the ground. The high had so overtaken me that I felt a body slumped mellowness as I headed toward the institution I had come to hate. Plus, being late March I knew the snow would melt in short order.

My mission was to drop off a few reports connected to the building sale. This completed the list of sale related items the bank needed. I could now celebrate Easter guilt free. They were very un-confrontational, minor reports. I just left them at the front desk and never saw Bert, Nick or Frank. Like most businesses on this holy day the bank had a skeleton staff that would leave at noon when its doors closed for the long weekend. For at least this one day, being home in blue jeans and a sweatshirt did not seem unusual.

During my drive home from the bank, Annie texted me to see if Francie and I would like to stop by their house for an hour to listen to

Bernie and her son informally play music. The building having been sold, listening to music with Dan and Annie—wow, the drug was making things seem right. Yes, I would love to listen and sing along with the boys for an hour. Exhilaration was swirling around in my head. We ended up staying at the Madigan's through dinner and then right into NCAA basketball games. When we finally left Dan and Annie's it was close to midnight. Was my life coming back into order? I thought it might be, but it was hard for me to see clearly through the blessed purple haze.

The following morning, Saturday, March 22, 2008, we woke up and met our running club for a downtown run. On special occasions we drove to Chicago and ran along its famous lakefront bike path. Running south toward the museums with the big shoulder skyline to my right had me close to a state of nirvana. I had been trapped physically and mentally for so long I could not fight the drug. I felt like I had been released from a thirty-year imprisonment. I was finally free. When we finished the run we had a light breakfast at Fox and Obel to begin Francie's birthday celebration.

That night we went with the Kellys and Madigans to Katie's apartment in the Ukrainian Village section of Chicago to continue celebrating Francie's birthday. We ate hors d'oeuvres and drank beers. Dan, Tim, and I snuck over to the TV with some of the kids to watch more basketball games. Annie joined us when the Marquette game came on. We drank, we cheered for Marquette, we told basketball stories, and we watched our kids mingle. Our children, who were quickly becoming adults, who were or would be in short order out in the world trying to make their own fortunes.

After a terribly disappointing Marquette loss to Stanford on a last-second shot, we went down the street to an organic pizza place called 'Crust's'. I asked for, "A table for eighteen please."

At first they thought we were joking. At ten thirty you want a table for *how* many? And you want us to have you out of here in less than an hour. When they realized we were not kidding, the wait staff was psyched. Why not? They anticipated—correctly—a huge tip for very little work. We laughed, drank some more, and ate pizzas with silly names.

On Easter Sunday we attended ten-thirty mass at St. Gertrude's, the Chicago parish of Francie's sister, Julia and our brother-in-law Dick Ryan. We have attended Easter Mass each year at St. Gertrude's since I have lived in Chicago. I like to call this mass the Super Bowl of masses. The ceremony includes dancing, songs, ballet, a short rendition of the resurrection, and a somewhat amusing homily from Father Connolly. I always purposely make an excuse to slow our family up on Easter morning so we would arrive a tad late. After mass, we set off for Julia's for an all-day Easter celebration. All the Madigans, plus every mass attendee, were invited. Julia had her traditional Easter egg hunt with the candy-stuffed three thousand plastic eggs, even though there were very few hunters left. We drank champagne and ate homemade muffins, cinnamon rolls, and bread. It was time to indulge after forty days of Lental sacrifices. I felt I deserved this indulgence more than most, if not all, at the party. I, like Jesus, was out in a desert for forty days. No one there with me except the devil.

A new life, a rebirth, I made myself believe the symbolism. I was like a Phoenix and had risen from my own ashes to fight again.

All that day at the Ryans' I had an air of relief that had to be evident. I drank and ate freely. I talked with a confidence that had been missing for four to five months. We watched more basketball games, and we discussed and solved all sorts of important issues. I bravely had opinions in spite of Annie's one-time advice to me. The BSD—building sale drug—had masked my fears. I was looking at the world through distorted colors. I believed the BSD had made me whole. I acted as if I had no problems.

Driving home from the 'Our Lord has risen' party I reluctantly recognized I had one major issue that had to be dealt with. I was unemployed. I was probably the only male at the Ryans' who would wake up the next day with no factory or office to go to. The BSD had worn off—I came crashing down, *hard*. I could not contain the withdrawal pains. I was visibly shaking and sweating. Francie could not see me, but must have sensed my feelings. She quietly said, "Are you all right?"

I lied and said, "Everything's okay."

It was the first time in my adult life where I had nowhere to go. I had tackled a major hurdle by selling the building, but I was far from being in the clear. I had to go bankrupt, get a job, and finalize the debt picture with the bank. All three were monumental hurdles to overcome. I woke up Monday depressed. From the weekend's brief respite of sheer joy and excitement, to a depression that was as much physical as mental—this was the overnight transition in my life. I stayed in bed feeling sorry for myself, worrying about money, people's perceptions of me, what to do next, and how to deal with all these problems. My chest hurt and my arms felt heavy once again.

I often wonder if there is a God and was this really His plan for me? Does He pay attention to me? Am I important enough to warrant a mention from God to His subordinates? Is heaven run like a corporation? Are angels middle managers running around with clip boards, Bluetooths in their ears, drinking heavenly lattés while enacting the strategies of the saints? Is there a bureaucracy, like companies on earth, running right up to executives like Mary and Jesus who report directly to

God?

"Yes, um, Jesus, Sir ... we have a situation in Wilmette, Illinois. We need a little suffering. I think we have a couple of small but perfect candidates. Can you arrange a meeting with Peter and some of the saints in the Department of Suffering? Have them strategize on which of the candidates to pick. Send me an email with the results, will ya?"

"Skip the red tape. Those committees take an eternity to make anything happen. I know just the right guy," Christ says, peering down on earth with His ubiquitous vision and pointing. "There—he's your man."

Why was I chosen? How did I become this person? Why did I try to be a company owner and not a manager, store owner, accountant, attorney, teacher? What made the packaging industry move to China and not paper or plastic? Did the God Corporation really have a hand in all this? It's one of the millions of questions I'm going to ask if I get to heaven.

"Oh, shit. Sorry, Mister Sabino, little oversight. Angel Bob over there was supposed to make packaging prices go up, not down. Woops, our bad."

I'll look over and Angel Bob will shrug his shoulders at me as if to say, *Sorry*.

Could I have made better decisions? Could I have better foreseen some of the pitfalls ahead? What if I made Francie move to New York, how would it have ended up? Was luck involved? Is our destiny in our own hands?

Does the butterfly theory really work? A butterfly flapping its wings in the Pacific Ocean may set off a chain of events worldwide. As a result of the butterfly a bee may fly in a different direction, annoying or stinging a different person causing a new and different chain of events to occur than if the butterfly did not flap its wings. In looking back, there was a series of events that could have easily sent me in a different direction. Why did I transfer to Manhattanville, where I met Francie? At the time I was looking at a number of other colleges. Manhattanville initially rejected me. Instead of letting it go and selecting another college I, very untypically, decided to investigate why I was rejected. The Manhattanville admission office immediately discovered that my high school had sent the incorrect transcripts. I had crushes on different coeds at Manhattanville, but ended up with Francie. Pullman Inc., the first company I worked for, was a 100-year-old solid company that was surprisingly bought out two years after I began working there. This made me look for a new job much faster than I had planned. I could go on and on about the countless events in my life that led directly to October 29, 2007. Could altering any one of the events have prevented my going bankrupt? Could the butterfly have flapped its wings setting off a different series of events that would have resulted in my being happy and satisfied?

***

Being home made it possible for me to hear Francie each morning on the phone with her older sister Janice. It was always a short conversation. Francie rarely talked, so I knew Janice was on the other end giving her words of support. They ended every call the same way. Together they chanted,

"God grant us the serenity to accept the things we cannot change,
the courage to change the things we can,
and the wisdom to know the difference.
Grant us patience for changes that take time,
gratitude for all that we have,
tolerance for those with difficult struggles,
and the strength to get up and try again one day at a time."

FORTY-FIVE

Looking for a job at age fifty-three after having watched your dreams blasted to hell in an exploding bonfire is humiliating and depressing at the same time. I was afraid to approach people and ask for help. It meant I would have to explain why I was looking for a job. When I managed to get the rare interview, it was difficult for me to get excited. Getting dressed up in a suit and sitting in interview rooms explaining why I would be a good employee and how I was a team player was demoralizing. The last time I had gone on a series of interviews was almost twenty-five years ago. Some of my present interviews were for jobs that offered less pay and had less responsibility than the ones I went on in the eighties. I was also being interviewed, for the most part, by someone the same age as my children.

Debra again suggested I come see her two times a week. I knew I would consider this second offer of hers differently than the first time it was offered months earlier. I wanted to see her more. It was the only time each week that I could open up. Ironic how Debra, for the longest time, reminded me my biggest problem was not opening up. Now I had enough to talk about to fill up at least two hourly sessions a week. Plus, I figured it would break the monotony of sitting at home on the computer all day searching for a job. But it also meant that I would be seeing Debra twice each week without paying. So, I declined.

Well into April I still received calls from ex-employees needing insurance or 401(k) help and from vendors and creditors demanding payment. The bank must have contacted me at least three times a week to discuss the Great Lakes commission check, forbearance agreements, or collecting receivables. Would I ever be allowed to let MPC go?

In spite of the plethora of depressing calls, all my April sessions, according to Debra, had become a lot more positive. Debra said my dreams were optimistic and showed great signs of hope. I often wondered if she was saying this as some kind of beneficial placation. She never said anything negative to me or about me. Whenever I mentioned that I believed she was correct in saying I had led a life that was not right for me, I could see her body tighten up and cringe—even though she originally brought the subject up.

She also instructed me that even though I had opened up some I still did a good job of hiding a lot of my true feelings. I know I confused her. I'd say the right thing, but saw that Debra wanted more. I should have been crying, complaining, or showing outright anger. I wondered if Debra thought badly of me because I didn't show these emotions. She said the grieving process for my situation should be very similar to a death. And, like a death, with time it would slowly become easier to accept. The problem was I had not yet died. Like a person who fights a terminal disease, I kept hanging on for years.

During April sessions I often sat in the chair and just looked across the table at Debra. I would lose myself thinking about her. How does she really perceive me? Does she like me? Does she talk about me with her husband? What does she think about me and my problems? I wish I was brave enough to ask.

Often I stared at nothing in particular while in the sanctuary, mostly daydreaming. When I looked over at Debra, I could see the compassion in her eyes. I wanted to tell her that she did not have to worry about me anymore. I knew that after the building sold I would not do anything rash. Thoughts of suicide had left me. Running away, however, was something I still considered. I always said to George things like "Maybe someday the bank will call and ask if you've seen me. Do you know where he is?" We'd laugh and joke that I'd be in California or New York. But it was always that sort of uncomfortable laugh. I know George well enough to sense he was wondering if I was really joking or not.

I wanted to tell Debra how much I loved going to see her. I wanted to hug her and thank her over and over. I have always been a giant sap for the movies with the great romantic endings. I love the imagery of Elizabeth and Mr. Darcy walking toward each other in the enchanting, perfectly filmed English garden in *Pride and Prejudice*. I want to jump out of my seat and cheer when Will decides to follow his heart and takes off driving to California to win back his girlfriend, Skylar, in *Good Will Hunting*. There is no greater smile in movies, one that makes me melt, than the one George Bailey has while holding his daughter as a bell rings signifying another heavenly Angel got his wings in *It's a Wonderful Life*. And yes, most of all, Holly Golightly in the pouring rain crying tears of joy in Paul 'Fred' Varjak's arms to end *Breakfast at Tiffany's*.

There were days during this time when I believed I too would have the happy romantic ending. I would find my great job, pull myself up by the proverbial bootstraps and get back on my feet. I would arrive home from work, see Francie, throw my suitcase down, and run to her as she jumps into my embrace for a long, slow, passionate kiss. Like all the heroes I loved watching so much on the big screen, Sabino the Great would have his day of glory.

Yet more often there were the days where I felt I had forfeited all rights to ever again have a normal—happy? Is happy normal?—life. But I was learning to cope with this. I have to admit there was a part of me that felt liberated. I was free to go and do as I please. I could be a lawyer, teacher, construction worker. I was twenty-one again—nothing tying me down, no home, no responsibilities outside of wife and marriage, just starting over fresh. Like the newlywed twenty-one-year-old, I once again had to decide what I wanted to be when I grow up. I was free but I again had the anxiety of going out into the real world. I was walking off campus, realizing I was 'ugly' once again.

There was another problem; the world is not as kind to fifty-year-olds as it is to twenty-one-year-olds looking for a job. I was realistic enough to know that a number of great movies end tragically. So I continued to worry about the one major factor that could hold me back from my romantic ending: my mental well being, the depression that had always been with me. The beating I took was not completely healed. I still knew I was fragile and could easily fall back into a depressed state. I frequently wondered—no, I know—I would have not been able to get this far without Debra. But now she must get me to the finish line. She was the only one who had a chance. It was the reason why every time I left Debra's office, I looked up toward the heavens as I opened the door onto Greenwood Avenue and thanked God that he allowed Annie to introduce me to 'this person she is seeing' and gave me her telephone number. I knew Debra would stick it out with me.

Yes, I could sit in my familiar chair as St. Teresa of Avila, Kwan Yin the Chinese goddess of mercy and compassion, Carl Jung, The Virgin Mary and the Dalai Lama all watch over me. We would continue to work on my feminine side, exploring my decision making. Continue we would, to try and make me see the good and enjoy life, and mostly she would continue to tell me stories. Our sessions would get lighter, but we both knew there was still a lot of work to be done.

Debra was prone to telling me, "Ken, we are in a constant state of development."

Who knows? Maybe it was just a matter of time before the screen silently fades to black as I ride off into the sunset.

***

I accepted the bank's request and met with them in April for one last time to discuss 'where we were at with everything,' whatever that meant. Since Bert Callahan was not there, Nick and Frank led the meeting. I was glad when Nick informed me that Bert got called away. It was my only fear going to the meeting. The fear of me possibly saying something uncalled for to Bert. I hardly listened as Nick droned on for the second time about the bank having agreed to drop late charges and accrued interest. Nick's needless, incessant yammering was mere white noise in the background as he expressed how the bank wanted to walk away from this situation with no hard feelings. I had better things on my mind when they discussed the remaining receivables and the Great Lakes commission. I wanted to tell them it was all a moot point, I went bankrupt and I don't have a job. I said nothing about business; I merely thanked them, asked them what they thought about the Cubs, and left. There was nothing more they could do to me, and I think they finally realized that.

FORTY-SIX

Crossing the street toward my car after an April session, as was becoming habit, I continued to think about Debra and what we worked on that night. She had again complimented me on being a good patient. She was proud of me and said I was beginning to get comfortable with the therapeutic process. My dreams and I had revealed a great deal about myself since I began seeing her. She said she knew it was difficult for me to get to this point and she appreciated the hard work I put into our sessions. She said that unlike her, I did not scream out. She told me, "Ken, I'm just not subtle." All I could say with a bit of a smile on my face was, "I know."

As I approached the silver Volvo Tim gave me, it smacked me. I was in complete awe at how much I learned about another person in an hourly session once a week. I had sat with Debra for less than seventy-five total hours. Seventy-five total hours! Just a little over three days elapsed time. I had played golf with customers that added up to over seventy-five hours. I had been on committees at various jobs that met for over seventy-five hours in total time. When I was in high school our football team went away for five days during the summer for practice. I was with thirty other guys for 120 hours. I had four college roommates that I lived with for at least one semester—about ninety days. I could go on and on. If I thought about how many people I had a seventy-five hour or three day relationship with or more, the list would probably be enormous. Yet if I pulled almost any one of these people aside and quizzed them about my life or me, they would fail miserably. They probably could not even tell me all my children's names, never mind intimate details. The amazing thing was how much Debra and I learned about each other in such a short period of time, considering that in the beginning of our sessions I was very guarded on what I said or told her. So for at least ten to fifteen of the hours I did not cooperate, rarely talked, and certainly did not reveal intimate life details. Yet, she knew me better than anyone alive except Francie.

Debra knew more than my kid's names. She knew more than my likes and dislikes. She knew more than little things—like what I may have said to the bank or about the person who was aggravating me this week.

I'm convinced that if someone saw us talking at a party they would've thought we were childhood friends or related. How else could we possibly know this much about each other's lives? This alone could wow you. But it was more. She knew a world of mine that I did not know existed up until a year or so ago. Debra had seen my unconscious world. She was the only person who had been let inside this world. She knew what makes me tick. She knew my true anxieties, my true fears, and my true feelings. She was aware that I thought of suicide because of this world. She knew that I wanted to run away because of this world. She understood I never lived my true life because of this world. When it came to true, intimate knowledge of my weaknesses and my strengths as they relate to this world … of all the people I know, my beloved Debra was the most aware.

FORTY-SEVEN

In early to mid April I contacted David Morales and assured him that all aspects of the company had finally been sold. It was time to declare bankruptcy. He outlined the remaining information I needed to complete the bankruptcy filing. Nothing he asked of me was difficult to gather. He suggested one more meeting and then we would be ready to file. I would join a long list of people who have filed for bankruptcy, trying to insure themselves a fresh financial start. Once, while job hunting on the internet, I decided to look up famous bankruptcies. I was amazed and shocked at the number of celebrities who had filed for bankruptcies. Included were: Abraham Lincoln, 16th President of the United States; Kim Bassinger, actress; Samuel L. Clemens who was known by his pen name as the classic Great American Novel writer Mark Twain; Walt Disney, Oscar winning film producer and animation and theme park originator of Disneyland; Henry Ford, who revolutionized the automobile manufacturing industry; Dorothy Hamill, Olympic Gold Medal Winner; Tony Gwynn, professional baseball player; Willie Nelson, country singer and songwriter; Rembrandt, historic genius painter; Anna-Nicole Smith, model; Donald Trump, billionaire entrepreneur; Johnny Unitas, famous NFL quarterback; Oscar Wilde, poet and author.

The list includes a great many more people and is easy to find on the Web. Included are males, females of all races, creeds, cultures, varying ages and economic backgrounds. I was in some pretty damn good company. I was the only one of my friends or relatives who could say he had something in common with such a host of historic and famous people. Equally surprising were the number of America's most well known large corporations that had filed for bankruptcy. Included were such companies as Bethlehem Steel, Delta Airlines, Enron, Fruit of the Loom, Montgomery Ward, Owens Corning, Pan Am, Polaroid Corporation, Texaco, Western Union, and Zenith.

When David called me on my cell phone to let me know the bankruptcy papers had been filed I was in a Kinko's making copies of my resume. He said I could stop by and he would fill me in on dates, numbers, amounts, etc. Having lost interest in details, I told him that he did not have to bother. I had mixed feelings about the filing. Due to the number of suits against me I had no choice but to file. My financial life had officially started over. I had no more debt, But it was not how I imagined, dreamed, or fantasized my life ending up. I wanted to be debt free for sure, but debt free because I had made millions. There was also a sense of relief. I did not know if I was happy or sad. I finished my copies and left Kinko's thinking that, like my son Dominic who would graduate from college in one month, I did not have a job, I pretty much had no money, and no home to call my own. Hopefully, like my brother Marty did years ago, I could now go out into the world and try once again to achieve the American Dream.

***

I read in the obituaries that on April 8, 2008, Stanley Kamel, the actor who played the psychiatrist on the TV show *Monk* passed away. He was only, what I now considered a young, sixty-five years old. Although fictional, I actually felt for Adrian Monk. News like this caused me to feel somehow broken. I resolved I was going to watch future *Monk* shows with great interest to see how they handled not only Kamel's death, but Monk's reaction to it.

***

It was six thirty in the morning and I was in bed half awake trying to plan the things I had to do that day. Who to call, where to look for a job? For some reason I was not as nervous as I should have been for a man who was jobless and soon to be homeless. Francie shimmied toward me, grabbed my shoulder and pulled me toward her. I let myself roll over onto my back. She leaned up on her elbow and looking down at me said, "Ken, I love what that woman has done for you. She must be a great person and she really has done a tremendous job."

Francie skirted away over to the edge of the bed, jumped out and walked into the bathroom. Francie, even though I had been seeing Debra for over a year and a half, still did not know her name. She called her 'that woman' and rarely, if ever, mentioned her or even bothered to ask questions about Debra or our sessions. I remained in bed, shook my head, let out a little laugh, and thought, Ken, maybe you really are nuts.

Later in the day I asked Francie what made her comment on the job 'that woman' was doing. She answered, "I can see her influence in the way you have reacted to this tragedy and by some of the comments you've made to me along the way. I'm so glad you found her."

FORTY-EIGHT

The day before my birthday in April, I was sitting on my porch reading a book. I was startled out of my book by the sounds of birds chirping, making me look up to try and catch a glimpse. It was the time of year when cardinals made their annual appearance. Red cardinals that swoop down onto a tree branch and look out majestically over the world with their heads slightly cocked to one side. They usually travel in pairs, a female and male cardinal. I placed my book on a small table and walked slowly to the porch railing hoping to catch a look at the birds. Leaning on the rail, I looked out at a neighborhood that I would soon be leaving for an apartment. The house where we raised our five children had sold two days after Sharon, our realtor, put the 'for sale' sign up on our front lawn. She later had said to me that while she was walking to her car, after the sign was posted, she looked back and saw a red cardinal perched on top of it. She knew then that the house would sell quickly in spite of the worst housing market in a number of years. A young couple from Ohio looking through rose colored glasses only saw the good in a house that had character. They wanted to start and raise a family in this wonderful home and neighborhood that they absolutely loved.

Leaning against the rail it suddenly occurred to me—the trees were starting to bloom, more people were about, but most of all ... no snow. The snow had finally melted. It was gone for at least another year. It finally melted! The 60.3 inches of the fluffy stuff that Chicago had recorded during the winter of 2007-2008 had at long last disappeared. Hopefully, as Francie once told me, like the snow my problems will slowly melt away. One day I will wake up and they will have gone away, relegated to an unsavory but remote and harmless memory.

I sat back down and began to think about the dinner planned for that upcoming Friday. We were invited to the Olson's to celebrate my birthday and Maria's. They were one day apart and we had celebrated together for at least the past ten years. Maria would cook one of her famous Italian meals. It would not be a big party, but instead just our closest friends.

I imagined walking into the party and seeing Annie. We had been seeing a lot more of each other lately. I still loved Annie, but only as a friend. I would run up to her and we'd start talking about our children and what was going on in our lives. I thought I might now finally have the courage to tell her I meet with Debra once a week and that she could never fully understand the importance of her having mentioned Debra to me back in what now seemed like such a long time ago. While we're chatting, Dan her husband might look over and smile seeing the two pals together again. After a while Annie would get up, kiss me on the cheek as she always does, say, "Love ya, Ken," and move on to her 'chick' friends. I would look over and see Francie talking to Mike and think of how Mike always sought out Francie at these events. How they always sat next to each other at our dinners and always chatted ... maybe she was his Annie?

After Annie had left me, I would walk over to Kevin and Rich who have already begun talking about golf now that spring and summer are fast approaching. The three of us, along with Francie, have played golf together at least ten times a summer for a number of years. I would tell them about how I played recently in Florida with my brother and friend Paul, adding some new golf stories to the old ones that we have been telling each other for years.

"Remember when our friend Cliff got a hole in one on the wrong hole. God, what do you think the guys on the green thought when the ball rolled in the cup? I'd loved to have seen their reaction when they realized it was from the man on the tee box one hole over."

Or, how Mike's cousin, Joe, in frustration, threw the ball toward the hole when he thought no one was looking? "Can you believe it landed six inches from the hole? The best is when Gary confronted him on the green."

"Joe, nice shot. What did you use, a five iron?"

"Yeah, got under it nicely."

"Stop lying, I saw you throw the ball."

"I didn't throw the ball."

"I saw you."

"No you didn't."

Anyone who has a brother appreciates that story. Two brothers rationally discussing an issue is a wonderful part of life.

Then there was how Andy Warner on the par three water-surrounded third hole at North Shore Country Club uncharacteristically hit his drive right in the water. He teed it up again and watched as his perfect shot bounced into the hole for a story telling three.

We would talk of our own golf failings and laugh at shots we made in the past. Now, when I am with Kevin and Rich, I often think of my own mortality. And I know that when I am on my death bed, Francie will walk in and announce that Rich and Kevin are here to see me. I will with great joy tell her to show my friends in. They both will pull chairs up close to the bed and we will tell these same golf stories. "What club do *you* think Cliff used?" We will laugh, joke, and at times sit silently. Perhaps I will pass away two days after they leave. But it will be with a smile on my face knowing that my friends came to see me.

I always remind Francie that I want my funeral to be like the funeral in the movie *The Big Fish.* All the odd characters that helped to make my life story meeting at my funeral service, their common bond being that they once knew Ken Sabino. I know Marty and Paul, with their wives Sally and Meg, will fly up from Florida. Murph will drive in from the east coast with his spouse Linda ready to hold court and eloquently tell of our college misadventures. My two sisters will be there with all their brood, jokingly telling everyone they were my parents' favorite child and not me. Maria, Mike, and Annie will greet the out-of-towners and make them feel welcome. Francie's family will be there in force. Most of all Debra, who has heard and knows most of the stories, but bound by law to not reveal such privy, will be there only to listen. Maybe she will bring the doll from her bookshelf—the one dressed in black. The doll with the white stole and gloves, the one the Mexicans call Katrina. The doll that supposedly reminds rich people that they someday, like the poor, will also pass away.

All my guests will only talk about the good times we had together, no sadness will be allowed or tolerated, just 'good ol' stories' of all the adventures we had together. They will, no they have to, embellish and exaggerate every story so that it either looks much better or, sometimes if it fits, a little worse than what really happened. They can make me a great man or they can tell a funny story at my expense. But there will be no forty-two regulars at this party. They have all heard stories about each other. When I am with Murph, I always tell Paul and Marty stories. I tell Marty and Paul, especially on the golf course, Rich and Kevin stories. All my friends will be there representing all the different stages of my life. Uniting to honor and remember me in stories and to tell all my fabulously outstanding life adventures. It will be just like some of the early dreams I shared with Debra where all my friends from every walk of my life are finally together. But, unlike my dreams, they will not be at odds with me. They will hug when they see each other, because through me they will all know each other intimately. One of my five children will lose the argument and have to get up and say a few words about me at the funeral mass. Hopefully, they will talk about what a good family man I was. How I was honest, loved sports, and especially loved my children and Francie. I will write in my will that the eulogist will only be allowed to talk for a minute or two. Of course that's probably the longest a Sabino would ever talk in public anyway. But my intentions will be well known just to insure that there will not be a long and boring speech. It would only cut into the wild celebration and story telling.

At the party, Dan Madigan and his Irish band will join forces with Bernie Sabino and his band mates and they will play all types of songs: Irish, rock, blues, and folk. Francie will cry because she knows how much I would've enjoyed this type of celebration. There will be plenty to eat, because like all good Italians cooks, Maria will have organized the food and she will make absolutely sure there is way too much to eat without becoming bloated. Everyone, especially Murph with his loud booming baritone voice, will sing along with the makeshift band, as they all drink beer and wine into the wee hours of the night and no one will mention how I went bankrupt in 2008. No one will talk about my failures. No one will really know the pain I felt when my life was unraveling.

FORTY-NINE

When our children were younger, Francie and I would often bring them to visit Francie's parents on their farm in Gurnee. The farm was known for the pink and yellow silos visible from route 94. Many times, in spite of the ninety-degree weather, I left everyone behind at the pool and went to the barnlike house to sit and watch the Cub's game with my father-in-law, Jack. Here was a lifelong Cub fan who had not been rewarded with so much as one World Series winner in his lifetime, sitting next to his Yankee fan son-in-law. Me, I have been alive for nineteen pennants and eleven World Series championships by my New York Yankees. Yet, this humble man would sit and watch the game with me, telling me stories of baseball's all-time greats, mostly the great New York Yankee teams of the late 50s and early 60s. The teams of Mickey Mantle, Yogi Berra, Roger Maris, and Whitey Ford. Those great squads that made my brother and me fall in love with baseball. It always brought back memories of sitting in our living room in front of our small black and white TV, next to my brother Marty, with Dad behind us in his recliner. Having our dad saying to us for what seemed like the thousandth time while we were drawing or playing, "Ken, Marty, pay attention. Mickey Mantle is up and I think he's going to hit a home run." And for the thousandth time his prediction would come true. Mantle would clock it for a mammoth home run. Marty and I would jump up and down in our living room as the heroic, larger-than-life Mantle with his Popeye arms hobbled around the bases on his bad knee.

We'd yell, "Way to go Mick."

Dad, leaning forward in his chair, would say, "That Mantle is something isn't he boys?"

Mom, always fooled by the commotion into thinking something was amiss, would run in from the kitchen asking what happened and then have a sigh of relief as Dad let her know, "Nothing, Sheila, the Mick hit another one." But she wouldn't go back to the kitchen until after she watched with us for a minute or two to catch a glimpse of that marvelous, handsome Mickey Mantle. Mickey Mantle, the larger than life 'Oh, golly gee, shucks talkin' Oklahoman who took New York City by storm.

My dad raised me on stories of Joe DiMaggio, Phil Rizzuto, Yogi Berra, and Frank Crosetti and other great Italian ballplayers. Especially Joltin' Joe DiMaggio, the Yankee Clipper. I remember with enthusiasm calling Dad in the late 90s when Francie and I went to see the future Baseball Hall of Fame manager, Tony LaRussa, inducted into the Italian Hall of Fame, just because Joe DiMaggio was going to be the guest speaker. The only thing I remember about Tony's acceptance speech was when he said the only way he could convince his own father into coming to see him inducted was with the promise of meeting Joe DiMaggio. That got a roar of laughter from the crowd. I thought it was pretty funny too.

So now there I was sitting with a born and raised Midwesterner telling me stories about my teams because he knew my love for those Yankees. It was always such a great reminder of my childhood. I felt like I was magically back in my living room with my dad and brother. An earlier more innocent time when I did not know better and thought all my dreams would still come true.

Jack would tell me how his fanatic Chicago White Sox loving friend, Bill MacNamara, would call him up all excited when the Bronx Bombers were coming to town and let him know that he had two tickets. They would take the El to 35th and Shields and file out with the rest of the loyal White Sox fans to crowd into old Comiskey Park to watch their Sox play those hated NY Yankees. He told me it always seemed like every game had the same result; the Sox would get a lead that they would eventually lose to the Yankees after the 7th inning. He would look up from the Cubs game and say, "I'd swear Yogi Berra batted a thousand after the seventh inning." He had one story I particularly liked. It started like all his Sox stories, getting a call from MacNamara, "Jack, I got two tickets; this is the year we will finally beat those damn Yankees."

And, once again, Jack continued, "It is the top of the ninth and the White Sox find themselves winning by a score of two to one. Up to bat comes Mickey Mantle with a man on second base. The pitcher, I think it was Early Wynn, works the count to one ball and two strikes. Clearly a pitcher's count. Wynn walks behind the pitcher's mound as the crowd works itself into a rage. 'Mantle you bum,' 'Not this year, Mantle.' The Mick is cool as a cucumber in the fridge. He steps back into the batter's box. The pitcher looks into the catcher for the sign, when all of a sudden Sherm Lollar, the White Sox catcher, pops up and runs out to the pitcher's mound."

I always felt like I was hearing the story of *Casey at the Bat* being told by Ernest Thayer himself. I wanted to yell right in the middle of my father-in-law's story, "Hang in there Mick, don't strike out Mick, you can do it."

Jack would get more serious as he continued his story, "Lollar gets to the mound and says something to his pitcher and quickly returns to his place behind home plate. Wynn looks in to his catcher, goes into the stretch, looks behind himself and checks the runner at second base. He winds up and delivers a fastball that was invisible and clearly impossible to hit by anyone in the world except for Mickey Mantle. Of course, Mantle smashes it, a towering drive way over the fence, and ... there was stunned silence in Comiskey Park. The Yankees went on to win by a score of three to two. It was the game that propelled them to yet another American League pennant. After the game a beat reporter goes over to Lollar and asked him just what did you say to your pitcher? "Well," Lollar answers, "I told him to forget who's at bat; it's your strength against his strength."

Jack would turn toward me, shake his head, and say, "Can you believe that, your strength against his. For god's sake it was Mickey Mantle." Jack told me that story at least twenty different times throughout the years while we watched his beloved Cubbies. I never tired of it. Over the past four to five months this story had found its way into my head many times as I was driving home from MPC. *Your strength against his*. I would give myself little talks of, "Don't let them beat you. Keep your dignity." I'd pray to Jack and Patrick and ask them, no beg them, to remove this burden from me.

My father-in-law had two great legacies: his family and his friendship with a group of Carmelite nuns. He loved his wife Margaret, his children, their spouses, grandchildren, and great grandchildren. He sincerely felt they could do no wrong. He always saw the good in all people, especially his family. Many times Tony and I found ourselves in the MPC office alone at the end of the day talking about Jack and this incredible quality of his. We told the story of when one of the grandchildren put a bike in his car trunk and the trunk would not close. The grandchild used his shoelace to tie the trunk down, using the same knot one would use to tie a shoe. Jack turned to his wife and said, "Margaret, it's like he's a navy seal." The two of us would then laugh and then make up stories. What if Tony ran up to Pa, pulled out a heroin kit, tied the rubber around his arm and shot himself up? Do you think Pa would say, "See Margaret, I told you he could be a doctor?" We'd laugh some more until there was complete silence as we quietly recalled our own little Jack stories before heading home for the night.

His second legacy was the friendship he formed with the Carmelite nuns. In the mid-1950s Jack had read about this sect of cloistered nuns stationed in Muncie, Indiana. He became interested in their mission in life which was, solely, to pray for people. Unlike other orders of nuns they did not teach, work in hospitals, or run missions. They had one job: to pray. Jack began sending money to the nuns. My father-in-law was known for his generosity. One year he was actually audited by the IRS for making donations in an amount larger than his income. Because of his honesty and generosity a friendship was formed with these nuns.

In 1956, as this friendship was taking hold, Jack's parents were tragically killed by a drunk driver on Edens Highway while returning home from Jack's cousin's wedding. Jack, being an only child, was bequeathed all his parents' assets. A few days after the funeral, Jack received a call from Mother Agnes of the Carmelites, offering her condolences. She also had another reason for the call—to ask Jack what he was doing with his parents' house. Jack answered honestly … he didn't know. To which Mother Agnes replied, "Then you will give it to us?"

Mother Agnes believed that Jesus taught us asking is not bad, in fact quite the opposite—it was required. We must ask of ourselves and of others to make sacrifices, to give to the poor, to do God's will. Therefore, asking for the house was something she felt she had to do. Jack understood Mother Agnes's request because, like her, he believed we are required to make sacrifices. He gave the house to the Carmelites.

They eventually sold the house and built a monastery in Des Plaines where the Carmelites continued their cloistered life of prayer. We visited the Carmelites from time to time. Francie and I had breakfast prepared by the nuns from behind their cordoned-off wall before our wedding. We showed up every St. Patrick's Day to hear Dan Madigan and his cousins play Irish music as the nuns sat and sang along.

We were there for a memorial service after our son Patrick passed away. I remember how after the service George came up to me in half-shock-half-awe telling me what he had just witnessed. As a legal requirement someone who knew Patrick had to ensure that he was in the casket when the top was sealed. Francie and I did not feel we could do this so we asked George to be the witness. As he walked behind the altar with the funeral director, Pete Finnegan, they thought they heard singing. As they got closer to where the casket was the singing grew louder. They turned the corner and saw the Carmelites dancing and singing around Patrick's tiny casket. George could not believe this incredible show of happiness on such a sad occasion. One of the nuns saw George and walked toward him as the dancing and singing continued.

She saw his confusion, smiled, and said, "George, Patrick has been blessed. He has been called to be with our God. He is lucky to be called. He will not have to stay on this earth and suffer. We are celebrating his entry into the Kingdom of Heaven. This is not a sad occasion."

As George walked over to the casket, looked in, verified to Pete it was Patrick and gently closed the top, the celebration continued.

Years later we sat in the same chapel, saying the same prayers during my father-in-law's funeral. When the mass ended we proceeded out to the backyard of the monastery. It was the first time that people were allowed on these hallowed grounds. We followed the slow walking priests up a small hill where Jack was being laid to rest. The nuns requested, and Jack agreed, to be buried on the grounds of his good friends. The gigantic former Notre Dame Football star, Father Moran, and our close friend and Rose's godfather, Father Eric, looking small next to the giant, stood in their priestly funeral robes preparing to start the graveside prayers when they suddenly stopped. We all turned to see what had caught their attention. Out of one of the back doors of the monastery, in two coordinated lines, reverently walking toward us were the Carmelite nuns. On this occasion they would break their requirement of isolation and stand with the crowd to see their best friend Jack Madigan go be with his God in the Kingdom of Heaven. The nuns in their brown habits with holy beads dangling from their necks crowded close to the casket. Once they were settled Father Moran began the graveside service. I wondered if the nuns would start to dance after he finished his prayers while the casket was lowered into the ground, as everyone, including the Carmelites, would be throwing white roses on top of it. They did not; instead they stood in reverent silence around the place of burial like the rest of us.

I went over and put my arms around Francie, thinking we would be leaving shortly to go to George's house for the celebration of Jack's life. This would be the last time Francie, or anyone for that matter, would see Jack's gravesite with the grave stone that simply read 'Jack B. Madigan 07/29/21-10/08/05, Our Beloved Founder.' We would not be allowed on these cloistered grounds again.

Margaret, as we were all beginning to start down the path toward the parking lot, half yelled, "Wait a minute." She then told all the great grandchildren and younger grandchildren to, "Go touch a Carmelite. They are living saints and this will be your only opportunity to ever touch one."

The children obediently ran up to Carmelites and touched their hands or their habits. Soon the older grandchildren joined in and then finally the adults. We walked with them as they showed us their grounds and as they recounted the story of St. Teresa of Avila. They showed us a certain special tree, giving us its background—when it was planted and why. The nuns pointed out all the different statues, explaining who it was who donated each one, and when. Adults asked to be remembered in prayer and what they needed the Carmelites to help them with. Margaret was right; for an hour we were allowed to walk with saints. Then, as if a bell began chiming in the distance, the Carmelites lined up in twos and silently, heads bowed, walked back into the monastery to return to their austere life of prayer. We left for our celebration, feeling renewed.

The Carmelites do not pray for things. If you ask them to pray for your son who is struggling in school, they will not pray for good marks. They instead will pray that you accept whatever God gives you—that you are able to handle God's will, good mark or bad. During the months leading up to October 29th I would arrive home after a tough day at MPC and ask Francie to call her mom and see if she can get the Carmelites to pray for me. Francie would always say, "Ken, I think it would be much better if you call." I'd tell her she was right and then never call. I must have approached Francie three or four times always with the same result, me not calling. Driving home on that fateful Monday in 2007, three days before all Saints Day, I picked up my cell phone, dialed 411 and asked the operator for the number to the Carmelite Monastery. After a few seconds of contemplation I dialed the number given to me.

"Hello."

"Hello, Sister, this is Ken Sabino."

"Hi, Ken. Of course I know who you are. We hear Dominic and Bernie are doing well in school and that Rose has made a lot of friends at New Trier. Does Katie still like working for Catholic Charities?"

"Yes, Sister. I am calling because I need you to pray for something. MPC is going to go broke. As a result family members are going to lose a lot of money. Francie and the kids are going to be put in a very difficult position. And, I'm worried about Tony. Will you pray that they all accept God's will during this troubling time?"

"Ken, the Madigans are a very strong and close family. This will not bring them down. We will instead pray for you."

I begged, "Sister, please, I don't want you to pray for me."

"Sorry, Ken, but you are the one who we will keep in our prayers."

I was about to hang up when the nun, I still do not know which of the Carmelites I spoke to, said, "Ken, you know that our God is a good God and when He closes one door, He opens another."

"Yes, Sister," I said, half listening.

She repeated almost admonishing me, "Ken, I want you to listen and understand what I am saying to you … that when God closes one door, He always opens another. He will open a door for you."

I thanked her and hung up.

Sitting on my porch the day before my fifty-fourth birthday I thought about all the doors God has opened for me since October 29, 2007.

He showed me the decency in many people; in-laws, ex-workers, acquaintances, and business associates.

He gave me loyal friends who stuck with me as I failed on every level.

He gave me parents and siblings who supported me unconditionally.

He gave me five healthy children who watched their father in a fight for his life and still kept their respect for him in spite of his losing everything.

He gave me a spouse who embraced a terrible situation and, like her parents, looked for the good in it.

He gave me the grace to accept what was being given to me.

As I was thinking of all these doors, I glanced at my watch. It was five thirty p.m. on a Wednesday. It was time to go see the biggest door that He had opened.

Debra, my therapist. Together we will continue to work on that sappy romantic ending I've always loved and want so badly.

About the Author

Les Russo was born and raised in Greenwich, Connecticut. After graduating from Manhattanville College, in Purchase, NY, Les moved to Chicago with his now wife, Patricia 'Petie' O'Connor. Les and Petie still live in the Chicago area, where they have raised their five children. The Biggest Door, is Les' first novel.

ALL THINGS THAT MATTER PRESS ™

FOR MORE INFORMATION ON TITLES AVAILABLE FROM
ALL THINGS THAT MATTER PRESS, GO TO
http://allthingsthatmatterpress.com
or contact us at
allthingsthatmatterpress@gmail.com